NOHARM
WENDY HORNSBY

W RLDWIDE®

TORONTO • NEW YORK • LONDON • PARIS
AMSTERDAM • STOCKHOLM • HAMBURG
ATHENS • MILAN • TOKYO • SYDNEY

NO HARM

A Worldwide Mystery/August 1989

First published by Dodd, Mead & Company, Inc.

ISBN 0-373-26030-X

To my Committee—
Raymond Obstfeld, Jason Frost,
Pike Bishop and Carl Stevens

ONE

ASHES FELL LIKE TEARS on the dull gray coffin.

Kate turned her head away from a hot blast of Santa Ana wind and saw the TV cameraman on the knoll behind her wipe his eyes. She knew that his tears, like those shed by the crowd standing around Mother's open grave came from brush fire debris in the air, not from grief. But it would look impressive on the six o'clock news, so many mourning the passing of Margaret Byrd.

Kate wiped her own eyes, and wished for privacy for the grief that raged and burned inside her like the brush fires devastating the hills above Santa Angelica. Looking around at the few familiar faces, she found some consolation in the knowledge that Mother would have liked this. It was a big crowd for a funeral.

Everyone seemed hot and miserable, except for the priest, who was in his element as he delivered his endless eulogy. It would be a long time before he drew a crowd this large again; murder along Santa Angelica's Gold Coast was a rare occurrence.

Wind stirred ashes into little flurries around Kate's trim legs, then dropped them into the cool stillness of the open grave. Poor Mother, Kate shuddered. All her plots and plans and wild machinations ended here, with the ashes in that hole.

Carl's big hand circled her arm, the scars on his knuckles standing out against the tanned skin. The scars looked fresh. The first time she remembered seeing them was in the lawyer's office when he signed their divorce decree. They turned white as his grip tightened around Kate's arm. "Can we goose up the priest?"

"What shall I do, faint?" Kate asked.

"If you don't, your Uncle Dolph will." Carl's voice was a soft rasp close to her ear. "God, he looks like chalk. He has to get out of this putrid air, pronto, or you'll be digging him a hole right here next to your mother's. And if that brush fire jumps the freeway and sets off the ridge above us I don't think we'll have time to get all these people into their cars and out of here. It can't be more than a mile away now."

"Then go, if you want." She pulled her arm away.

Carl shrugged. "I can wait if your uncle can."

Another hot blast of wind came over the crest of the hill, carrying with it the rank odor of the fire. Kate bowed her head against the wind, dark hair falling like a shield around her face. Beside her, Uncle Dolph seemed hopelessly exposed to the relentless wind as it flapped the vents of his lightweight suit and whipped up tendrils of his sparse white hair. Kate moved closer to him, making herself a windbreak for him. "You okay, Dolphy?" she whispered.

"Don't worry about me," he said, but he leaned into her, hunkering down out of the wind.

Runnels of perspiration tickled down between Kate's shoulder blades. Kate's maid, Esperanza, had insisted she wear this black linen suit, but it was stifling. At least she had gotten out of the house without pantyhose. She unstuck her black pumps from the little divots they had made in the wet grass and tried to find a more comfortable position.

Though thoroughly miserable, Kate would tolerate the heat and soot and the droning of the priest out of love for her mother and respect for her mother's sense of propriety. But why didn't all these other people, strangers for the most part, go home? She knew there weren't this many people in Santa Angelica still on speaking terms with Mother, not since the press started covering her case against Uncle Miles, trying to have him put back in the institution. Maybe, like Carl, they came to be sure she was gone. Or maybe the brutality of the murder drew them, like dry brush into a fire.

"... and help us to comfort the family of our dear Margaret." The young priest seemed oblivious to the discomfort of the assembled crowd. "... her cherished daughter, Kate. Her beloved brothers-in-law, Miles and Dolph. Dolph's loving wife, Mina." The priest drew a deeper breath than Kate could have managed. "And in memory of her dear husband, Cornell, who lies here beside her for all eternity."

Kate watched the color drain from Uncle Dolph's face, as if a shade were drawn down from his balding crown to his chin. Proprieties or not, she had to get Dolph away. She caught him as his legs buckled, supporting his weight against her. She nudged Carl. "Let's go."

"Right." Carl hoisted Dolph up in his arms like a sleepy child and carried him away.

The priest, still talking, scarcely glanced up. How could a priest who had never met Mother find so much to say about her?

Kate made a perfunctory sign of the cross and turned to follow Carl. As she walked across the uneven grass, she avoided the headstones and sunken ground that marked old graves. Thinking of the coffins beneath her, collapsed under the weight of earth and time, and her mother's coffin slowly descending into its hole behind her, she hurried to catch up to Dolph and Carl.

Then she remembered the yellow roses in her hand. She had picked them for her father, just as a token to show she still had some memory of him. But his headstone was buried under the earth dug out to make Mother's grave. It would be too awkward now to turn back, to put these rapidly wilting buds among the flowers heaped by Mother's bier.

The thorns pricked her fingers. Quickly, she knelt, her slim back straight, and dropped the flowers on the closest marker. The name on the headstone wasn't familiar.

"Ashes to ashes, dust to dust," the priest was giving his benediction. The idea of Mother being so involved with dirt caught Kate as ludicrous, funny even. The alternative, cremation, was unthinkable in this weather. Kate wished her mother had left funeral instructions; she was usually more thorough. But of course, under normal circumstances, Mother would never have allowed her own death. Kate stood up and brushed the wet grass from her knees.

Carl, with his long strides, had already reached Dolph's big black Mercedes. The driver sent by the mortuary took off his hat and helped him put Dolph in the front seat.

Kate watched them, the smoky haze like a curtain in front of her. Seen there in blurred outline, Dolph looked so much like her father, or what he would have been like if he had lived past thirty. It was at the same time reassuring and a little spooky. She touched the tiny lines under her eyes and thought about how she looked more like them all the time. She had the slender, straight body typical of the Byrd family, saved from austerity in her case by a promising roundness at hips and breast. The angularity of her face was softened by the great gray eyes, thickly lashed in black; a legacy from her father.

"Now, was that nice?" Aunt Mina caught Kate's arm in a white-gloved hand. Ashes, like a parody of snow in the heat, settled on her white hair and lined face. "I suppose you'll burn in hell for walking out on the priest. I thought that man would never shut up. Who is he, anyway? He isn't Margaret's regular priest, the one who wheezes."

"The diocese sent him," Kate said, falling in step with Dolph's wife. "Father O'Banyon has asthma. He couldn't come out in air like this."

"At least *he* would have kept it short."

"Big crowd, huh? I don't recognize half the people here. Who are they?"

"Vultures." Mina flared her fine nostrils. "Murder brings them out. Look there." She nodded toward the car where a big-bellied man, panting heavily from the exertion, was making a show of helping Carl. "Sy Ratcher. He's gushing over Carl today. Next week he'll call you and remind you of our old family connections and offer to help you get your real estate through probate."

"There won't be a probate. The house is mine. According to Grandpa's will it simply reverted to me when Mother died."

"I'm sure Sy knows that. But maybe you'll want to sell."

"Maybe." Kate watched Carl clap Sy on the back, a gesture of superiority. "But I'd never have Sy help me."

Mina leaned closer to Kate. "Is Carl staying over again tonight?"

"Yes." Kate smiled. "His mother is coming, too."

"Young people!" Mina's lavender eyes, the last relic of once astonishing good looks, flashed like opals in the eerie orange light. "A long time ago I got used to the idea that people might sleep together, hell, even live together, before marriage. But it will take me a while to understand people who sleep together once the marriage is over."

Kate laughed. "I said he was staying over. I didn't say we were sleeping together."

"Now that," Mina said, "I don't understand at all."

"Me either. Frankly, sex was the best thing we had going."

"So why does he invite his mother along? For a chaperon?" Mina didn't wait for an answer. She hurried Kate toward the car where Carl stood, his square jaw clenched with impatience. Pausing by the open car door, Mina turned and sniffed at the dull orange sky. "Smells," she said.

"And spreads." Carl waved for Kate and Mina to hurry into the car. "Meaning no disrespect for the occasion, ladies, but let's get moving. Dolph needs a drink and I need to piss."

"I'll have one of each," Mina said, sliding across the back seat to make room for Kate and Carl.

"Wait," Kate stopped. "Where's Reece?"

"I asked him to stay behind," Mina said, "to shake hands and wipe noses in our absence."

"Then let's go." Kate sat on the edge of the seat, leaning forward close to Dolphin in the front. She watched Sy Ratcher dissolve into the smoky horizon as the car drove away. Dolph turned to her. He was sitting straight and there was reassuring color in his cheeks again. She bent closer to him. "Dolphy, are you surviving?"

"Oh Kate, my Kate, my pretty Kate," he intoned in a bluff, wavery tenor, trying to seem strong, she thought. He punctuated the end of his ditty by kissing her cheek. "What did you think when you saw your old uncle bundled off like a baby? I haven't been carried like that for half a century."

"Or more," Mina added with typical dryness.

"Some help we've been to you," Dolph said. "You've been through hell the last few days, baby. I would give anything if we could have spared you some of it. It sickens me to think of you having to see your own mother on a slab in the county morgue." He widened his pale eyes to keep the tears from spilling down his cheeks.

"Dolph, please," Mina reproved. She wrapped a thin arm around Kate's shoulders and drew her back. "It was an awful, awful thing that happened to Margaret, but it's time to put it aside and get on with our lives. We're still just one big happy family, you and me and Dolph and Miles, all living so close together. Things might seem bleak right now because you're sad, but everything is going to be fine."

"Thank you, Pollyanna," Dolph said.

Kate settled back, resting against Carl's hard shoulder. It surprised her a little how good it felt to be close to him, in spite of the bitterness that lingered after the divorce. But then, tragedy had always brought them closer. He'd come to help her with the legal mumbo-jumbo of death one afternoon, and when it got late she'd offered him the guest room. Three days later, he was still there, more a part of the family than ever. Yesterday, after years of talk, Dolph had finally persuaded Carl to leave the district attorney's office and join the Byrd family law firm. The marriage was over, but the partnership begun. The arrangement made a strange and sexless *ménage à trois*.

"Damn!" Dolph spat, startling Kate. "If the police believe it was just an ordinary mugging, why can't they find the punk?"

"Shush, now." Mina thumped him on the shoulder. "That talk won't help anything."

Kate closed her eyes, not listening to them, and took a deep breath of the cool, stale car air. If the police were really looking for a street criminal, she thought, why had they spent so much time questioning her? Like ants in a heat wave, they were everywhere; in the house, around the grounds, swarming on the beach, and worst of all, handling Mother's private things. Kate wanted the person found, but the process was so painful, keeping alive the first moments of terror and anger she'd felt after she'd identified the body.

Again she saw Mother's crisp white hair caked with dark blood, and her sweet, smooth face, now locked away forever in the gray coffin, ruthlessly bashed to shapelessness. The police thought the mugger was probably a young, drug-starved punk who took Mother's purse and her life to get himself through another day. It made so little sense when so many people were really mad at her.

The driver swung the heavy car onto Ocean Boulevard and Carl lowered a window and let in the comparatively fresh sea air.

Leaning across Carl's chest, Kate looked back at the blaze-colored sky. She had embroidered a sampler for her grandfather when she was little, "Red sky at morning, sailors take warning. Red sky at night, sailor's delight." It was a peace offering when she and Mother moved back into Grandpa's big house after Kate's father died. Mother had framed the little scrap of linen and presented it to Grandpa Archie and he had patted Kate on the head and tucked the thing in a desk drawer. Just for an instant she could see it again, feel the uneven sailboats stitched along the border. For no good reason, she wondered what had happened to it.

The driver took the curve around Angelica Point too fast and Kate braced herself against the seat. As the car straightened out, she shielded her eyes against the sun to catch a glimpse of the house standing at the highest point of the ocean bluff. It was the centerpiece of three massive, whitewashed adobe California-Moorish houses planted by her grandfather during the thirties, when bootleggers still ferried customers from the beach to floating casinos beyond the three-mile limit. With the sun behind them, they looked to her like a giant mother bird in her aerie, flanked by two huge chicks grown too heavy to fly from the nest.

The houses were grand and elegant, built before property taxes and coastline conservation laws made such places prohibitively expensive. Outside the iron front gate, painted white to hide its heaviness and function, was the usual variety of beach-front businesses: a pizza parlor with billiard tables, an ice cream store, and a kiosk renting roller skates. They were a homely contrast to the estate behind the gate.

Dolph reached in front of the driver to push the electronic gate opener. Silently, ponderously, the gates parted, revealing the courtyard like an oasis in a blacktop desert. Skaters and sandy children dripping ice cream stopped to peer in, stealing glances of a secret garden.

The driver sounded the horn as a warning to sidewalk traffic before driving across. The hot pungency of the densely planted hawthorne and eucalyptus, a barrier to outside noise and vision, cut through the smell of brush fire and signaled the transition between the world outside and life inside the compound. The buffer zone, Kate thought, or maybe the no-man's land. She felt tension slide up her back as the driver parked in the brick courtyard that served as the common drive for the three houses.

"When the law says a man's home is his castle, this is what they're talking about," Carl said, eyes riveted on the center house, like a child selecting dessert from a pastry cart.

"This is *your* house now, Kate," Mina said pointedly.

"Yes." Kate looked at it past Carl's profile. A big house to live in alone.

"Look, Carl," Dolph said, "the troops are storming the bastions."

Mina sat up abruptly. "What are you talking about?"

"Police," he said, pointing toward the beach stairway. "They're over the beachhead and up to the gates."

TWO

MINA STRAINED FORWARD, nose pressed against the car window. "How do you know they're police?"

"I can tell by the cut of them," Dolph said. "All the putzing around they do, they can't keep a press in their suits."

"What were they doing down on the beach?" Kate leaned forward to see the two men at the top of the beach stairs. They stopped to dump hot sand from their shoes and cuffs, looking like passing tourists who were seduced into a quick toe-dip in the surf. The taller man waved, straightened his jacket and tie, then loped easily across the grassy bluff toward the car. Kate liked the looks of him, relaxed somehow, without the bulldog eagerness of the police investigators she had met since her mother's death.

"Wait here." Carl opened the car door. "I'll see what's up. I know this guy."

Hands in pockets, Carl walked to the edge of the courtyard, perched one foot on the curb and waited for the other man to come to him. Kate knew the ploy well, part of the jockeying for dominance Carl used so skillfully in court. Usually confronted by Carl's imposing size, other men shrunk into their jackets, slacked back a pace. But this one didn't. He extended his hand to Carl, letting Carl reach for it. It looked like an even match.

"Nice looking fellow," Mina said in her stage whisper, "if a little darkish."

"Darkish?" Dolph laughed. "That's somewhat better, I suppose, than black as the ace of spades?"

Mina nudged him. "You know what I mean."

"Only too well, my love. Only too well."

Carl walked the policeman over to the car, his arm vaguely behind the man as if he were an usher at a formal gathering. The man was tall, maybe a little taller even than Carl, but narrower, not as solid. He looked Latino, and walked with an easy, unhurried sort of grace, forcing Carl to trim his normal full-speed-ahead pace. Kate smiled at the annoyance on Carl's face.

"Kate," Carl said, "this is Detective Lieutenant Roger Tejeda from the Santa Angelica police."

"Lieutenant?" She offered her hand, smiling to cover the prickly feeling of dread growing inside. "What happened? We haven't rated anyone ranked higher than sergeant yet."

"Maybe you just got lucky." He gave her hand a little squeeze before he released it. A small gesture, she found it reassuring, until he put a sudden brake on the smile that started to light his face. He smoothed his tie, leaving a faint dark tracing on the red silk. "We found something down on the beach we hope you can identify."

She held her breath, remembering the last time the police had politely asked her to come and identify something; it had been her mother, laid out on a cold slab in the county morgue. Her throat seemed to clench shut. She tried to clear it, to break through the tight knot. "Is it a body?"

There was a collective gasp around her.

"Oh, God, no." Tejeda touched her arm, seemed embarrassed. "It's just a handbag."

"Ah," she breathed, feeling a little chagrined by her reaction. "It's Mother's?"

"Think so," he nodded. "Maintenance people found it when they cleaned the beach this morning."

"Our beach?" She stepped away from the car to look down toward the beach, straining as if she might still be able to see some impression on the sand, find some reality there. "Where?"

"Just down there." He pointed in the direction of the beach stairs.

Carl edged between them. "If Kate needs to see the purse now, Lieutenant, why don't you bring it up to the house. We'll all get something cool to drink."

"Thanks just the same," Tejeda said. "This is only a formality. If the rest of you folks will excuse us, my partner will bring the bag over for Mrs. Teague. Save you a trip downtown. I know the timing is bad, but I thought you'd rather take a look at this thing now and be done with it."

"Carl, darling." Mina took him by the elbow and gently turned him. "Would you please help Dolphy up to the house? This heat is just more than he can bear."

Kate sensed Carl's hesitation, as he looked first at Dolph, then at Tejeda. Then he shrugged, dismissing the importance of the dilemma. He gave Kate a possessive kiss on the cheek. "Yell if you need me. We'll be at the house, waiting."

Kate recognized how skillfully Mina had gotten rid of Carl by giving him a graceful way out. Maybe Carl knew it, too. He solicitously held both Dolph and Mina by the arm so that they formed a little cluster as they walked to the shady portico of Kate's house and stopped there by the big front door, watching Kate and the lieutenant in the same way that gulls hover over crumbs on the beach.

Tejeda motioned to his colleague, who picked up an untidy plastic bundle and brought it to him. The bundle trailed a thin stream of sand as he crossed the courtyard.

"This is Sergeant Green, Mrs. Teague," Tejeda said.

"We've met." Kate recognized him from the beginning of the investigation into her mother's death.

"Mrs. Teague." Sergeant Green gave her a Boy Scoutish salute. "Sorry to put you to more bother."

"It's okay," Kate said, nodding toward the bundle in his arms. "Is that it?"

"'Fraid so," he said, futilely trying to clean sand from it.

Tejeda took the bundle from him and set it on the hood of the Mercedes, spilling sand among the ashes that dulled the hot surface. He unrolled the leaves of plastic, exposing a black handbag with a dazzling gold clasp.

Kate drew in a painful gasp of searing dry air, reeling a little as she recognized it.

"Can you identify this?" Tejeda asked.

"It's my mother's." Her voice was a dry whisper. The Mark Cross handbag had been such a beautiful extravagance, even for Mother. It was certainly worth more than its contents. Now it hung like a filthy derelict from Tejeda's hand, bringing back the rush of horror she'd felt when she saw her mother in the morgue; the beautiful and immaculate woman who had been soiled and discarded on the dark city street.

Lieutenant Tejeda removed the bag's contents, laying Mother's personal little collection of necessities in a precise row on the hood of the car. Heat shimmered around them, blurring their outlines like shadows on a mirror.

Kate reached out for the wallet, then pulled back her hand, afraid almost to touch it, as if the murderer's taint lingered there.

"Go ahead," Tejeda said. "We've already lifted prints."

Kate picked up the wallet and opened it. She leafed through the folder of photographs. Most of them were her school portraits, carefully encased in plastic, following her as she changed from sweet, sometimes toothless, awkwardness into blooming young adulthood. The most recent picture was twelve years old, a quick snapshot taken outside the courthouse after her wedding. In the picture Carl towered over her, beaming at the camera.

"You were a cute kid," Lieutenant Tejeda said, smiling. He pushed a well-gnawed thumbnail at Carl's face. "I see your husband in court sometimes. I'm glad he's on our side."

Kate hardly heard what he said, aware only that his conversation was meant to put her at ease. She opened the bill compartment of the wallet and pulled out a thin sheaf of currency, then a checkbook and a folder of credit cards. She held them out to Lieutenant Tejeda. "These shouldn't be here, not if..."

"Changes things, doesn't it?" He took them from her. "Credit cards and checks your standard-issue purse-snatcher won't always bother with. But cash? What worries me is your mother was found downtown and this handbag turned up almost in your backyard." He focused his brown eyes on her face. His voice became very soft. "Could she have been carrying anything else—jewelry, bonds, anything of value that might make someone overlook a bit of cash?"

Kate shook her head; it all seemed so fathomless, ludicrous even. "Secret codes, blackmail letters?"

"Right." The corners of his mouth rounded in a tentative smile. "Anything like that. If her death wasn't a random thing, then we have to start looking for reasons."

"Where do you start?"

He glanced toward the group still assembled in front of the house.

"You can't be serious!" Kate felt the heat rise in her face. After a moment needed to compose herself, she explained, "I saw what was done to my mother. She was no angel, but no one who knew her could have hurt her that way, could have hated her enough to club her so viciously." Looking again at Tejeda she continued uncertainly, "No one had enough to gain to do *that* to her."

"We'll find out," he said. His hand was a warm patch on her arm. When he took his hand away she could still feel its residual heat.

Tejeda turned back to the objects on the car hood, biting his bottom lip as he slowly returned Mother's things to the sandy handbag. He folded the bag into the plastic wrapping and tucked the bundle under his arm. Reaching into his breast pocket he pulled out a crudely hand-laced rawhide card folder with "Lt. Daddy" burned in childish letters on the cover. Awkwardly shifting the bundle he pulled out a card and handed it to Kate. "I'll be in touch with you, but if you need me, call me at this number."

She met his eyes. "Please come in for a drink." Then she remembered Sergeant Green standing beside her. "Both of you."

"Thanks," Tejeda smiled. "Maybe another time."

"Yes." She curled his card into her palm, closing her fingers around it. "You'll let me know what you find out?"

Sergeant Green took the bundle. "We through, Rog?"

He nodded. "For the moment."

Kate watched their retreating backs for a moment before she turned away. With a sense of *déjà vu*, she walked toward her family, waiting for her in front of the house just as they always had when she came home from boarding school on holidays.

Mina walked down the front steps to meet her. "What did he want?"

"They found Mother's purse."

"Oh, good," Mina said. "Be a shame to lose it. Margaret spent a fortune for it. It's a real Mark Cross, you know."

"But..." Kate started, then decided there wasn't much point in arguing the implications of the find with Mina. At least, not now.

The tall front doors behind Dolph and Carl opened slowly. Esperanza, as always in a starched white uniform, emerged from the dark interior. Her silver hair was pulled back from her flat, Mexican-Indian face and twisted into a tight bun at the nape of her neck. She moved gracefully, standing so that her shoulder covered the mismatched panes of the stained glass clipper ship set into the door. Kate had broken the window when she was seven years old and the repairman hadn't been able to match the original colors. The old house and children had never been very compatible.

Esperanza opened her arms and folded Kate against her.

"Oh, Esperanza. I'm so glad you didn't come to the cemetery."

"I stayed because I was worried about Mr. Miles," Esperanza said, nodding her head toward the companion house across the courtyard where Kate's invalid uncle lived.

"Is he okay?" Mina asked.

"I think so," Esperanza said. "See there? As always, he is watching."

Carl glanced toward the window where Miles kept his constant vigil. Heavy drapes fell into place as Miles retreated from view. "Did he say anything to you?"

Esperanza shook her head. "I think he is too sad to talk." Only a slight softening of the consonants betrayed her Mexican origins.

"Such a waste," Dolph murmured. "He had a brilliant legal mind once, Carl. I'm sorry you'll never be able to work with him. He could be such help to us on the oil leases."

"Don't talk shop, you two," Mina said sharply. "Now that you're working together, there's one of Grandpa Archie's rules I intend to enforce. He built three houses on this bluff for his family and no legalese or office chitchat is allowed in any of them. Right, Kate?"

"Right," she said, straightening up and wiping her eyes with the back of her hand. "But we're going to break another dictum right now. I'm hot and I'm tired and I'm thirsty. The new management is offering drinks all around even though the sun hasn't passed below the breakwater. Esperanza, is there anything very tall and very cold?"

"I have chilled some nice wine for you." Esperanza smiled tenderly at Kate. "I will bring it into the study where it is cool and you can watch the sun go down." She patted Kate's hand and went back into the house.

"She's always so Zen," Mina said when Esperanza was out of earshot. "So inscrutable. Wouldn't you like to know what goes on in her mind?"

"No," Carl said, "I wouldn't. Let's go inside."

"You and Kate go ahead." Mina grabbed him by the arm and stretched up to give him a peck on the cheek. "We're going home. If Carl's mother is coming tonight you youngsters need some time alone. See you at eightish for dinner. Come, Dolphy," she led Dolph down the steps and toward their house. Abruptly, she turned.

"Miles," she called across the courtyard in a strong voice, "we're home from Margaret's funeral. She's buried up on the hill next to Mother and Father Byrd and Kate's daddy. Your flowers were lovely, dear." Turning again, she walked briskly home.

CARL EMBRACED KATE inside the great arched doorway. "I wish I could spare you the grimness of all this murder business."

"Did Tejeda tell you about Mother's handbag?"

"Yes."

"You know what it means?"

He nodded.

"It's scary," she shuddered, "scarier than when I thought Mother was just a victim in a random killing, even if it makes more sense. If this was a premeditated thing by someone Mother knew, then chances are I know him, too." She looked up at him. "Who? Why?"

"I don't like the way you're looking at me." His smile was forced. "Those are just rhetorical questions, right?"

"Yeah." She patted his damp cheek. "Just don't leave town for a few days, mister."

"Count on it," he said, holding her close. "Now, about that drink?"

"You go ahead," Kate said, stepping away. "I feel restless. I need to walk a little. Meet you inside later."

"Don't be long."

Kate walked down the hall and out through the back terrace
door. She stopped at the corner of the house to take a quick
drink of water from a garden hose and to shed her black
pumps. Barefoot, she crossed the cool lawn to the beach stairs.
She raced down the stairs, the hot, green-painted wood burning the soles of her feet. At the bottom she stopped in a straggly
patch of ice plant to relieve her feet and to catch her breath.
Coughing what felt like chunks of the smoky air, she surveyed
the nearly deserted beach.

Twenty feet from the bluff a patch of the smooth white sand
was disturbed, as if churned by wrestling giants. Kate followed
the trail of one of half-a-dozen sets of footprints leading to the
place. Standing there, she turned and looked up, searching for
the place where the murderer might have stood when he threw
her mother's handbag over the bluff. She narrowed it down to
a fifty- or sixty-foot section of the craggy bluff, including the
beach stairs. Surely, she thought, the handbag was meant to be
found. On a public beach in the middle of a heat wave, someone would see it.

She counted on her fingers; Tuesday, Wednesday, Thursday. Three days since the murder. She doubted that the handbag could have been there, undiscovered, for three days, and
the realization gave her a cold chill. The murderer had been
around here after the murder, and maybe no one had been
alarmed because it was someone they all knew.

Lost in thought, she swept her toes in long arcs, smoothing
the disturbed sand. She turned up cigarette butts, bits of pop
can tops, shells, little chunks of driftwood, the usual beach
detritus. She hardly noticed any of it, until a dull shine caught
her eye.

Bending closer, she found, sticking out of the sand, a torn
corner from an old black-and-white glossy photograph.
Browned by time, the fragment showed four feet standing on a
brick pavement; a pair of slender ankles in thick 1940ish
pumps, and a pair of child-sized dark oxfords and dark socks.
The woman's feet were angled smartly, posed. The child's feet
were planted solidly apart, the left foot turned in slightly.

She turned the photo over. There were no markings on the back, but the paper was clean and dry. It couldn't have been in the sand very long.

"Shelling?"

Startled, she spun around, slipping the fragment into her pocket. "Dolph! Where'd you come from?"

"I saw you down here alone. Thought you might want some company."

"Thanks." She looked him over, standing there in his usual beach attire—shorts, bare feet, sand clinging to the hair on his still-muscled legs. "You look okay. Thought you were ailing."

"Good as new. It's just low blood pressure; can't stand still too long." He turned in a half circle, leaving deep prints in the sand. "Is this the place?"

"Guess so." She shrugged. "What's it all about, Dolphy?"

"Wish I knew. Your mother had more than a few people mad at her, but to think someone would kill her. It's crazy."

"Who was mad at her?"

"You want a list?" His question was a short bark of laughter.

"Yes."

"In addition to the immediate family, about every second name in the Santa Angelica phone book."

"Be serious," she sighed.

"I am. Since your mother filed suit to be named Miles's conservator, she's had a lot of bad press. Miles did a lot of good things for the town, and people still remember him."

"You're just trying to cheer me up, right?" She turned away from him, hands plunged deep in her pockets. The torn edge of the photograph scratched against her thumb. She pulled it out and thrust it in front of him. "Recognize these people?"

Dolph took it from her and angled it under his bifocals. "Nice legs. Where's the rest of her?"

She shrugged. "That's all I found."

"Here in the sand?" He turned it over. "Doesn't show much. Still . . . Maybe you should give it to that lieutenant."

She took it back. "Maybe."

"Kate." He lifted her chin. "You're mad at me. I spoke out of turn."

She shook her head. "I'm not mad."

"What then? You look like you've lost all your starch. Where's my old sparring partner?"

She laughed softly. "Maybe I've taken one too many on the chin."

"Tell your old uncle, Kate. Remember how you used to come and pound on my shoulder when you were mad at your mother? I'm still here."

"I'm not angry." She looked away. "It's something else. I have this sort of empty feeling inside sometimes that's somewhere between loneliness and not enough sex; like indigestion that won't go away. When things settled down after the divorce I started noticing it. And the last few days since Mother died, it's been so intense, like a big rubber eraser came by and scrubbed out some essential part of me. I don't like it."

Dolph wrapped her in his arms, folding her head against the hollow under his chin. "It's just loneliness, Kate. It'll pass. Do you know how lucky you are right now? May sound awful, but without Carl, without your mother, there's no one to stop you from doing anything you want to do." He held her away and peered into her face. "No one but yourself, that is."

"Funny thing to say, since you've just asked Carl to come and work with you."

"He may not be great husband material, but he's the best litigator I've ever met."

"Dolphy," she smiled again. "You're not like anyone else I know."

"How's that?"

"You always cut right through the shit." She stayed beside him a few moments longer, taking from him a dollop of emotional sustenance. They stood in the circle of churned sand, watching the horizon, where thick plumes of white occasionally broke through the shroud of black smoke. Kate followed the curve of the bay until it intersected the range of low, round coastal hills, fuming now like loaves of bread fresh from the oven.

"See the fire?" she asked. "It's breaking over the ridge near where the cemetery must be."

"Cemetery's a good firebreak," Dolph said. "Fire'll never get down this far."

"Maybe," she said doubtfully. "Just the same, I'll go ask the gardener to put some hoses out by the bluff."

"And while you're up there, get out of those black clothes. You've done your duty."

"You're not telling me what to do, are you?"

She could hear him still chuckling as she climbed the hot stairs.

Back in the house, Kate retreated into the small powder room off the foyer and took off her jacket. She turned on the cold water, letting it run over her bare arms as she looked at her face in the mirror. The hot, dry wind had taken its toll, emphasizing the fine lines around her pale gray eyes, messing her hair to expose the perversely stiff strands of silver that grew in a clump from the crown of her head and stood in stark contrast to the black. Usually, she paid no attention to these small symbols of aging, but today they were niggling reminders that time was running out, both for Kate and the children she hoped to have. With her damp fingers she combed her hair to hide the thin thatch of gray. The water glistened darkly on her hair, like the dried blood caked on Mother's scalp. She swallowed back the bile in her throat.

"Kate?" Carl called from deep inside the house. "Is that you?"

"Coming," she said. Moving quickly, feeling the bogey behind her, Kate turned out the bathroom light and followed the sound of Carl's voice. She found him in her grandfather's study, stretched out on a well-worn leather sofa, a glass of straw-colored wine in his hand. Light from a beveled glass window cast a rainbow across his handsome, smooth face.

He sat up to pour her some wine from the half-empty bottle. "Where you been?"

"Walking." Kate stood in the middle of the room, a little nervous to be alone with him.

"Sit down, Kate. Relax. We have a few minutes before we have to get Mom at the airport."

"I forgot," she said, sinking into a deep burgundy velvet chair. She wondered how he'd managed to slip in this visit from his mother, since Helga had never come to see them while they were married. The prospect of entertaining her ex-mother-in-law was grim. "How long is Helga staying?"

"Don't know. I was so shocked she said she was coming I forgot to ask." He looked up at her. "Now ask the next question."

"Which is?"

"How long am *I* staying?"

"Okay. How long?"

"Till you tell me to go. Forever, I hope."

She felt that knotting inside again. "Carl, I . . ."

"I know, I know. I won't say anything about it again. Just so you know where I stand. We'll talk about something else." He sipped his drink.

In the uncomfortable silence, she drank some of the dry wine and surveyed the room, all leather and mahogany, and thought about changes she would make to brighten it, make it her own. It would be fun, but a lot of work. "This is a big place," she said.

"For one person, it is." When she started to protest he made a time-out sign with his hands. "Don't get your back up. Point of information only. Just explain something to me. When your grandfather built houses for Dolph and Miles on either side here, why didn't he build one for your father, too?"

"For his baby, Cornell?" Kate shrugged. "I suppose he just assumed Daddy would never leave home. Grandpa never could separate himself from Daddy, or the mischief he got into."

"Vicarious thrills," Carl mused.

"Probably." Kate agreed. "I wish I remembered him better. He seemed to spend most of his time on his sailboat, tacking through the inner harbor, drinking himself into a stupor. Probably couldn't have managed a place of his own. Or didn't want to be bothered."

"Your mother could have managed. Your grandfather could have made her a sort of guardian. *In loco parentis*."

"He didn't trust her."

"Why not?"

"Because of her birth defect."

Carl perked up. "I was never aware of any birth defect."

"She was born female."

"Oh. *That* defect."

"After Daddy died, Grandpa was always afraid some man would take advantage of her, gain control of his estate. So he only gave her use of this place during her lifetime. I was the owner of record.''

"Wasn't he afraid you'd be taken advantage of?''

"What choice did he have? I'm the last of the line. And besides, he never met you.''

"Shrewd old bastard.''

"De mortuis," Kate said, pulling herself out of her chair. "Look. You wouldn't mind, really, if I don't go to the airport with you?''

"Not if you don't want to go." Carl sounded stiff.

"I have some things to do around here. School starts next week and everything is such a mess. All my books are just where the movers dumped them when I moved in here with Mother last June. I'm going upstairs to see if I can get myself organized. You relax," she passed a cool hand over his forehead.

Carl caught her hand and brought her down beside him. "I can't believe you're going back to work, after everything you've been through. Call the department chairman and have him find a replacement. Take a trip. Get away for a while.''

It was an old argument, one she thought the divorce had settled forever. "I'll think about it.''

"No you won't." Carl sighed with deep frustration. He ran his hand through his sun-lightened hair. Kate noticed with annoyance how perfectly the hair fell back into place.

A STIFF OCEAN BREEZE began to soften the searing heat of the day. Kate went up to the small room that had once been her nursery. Originally her grandmother's sewing room, it was like a small-faceted jewel set in the ocean side of the house. Three tall mullioned windows angled in an oriel filtered soft southern light into the room. Ancient cypress trees on the bluff below reached up past the oriel sills, making the room seem like a treehouse suspended on a branch over the ocean.

Kate pulled her desk into the oriel, turning it so her back would be to the light when she worked. She leaned against the desk, and, with her finger, she traced the words "safe harbor" that were wrought into the middle window.

Sometimes, as a child, the oriel had been her ship, carrying her out through the breakwater to the open sea towards sailors' heaven. Miles always told her, "If there's a heaven for sailors, your father's there." She wanted to be there with him, away from the strictures of her grandfather's house and his arguments with Mother.

Kate opened the long middle drawer of her desk and very carefully removed a small framed sampler. The sampler was her only memento from the grandmother she had never known. Embroidered on linen in intricate stitches with silk thread so faded by time that its original color was lost, was a brief Whittier poem. It had been a talisman to her as a child, protecting her from the angers of her grandfather. She tapped a small nail into the window frame and hung the sampler on it. It seemed to belong in "safe harbor":

> *And so beside the silent sea,*
> *I wait with muffled oar;*
> *No harm from Him can come to me*
> *On ocean or on shore*

Kate looked out to the narrow spine of wooden steps leading down to the beach. Halfway down was the small landing where her grandmother's body had been found so many years ago. A suicide; no one ever mentioned her. Now only two of her grandmother's three children were left to remember her life and grieve her passing. Grief for her mother's death washed over Kate, carrying with it sadness for her own daughter who would never be born to remember.

THREE

"So, Kate." Reece put his skinny rump down beside her on Mina's velvet settee, forcing Kate to juggle her after-dinner coffee. "How's our little heiress?"

"All right, I guess." Kate moved over to make more room for her cousin-by-marriage, Mina's nephew. His freckled face shone from too much sun, too much scotch. "You still working on *War and Peace*?"

"No."

"Heavy going, huh?"

"Right. Fall asleep holding that sucker, it could kill you. I'll stick with *Architectural Review*." Reece gave the others in the room a quick glance, as if to make sure they weren't listening. "I want to ask you something."

"You've lost your new job and you want to borrow my checkbook until something turns up?"

"Be serious. Listen. Sy Ratcher said something at the funeral that really bothers me. Did he talk to you?"

"No. About what?"

"A deal he was working with your mother. He seemed awfully nervous, wondered if you would honor her agreements, mentioned the 'old family ties.'"

"My mother and Sy Ratcher? That's a laugh. He's a real estate developer. What would he want with Mother? She didn't have anything to develop."

"But she had influence to peddle."

"True. She had." It was the use of the past tense that jarred her, made her aware of the emptiness in the air around her, the space usually filled with her mother's low voice, perfect-pitch laughter. Kate turned her head, half-expecting Mother to come in from the next room and fill the space, just as she always had, holding someone with power to be brokered close by her side. But Mother wasn't there. Kate felt let down, then a little foolish that, even for an instant, she had expected Mother would ever again come through the door.

"You're the architect," she said to Reece. "You work with characters like Sy Ratcher all the time. What do you think he's up to?"

"No good." Reece sipped his drink, surveying Dolph and Mina's richly appointed drawing room over the rim of his glass. "I love this place. I love all three of them. They're just about the only beachfront property left in Santa Angelica that hasn't been ruined by developers. It occurred to me this afternoon that pretty soon they'll all be yours. What are you going to do with them?"

"Tear them down and build condos."

Reece blanched. "You wouldn't really?"

"Relax," she patted his shoulder. "I'm not going to do anything for a long, long time. The property can't be sold or changed unless Dolph, Miles, and I all agree. And none of us would ever sell to a character like Sy Ratcher."

Reece caressed the placket of his green silk shirt. "Everyone has a price."

"Not Mina. You couldn't get her out of here if you set a bomb off under her."

"She doesn't have a vote, remember? Wrong side of the family."

"Just the same," Kate said.

"They came close once, trying to raise money to keep her old man out of the clink."

"What happened?"

"The old boy died." He raised his glass to his aunt's back in a silent toast. "Gone to embezzler's heaven. Then there was the claim against the estate in behalf of your father's bastard."

"My father's what?" Kate bolted to her feet, knocking Reece's glass on her way up.

"Hey, watch it! This shirt has to be dry cleaned." He tried to sponge himself with a minuscule linen napkin. "We don't all have your money."

"You're so full of it."

"Shut up." He patted the seat beside him. "Sit down. Behave yourself. Your mother-in-law is eyeing us. Do you want Helga to think we're a bunch of heathens?"

"Maybe we are a bunch of heathens. It wasn't Daddy's bastard, anyway. It was Miles's."

"That's not what Mina says."

Kate watched him carefully, looking for the curl at the corner of his mouth that always gave him away. "You're making it up, aren't you? You're pissed that Mina stuck you with handshaking duty at the cemetery today and you're just getting some digs in."

"Mina's the authority about the lurid past. Ask her."

"Why bother? Who needs a bastard when we have you?" She punched at his concave midsection. "Where's Lydia? Someone needs to be here to keep an eye on you."

"You forgot about the faculty meeting?"

"Oh, yeah. Missing that is the one good thing that happened to me today."

There was a rustle and stir in the far corner of the room as Dolph and Carl mixed fresh drinks. Dolph came offering Kate a dry sherry in a tiny crystal glass. "Did you bring your picture?"

"Just as you asked." She took the fragment out of her pocket and traded it for the sherry. "Think you know who it is?"

He shook his head. "Mina," he called across the room, "would you take a look at this please?"

"What is it?" Mina came closer, bringing Carl and Helga with her. She looked at the torn picture. "It's feet, dear. Four of them."

"I can see that," Dolph grumped, "but whose?"

Carl bent over Dolph's shoulder. "Not much to go by."

"The important thing," Kate said, "is figuring out if this picture was in Mother's handbag, if it was someone she knew. It might be just beach trash."

"Let me look again." Mina tweezed the fragment between thumb and index finger and held it out to Helga. "Look at those dumpy shoes, Helga. Had to be during the war."

Helga narrowed her eyes. "Had to be after the war. We couldn't get nice oxfords like those for children during the war. I used to stand in shoe lines for hours to get Carl the most wretched little shoes."

"Shoe rationing," Mina groaned. "What a nightmare."

"Go ahead, Mom," Carl encouraged. "What about the woman's shoes?"

"They're nice quality. Suede. My guess is they're postwar, too. But not much after. Look, Mina." Helga outlined the ragged top edge of the picture. "You can see one of her legs almost to the knee, and there's no skirt. If this was taken after forty-seven or forty-eight, you'd see some skirt."

Mina smiled up into the taller woman's face. "You're wonderfully observant, Helga."

"She is, isn't she?" Carl hugged his beaming mother roughly. "She'd make a damned good detective."

"Not me," Helga demurred.

Kate noticed that Helga seemed to relax a little whenever Carl was beside her. How awkward it must be for her here, she thought, caught in a mass of shifting relationships and alliances; just as Carl was dissolving his relationship with Kate, he was forming a professional partnership with her Uncle Dolph. Kate didn't really know Helga intimately enough to know how she felt about it all. Helga always seemed to enjoy Kate and Carl's regular treks to northern California to see her, but she had never returned a visit, until now.

Kate looked between them, searching for the family resemblance. There was a refinement in Carl's features that set him apart from Helga. The high, thick cheekbones that gave her an almost horsey look were broadened and softened in him, the intelligent pale eyes set farther apart. Helga, in her simple, well-tailored dress, a coronet of silver-gray braids around her head, didn't look out of place in the formal surroundings. But Carl, open-necked shirt tucked into chinos, belonged.

Dolph had opened his wallet and was carefully sliding the bit of photograph into a plastic sleeve. "Miles always had a good eye for a pair of ankles. Maybe he'll recognize these."

"Miles?" Helga said. "He's the third brother? He's been ill, hasn't he?"

"Ill? Yes." Mina looked around the circle, helpless. "How do you say it nicely?"

"Flipped is about as nice as you could get," Reece said.

"That's cruel, Reece." Dolph sounded offended.

"I'm sorry," Helga blushed. "I didn't mean to be nosy."

"Forget it. It's hardly a state secret." Mina gave a wave of dismissal, the big stones on her fingers dancing sparks of light across the room. "The doctors call it 'profound melancholia.' Sounds very poetic, doesn't it? What it means is he likes to be left alone. Miles has had about half-a-dozen 'episodes,' as the doctors call them, when he just sort of caves in on himself. The first was during all the excitement when Kate and Carl were planning their wedding."

"Wait now," Dolph protested. "Don't blame the kids for what happened."

"Well of course not." Mina's denial was theatrically anguished. "Kate and Carl were lovely about the whole thing and zipped down to the courthouse for a quiet ceremony. Miles was in an institution for about a year that time. Since then the stays have gotten shorter and shorter and the treatment rougher and rougher. The last time he was in he had so much shock treatment that Dolph says his brains are permanently fried." She took a breath. "That's not nice to say, but we're all family here."

Kate cringed. Just like Mina, she thought, to find exactly the wrong thing to say. They weren't all family anymore. As if sharing the thought, Helga moved away a step, to put her hand on Carl's arm, defining where the family lines were drawn.

Carl took the hand and kissed the palm. "Getting tired, Mom?"

She nodded. "A little."

"I think that's my cue." Reece leaned heavily against Kate's shoulder. "I'm all in, Aunt Mina. May I camp out here? Don't think I could navigate home."

"Of course, darling." Mina patted his cheek. "Your room here is always ready."

Carl reached for Kate. "It is late. Maybe we should all turn in."

She hesitated, wondering how much invitation was in the remark.

Dolph was behind her, hand on her elbow, drawing her away from the group. "You folks go on ahead. If she's up to it, I'd like to talk to Kate about a thing or two."

Kate had the feeling Dolph was responding to Carl's suggestion that it was bedtime, giving her a graceful way out, if she wanted it. Staying behind did make things easier for her. Not sleeping with Carl, especially while they were in the same house, had been awkward, unnatural. But sex had such power. She knew that it could never be a casual thing between them again, not after all the years and beddings they'd shared. Just thinking about it, she felt the familiar stirrings that at that moment seemed a threat to all the independence she had gained since she filed for divorce. Kate glanced up at Carl, caught him watching her.

He smiled expectantly. "Kate?"

There was a little crease across the hollow of his temple, and she remembered how it felt to kiss that place, soft and velvety against her lips. She clenched her fists, digging her nails into the palms of her hands, using the pain as a diversion. "Good night," she said. "Don't wait up. I'll let myself in."

Dolph gently squeezed her arm. "It's so hot tonight. Let's talk in the next room. Cooler in there."

"If you like." She walked along beside Dolph, across the room, and down the passage toward his study.

Dolph didn't say anything until they were out of earshot of the others. "Reece seemed out of sorts tonight. Not been drinking too much, has he?"

Kate shrugged. "I don't think so."

"After what happened to your father, I hate to see a man controlled by his drink." He opened the study door. "After you, ma'am."

"Thank you." She paused to look around. Even though Dolph's study was a smaller version of the room now called "Grandpa's study" in her own house, it seemed larger. Where Grandpa had used dark mahogany paneling and leather chairs to give an air of solidity to his private lair, Dolph had preferred thick, pale green carpet, cream-colored walls, gilt-framed watercolors. She could see Mina's hand here, her unerring sense of line and color. Kate found it a very personal room, sexy even, the way Mina's selections were so intimately geared to Dolph's taste.

Kate waded across the carpet and opened the French doors onto the terrace, filling the room with cool, salty-fishy air tinged with smoke from the brush fires. She listened for a moment to the pot-and-pan clatterings coming from the kitchen as

Mina's housekeeper finished the dinner dishes. Every sound was both carried and softened by the breaking of waves on the beach below the bluff.

On the far side of the house, the front door closed, and she heard Carl and Helga in quiet conversation outside, the sound ebbing as they walked away from Dolph's house. Then Mina was in the kitchen, giving quick instructions about putting away the silver. Kate relaxed against the doorframe, eavesdropping, finding comfort in the humdrum details of the household. So quiet and normal after all the uproar. A breeze ruffled her hair. She turned to Dolph. "What did Ishmael say about the draw of the sea? 'There is magic in it.'"

"You remember that?" He eased into a print-covered wing-back chair, his legs propped on a matching ottoman. Chin resting on tented fingers, he smiled dreamily at Kate. "'Let the most absent-minded of men be plunged in his deepest reveries—stand that man on his legs, set his feet a-going, and he will lead you to water . . . as everyone knows, water and meditation are wedded for ever.'"

"When I was little, I always liked your little bits of wisdom from *Moby Dick*, even when I missed the message."

He threw back his head and laughed. "You're a good egg, Kate."

"So are you, Ishmael."

"Oh, no." He wagged a finger at her. "I'm no Ishmael. I've always been happy to stay home, slogging through the dull routine. Your father was Ishmael, meant for a life of adventure."

"Not much of an adventurer," Kate said. "He never went anywhere, except day-sails around the bay."

"And it killed him. That's exactly what I was trying to tell you this afternoon." He narrowed his eyes, the light of his pupils a tiny pin aimed at Kate. "Live your own life."

His warnings brushed by her like the moths batting their wings against the light. She stepped into the open doorway and let the breeze envelop her. Talking about her father reminded her about the crack Reece had made, and it led her thinking about her mother's death in a new direction. What if her father *had* left an illegitimate child behind?

"Kate?" Dolph came and sat beside her on the low brick planter surrounding the terrace.

She took his hand and held it. "Reece said something bizarre tonight."

Dolph sighed. "I can only imagine. That boy has a talent for stirring things up. What now?"

"About the family bastard."

"Oh, dear God," he laughed nervously. "Won't we ever put that one to rest?"

"Was there a child?"

"Could be. At any rate there was a pregnant girl, Miles's housekeeper."

"I've heard people whispering about Miles's 'bastard' all my life. It was supposedly the reason his marriage to Susan broke up."

Dolph nodded. "That's the way I understand it."

"Reece said the baby was my father's."

"I wish sometimes Mina could let go of a juicy piece of gossip. That tidbit is more than forty years old. Remember now, it happened during the war and there were a lot of pregnant girls in town. Hell, the navy was bivouacked at the park down the boulevard."

"I only want to know about that one girl's baby."

Dolph shrugged. "I wasn't here at the time so I can't tell you much. I was still in Europe with the adjutant general's office, hanging war criminals. The story was two years old by the time I got back."

"Didn't Mina write to you about it?"

"Bits and pieces; most of that time she was away on some ambulance corps training program. Why is it important?"

"The picture," Kate said. "The bastard would have been roughly the same age as the child in the picture."

"I see." He pinched the bridge of his nose, thinking. When he spoke again, the words fell in a rapid monotone, a lawyer giving a summary. "The way I understand the sequence of events, this young hired girl found herself pregnant and blamed Miles. He wanted to get a divorce and do the right thing by her. But Susan contested the action, and I suppose it was all taking too long, so the girl came back and claimed that, actually, it was your father who'd 'seduced' her. Took a lot of balls for a seventeen- or eighteen-year-old girl.''

"Balls?"

"Whatever. Dad filed a complaint with the Navy Department about the morals of their young men, paid the girl off, and sent her packing."

Kate was skeptical. "That's it?"

"As far as I know. By the time I got home from Europe it was all over. Your parents were married by then, and Miles and Susan had split up. Susan remarried shortly after."

"To Sy Ratcher's father. That's the old family tie Sy claims." Kate stood up to pace the terrace. "Reece mentioned a claim on the estate made on behalf of the child."

"I vaguely remember something about that when we settled your father's estate. Nothing came of it. It's hard enough to make a paternity claim stick to a man when he's alive. But after he's dead?"

"What if he tried again? If he, or she I suppose could prove who his father was, would he have any legal claim to any part of the estate?"

"Might." Dolph shrugged, forcing a smile. "Depends on a variety of things. Of course, he'd have a better case if you were out of the picture."

"Thanks a lot." She stopped pacing. "Very reassuring."

"What you're looking for is a murder suspect outside the family, aren't you?"

"Yes." She leaned forward, closer to him. "Dammit, Dolph. The whole thing's so maddening. Will you help me find the bastard?"

"I can try." He didn't sound encouraging. "I can dig up the old files, see if there's anything there."

"Mina would probably help."

Dolph let out a slow puff of air. "How much could you trust what she told you?"

"We'll find out, won't we?"

He reached for her hand and held it tightly. "Personally, I think this idea is for the birds. Otherwise, I'd be talking to the police. But just in case I'm wrong, you be careful."

"What has being careful ever got me?" She kissed his cheek. "You look tired. I'm going home."

"Would you mind checking on Miles on your way?"

"Sure. Good night." She waited at the edge of the terrace until she heard the study door click shut behind Dolph, leaving her in a checker of light from the windows. Eyes down, intent on the uneven surface in the dark, she crossed the lawn to the brick path. Glancing up once, she saw the triangle of light showing at the edge of the drapes where Miles stood, as always, watching the courtyard until someone came to check on him, to make sure he took his anticonvulsion medicine.

Her sandals made a racket on the path. She slipped them off and tossed them onto the front steps of her house as she passed. The damp bricks felt cool on her feet, still tender from walking in the hot sand that afternoon.

Halfway across the courtyard, Kate waved toward Miles's window. The gap of light disappeared as the drapes swayed heavily into place. She knew he would head for the front door. Without knocking, she waited at the door until she heard him release the dead bolt. It was a gesture of trust; he rarely actually opened the door after dark.

"Uncle Miles?" She put her palm against the smooth, polished wood, imagining his hands pressed against the other side, wishing she could make closer contact. "It's late. Are you ready for bed?"

There was a reedy little cough. "Pretty soon, I think."

"How are you feeling?"

"A little dizzy, dear."

"Did you take your medication?"

"Yes, dear."

"Did it make you feel sick?"

"No, dear. Just a little dizzy."

"Shall I come in and call Dr. Janss?"

"No, dear. It's not worth disturbing him for. Tomorrow is soon enough."

"Do you feel dizzy like before a seizure?"

"No, no." There was a thin laugh. "More like hot sun and pink gin."

She hesitated. "You're sure?"

"Yes, dear. Good night."

"I'll be out here for a while, walking. If you feel any worse, turn on the front light and I'll come back."

His only response was to shoot the bolt home and flick off the light overhead.

Kate felt sleepy, ready to go inside. But she wanted to give Miles time to get into bed, to make sure he was all right. She debated with herself about calling Dr. Janss anyway, and didn't only out of respect for Miles's right still to make that decision. She yawned and stretched, then walked slowly toward the bluff, trying to muddle through the events of the last few days.

Lights were on in two of the upstairs bedrooms of her house. Occasionally she could see shadows as Carl and Helga moved about inside. Their movements seemed so private, exclusive to a family that wasn't hers anymore, it was more comfortable to be outside until they were settled.

A stiff offshore breeze cut paths through the smoky pall overhead, revealing a few pale stars. Trying to relax, Kate concentrated on the sounds of the night: ships moving into the harbor, palms and cypresses stirring in the wind, the muffled throb of traffic on the boulevard. She paused at the edge of the bluff to rest against the railing, enjoying the cool and solitude.

The light in Helga's room went out, and the lawn seemed darker. Kate straightened and stretched and then walked along the bluff, skirting the lath gazebo, looking like black lace in the dark, until she reached the beach stairs.

The top of the stairs gaped like a giant black maw leading to the dark beach below. Only the phosphorescent plankton caught by the breakers defined sand from water. A long green roll formed, then disappeared, ending with a muted splash.

Kate went down the stairs to the first landing, ten feet below the edge of the bluff. Leaning against the banister, she could see the hills, dully lit in patches by faint orange fire-glow in the moonless night. The ocean end of the hills narrowed into a wedge that disappeared into the black water.

Kate turned around and looked up to see if Miles had turned on his front light. But there was only dark around his house. She decided he was probably already in bed, and she relaxed. She stood there in the dark for a while, lost in thought about her conversation with Dolph.

Something disturbed the ice plant beside the stairs, but it took a moment for her to react. She heard it again, a little closer, like some animal shifting in the sparse growth. With a sharp clink, something cracked against the wood banister a few inches from her, shooting sharp splinters into her bare arm. Instinctively, she grabbed her arm where it stung and pivoted around to look up at the dark bluff for the source of the projectile. She saw nothing but the vague outlines of the houses.

"Stop it," she screamed up toward the bluff at whoever had to be there. "I'm down here."

A marble-sized rock smashed into her cheek, sending fingers of pain through her eye socket and over the top of her head.

"Hey! Knock it off!" she yelled, but the rain of stones intensified. Arms shielding her head, she dove for the banister, intending to climb over it to find shelter under the stairs. At that off-balance moment, something the size of a fist smashed into the point of her shoulder, sending her backward over the edge of the landing. Then she was airborne, sailing into the blackness below.

The steps rose, ghostlike, in front of her as she fell toward them. The edge of a riser caught her hard on the ribs and she began tumbling headlong down the stairs, striking first her face then her knees as she tried to reach through the darkness for something to grab onto. She clutched at a baluster and missed it painfully, filling her hands with splinters from the old wood.

Again she reached, catching a corner support in both hands. The weight of her body, still rolling through its frightful somersault, pulled against her grip, wrenching her shoulders until she thought her arms would be torn from their sockets. But she held on until she was lying still, curled up on a riser, holding onto the peeling support as a child clutches a favorite blanket.

The horrible sounds of her body crashing against wood still filled her head. She lay there for what seemed a long time, knees drawn up to her chest, unwilling to explore the extent of her injuries. There was no awareness of pain until cool hands gripped her wrists, trying to pull her free. Kate held on desperately, too frightened to scream.

"*Hija*, it is all right. Let go." Esperanza pulled Kate against her soft bosom and rocked her, cooing the same unintelligible words she had used when Kate was a baby. She turned on a flashlight and ran its beam along Kate's body. "Are you hurt?"

"I don't know," Kate sobbed. She didn't want to move to find out.

"I heard you yelling like you were being attacked." Esperanza stroked Kate's back. "You stay here while I get someone to help."

"No." Kate held on to her. "Just help me up, please."

"Slowly, *hija*."

Kate unfolded her legs, feeling the torn skin and bloodied knots. Every bony point of her body throbbed painfully.

"No broken bones, hey?" Esperanza smiled bravely into Kate's face. "But you will have a shiner. You're a grown-up lady and still you fall and get a black eye."

"Shit."

"That's what you always said. You should be more careful."

Kate managed to stand up. "Esperanza, I didn't fall. Someone tried to kill me."

FOUR

"NICE SHINER, KATE."

"Thanks." Kate moved her feet out of the way as Lydia, her office mate, trailed coffee into their tiny shared cubicle in the history department's office wing.

Lydia lounged with athletic elegance against an institutional gray filing cabinet. She brushed her pale brown hair away from her face, green eyes sparkling. "I hear Carl has moved back in."

"Yeah. But I got this walking into a door."

"Really?"

"No. But I didn't get it from Carl, either."

Lydia looked down into her coffee cup, and Kate wondered what made her seem so hesitant. "Look, Kate, I'm sorry I wasn't at your mom's funeral yesterday. I wouldn't have been any help to you. I'm always such a mess at funerals."

"Don't worry about it. I did miss you at Mina's little dinner last night, though. So did Reece."

"So are you going to tell me what happened to you? You look like you were in a wreck."

"Professor Teague?" A girl hesitated in the open doorway. When Kate glanced around, the girl got a look at Kate's black eye and abrasions. Her mouth dropped open in a silent "ahh."

Lydia plunked down her cup, annoyed by the interruption. "So it begins."

Kate studied the interloper for a moment, not immediately recognizing the face framed by flame-colored spikes of hair tipped in turquoise to match her eye shadow. Then she brightened with recognition; during the spring semester the girl'd had a black Mohawk. Despite appearances, she was a serious enough student. "Hi, Lisa. Have a good summer?"

"It was okay."

"How can I help you?"

"I'm trying to register for your Tuesday—Thursday Western Civ. But it's full."

"Is it?" Kate shuffled through the litter on her desk until she found the appropriate enrollment sheet. "You're right. There are fifteen on the waiting list already, but you can sign it."

"Registration is such a rip-off." Lisa looked dejected. "All the good classes are already taken."

"No they're not," Lydia interjected. "I have lots of room in History of Third World Industrial Economies. And I have two slots on the women's volleyball team."

"Oh." Lisa looked doubtful. "What I really came to say was, I read about your murder, I mean your mother." She blanched. Before she could recover, down the hall the elevator door whooshed shut and immediately the passage outside the office was filled with a racket something like a combination hailstorm and earthquake. Three young behemoths in football cleats and cut-off jerseys pressed into the office around Lisa, impelling her farther into the already cramped room like a bit of chaff before a wind.

Kate knew the hulking figure hanging back behind his teammates. "Mr. Christopher?"

"It's Columbus." He corrected, his brow furrowed in a theatrical scowl. "Coach is pretty mad about the grade you gave me."

"Is he?" She exchanged a knowing glance with Lydia. They had both played out this scenario before.

"I can't play ball unless you change my grade."

"You think I should change it?"

"An F?" His voice rose half an octave. "Man, I came to class every day."

"Did you take the exams?"

"No." He puffed up his chest for the challenge, the jelly-roll of baby fat around his middle quivering.

"Did you turn in a term paper?"

"No, but . . ."

"I wish I could help you, but," she threw up her hands, "the college has rules about these things."

He shuffled back and forth, looking hopelessly childish in spite of his size. "I just never thought you'd give me an F."

"The baseball coach teaches history." Lydia smiled wickedly at the boy. "You should have taken the class with him."

"That's what I told him." The mammoth in front turned and grabbed Columbus by the arm. "Asshole, why didn't you take the class with the rest of us?"

Columbus pulled free and looked at Kate. "What do I have to do to get you to change the F?"

"Take the class again."

"Look, lady," he leaned menacingly near Kate, close enough so she could see the tears brimming in his eyes. "I don't think you understand."

"Cool it, Columbus." His teammate pulled him back out of the doorway and gave him a shove out the door. "You get her mad and she'll cook ya." He turned and winked at Kate. "Let the coach handle her."

"Eric," Lisa pushed at him in disgust, "you're a total wimp."

"Yeah?" He thrust his chin out with fierce belligerence. "Says who?"

Lydia jumped to her feet. "Out. All of you. You bunch of clods. Don't you know this woman is in mourning?" She hooked the edge of the door with her foot and slammed it shut behind them.

Kate burst out laughing. "I'm in what?"

"Sorry. First thing that came into my head." Lydia dropped back into her chair. "So, anyway, what happened last night? Looks like you had a few drinks."

"Not as many as Reece."

"He's not my problem. We aren't officially engaged or otherwise encumbered. Yet." Her long legs spanned the distance between their desks. "Did he tell you? I proposed to him again."

"What did he say?"

"He said I can't afford to get married. Last time he said *he* couldn't afford to get married. Do you think that's progress?"

"Do you?" The telephone on Kate's desk buzzed. She shoved the piles of books and papers away so she could reach it. "Hello."

"Kate?" The department secretary sounded doubtful. "Call for you. I didn't expect you to come in today."

"I'm here. Patch me through." She waited for the three clicks on the line as the call was redirected.

"Professor Teague?" The voice on the line was impossibly high-pitched and Kate groaned a little inwardly, not having the patience at the moment for another special-needs student.

"Yes."

"I want you naked."

"Excuse me?"

"I want to press my throbbing member against your bare flesh."

She handed the phone to Lydia. "It's for you."

Lydia listened, fascinated, her green eyes round and fiery. "Throbbing member?" she laughed. "This is the history department. What you need is someone in creative writing. 'Throbbing member' has already been done. Overdone, really." She hung up. "Lucky you. Another telephone breather. Except this one talks. Sounded like Mickey Mouse in mid-puberty. Do you think it's the same guy?"

"No. Security found that one. He worked in media services. Used to deliver projectors to my classes. He was fired, and I'm sorry."

"Why? He was a creep."

"Maybe. But he always got the projectors there on time."

Lydia shook her head. "I suppose weird calls are one of the perks that come with tenure?"

"Wouldn't you like to find out?" Kate teased.

"I'd kill for the chance." There was a pregnant pause. "Shit. Open mouth, insert foot."

"You do have a way with words." Kate stood up and began gathering piles of clutter from her desk. "I'm getting out of here. I seem to make everyone edgy. Besides, Esperanza promised me something that will fix my black eye. Want to come see?"

"No thanks. It's probably some voodoo ritual, and I'm squeamish. I'll see you later, maybe. I'm running on the beach with Reece." Lydia got up and held the door open for her. "You are still planning to run in the volleyball team's fund raiser, aren't you?"

"I guess." Kate juggled the stack in her arms to squeeze past Lydia. "I've never run with a pack before. And I hate wearing shoes."

"You'll do okay." Lydia caught Kate's arm, her mood suddenly serious. "I'm sorry about everything that's happened to you. If there's anything I can do to help you, you will ask, won't you?"

"Sure. Just one thing."

"Name it."

"Take my calls."

FIVE

"LEECHES?" Kate squinted against the reflected glare on the polished kitchen table.

"Yes, *hija*. For your black eye." Two long black leeches slithered through thick green water in the mason jar Esperanza thrust into Kate's hands. "I had to go all the way across town to my cousin's *bodega* for them."

Kate shuddered, setting the jar down on the table. "They're awful."

"Si." Esperanza thumped the metal lid with her knuckles. "But you put one on your black eye and it will eat the bad blood. My mother taught me this. You'll see *hija*, by tonight, no one can see it anymore." Gripping the jar, she began to twist off the lid. "Let me help you."

Kate took a step back, revolted. "Let me think about it. I'm going for a run. Maybe when I get back."

"How can you run, all busted up like that?" Esperanza scolded. "Here, put some more of this goo on your knee. It is bleeding again. I told you not to go to work this morning. But no one listens to me." Esperanza gave her a hard pat, like playing a drum tattoo on her shoulder. "You should go to bed."

"I should get moving, stretch out the kinks." Her back to the jar on the table, Kate pulled out a chair and sat down to rub more sticky brown salve on her knee. Bending her scabbed knees hurt, reminding her how ridiculous it was to be scraped up like a child who fell on the sidewalk while roller-skating. She leaned toward the nearest counter and examined her reflection on the side of the toaster. Distorted by the curve of the toaster and imprint of the manufacturer's logo, it was easier to look at the damage than to see it straight on in a mirror.

The point of her chin shone like a bright maraschino under Esperanza's salve. Carefully, she touched the blue swelling under her left eye.

Esperanza tapped the jar lid with a bit of menace. "When you get back, we fix the eye."

"I'll think about it." Kate headed for the back door. "Uncle Miles was asleep when I left this morning. Did you check on him?"

"Si. He's okay. A little headache, that's all."

"See ya." Kate went out.

"Be careful," Esperanza called after her. "And don't get in the way of that handsome policeman."

Kate stopped. "What handsome policeman?"

"You know. Big cow eyes."

"The lieutenant," she teased. "Go change your dress, I'll send him up for tea."

"Shoo," Esperanza laughed.

Trying to walk as if her knees weren't stiff and painful, holding her head up when she wanted to cover it with a paper bag, Kate went down to the edge of the bluff. She found police swarming the stairs and steep bank.

Barefoot, pants legs rolled up, Lieutenant Tejeda stood in a tangle of ice plant holding one end of a tape measure. The other end of the tape stretched to the stairway where Sergeant Green held it against a nick in the wood railing.

"Morning, Lieutenant," she called.

"Morning." He waved with his free hand. He turned to a photographer crouched in a patch of dry weeds below him. "This is it, Ernie."

There was a quick flash from the camera. "Got it, Lieutenant."

"Thanks. You can go back to the barn, then. Unless Green over there wants a portrait for his Christmas cards." Tejeda dropped the tape and struggled across the bank toward the stairs, then clambered over the railing. Kate noticed his jacket and tie draped over the banister, his shoes neatly aligned under them. While the other police collected their gear and reassembled their wardrobes, Tejeda rolled up his sleeves and undid another shirt button. He wasn't finished here.

Kate went down to meet him, stepping over a variety of tape and chalk markings; "A" where she started her fall, "B" where she landed. She shuddered. All that was missing was the chalk outline of a body.

Tejeda's grin widened as she came closer. "Nice shiner."

"Glad you like it." She extended her hand. "It's Robert Tejeda, right?"

"Roger." His hand was warm and she let it linger just a moment. He opened his smile, a flash of white teeth in beautiful honey-colored skin. Blue-black hair generously flecked with stiff silver.

"Roger." She avoided the obvious joke.

"Actually, it's Rigoberto, but there wasn't room on the police academy forms for Rigoberto, so it's Roger." Something about him caught her off-guard. He seemed so relaxed, but there was a disturbing intensity behind his big brown eyes. "Doc says you're not seriously hurt?"

"Not hurt. Just scared, embarrassed. I mean," she held up her elbows, "is this any way for a grown woman to look?"

"Definitely."

"Find anything down here?"

"Rocks and sand fleas." He rubbed one foot against a hairy ankle. "What can you tell me about last night?"

"I told it all to the police last night. Someone threw rocks at me." It sounded almost funny to her now, like tattling on other kids. Her hands described a watermelon. "Big ones."

He pointed to a little pyramid of rocks in marked plastic bags amid the investigators' clutter. The largest rock was about the size of a football. "How big?"

"Big enough." She pulled up the sleeve of her knit shirt to show him the big bruise on her shoulder. The bony ridge had an egg-sized knot where she had been hit.

"You didn't see anybody?"

"No. You can't see over the top of the stairs from the landing. But where I was standing, it was like being a pin in a bowling alley."

"You're lucky you didn't get hit on the head." He tapped his temple with the end of his pencil and looked at her clinically, surveying the damage, she thought. "Do you have any idea, suspicion, or wild guess about who might have been up here last night?"

"Sure. Who killed my mother?"

"That's the million-dollar question, isn't it?" He squinted toward the horizon, clicking his tongue while he thought. "Where're you headed now?"

"A run on the beach."

"Okay." He started off down the stairs. "Let's go." She stood there, mystified. "Go where?"

"You said we're going for a run on the beach."

"We?"

"Not if you don't start moving. C'mon."

"Sure thing," she muttered more or less to herself, following him down to the beach. "But don't you want your coat and tie? The detectives I usually run with wear a coat and tie."

"Normally I would, too. But I'm going incognito." Chuckling, he waited for her to catch up. He used the time to take off his white shirt, tying its sleeves around his waist.

They fell into step together, running at an easy pace on the hard sand at the edge of the breakers. She glanced at him once or twice, quickly, trying to fathom what he was up to. Maybe he just liked to run. He was lean and tan and, although there was a little softness in the middle where Carl's muscles lay like a row of petrified Parker House rolls, he ran like he knew what he was doing.

"What do you do," she asked, keeping her eyes on the beach ahead, "when your crime victims are sky divers?"

"I fall for them."

"That's terrible," she groaned. "Now are you going to tell me what's going on?"

"It's my lunchtime and I'm taking a little exercise." His words came out with soft puffs of air as his feet pounded the sand. "And I'm giving you the third degree. Seems to me there's a bit of money around here. Thought we might talk a little about it. For instance, you're your mother's chief heir, right?"

"Yes, but other than some jewelry and personal things, she didn't have much." Kate's words fell into rhythm with her running breathing pattern; pauses when she inhaled, bursts when she exhaled. "Mother lived on an annuity that expired with her death. It doesn't seem likely anyone would kill her for money, because, basically, she didn't have any."

"And you? Who inherits from you?"

"Most of my money is tied up in trusts that I share with my uncles, Dolph and Miles. The way I understand it, if one of us dies, the other two just get bigger pieces of the pie."

Water splashed the folded edge of his rolled-up slacks. It didn't seem to bother him; he stayed on the water side of Kate, his pace and breath regular. "In the event both your uncles die, who inherits from you?"

"That gets tricky. I've just gone through a divorce and haven't sorted everything out yet. So far, I've created a pension for Esperanza, my housekeeper. And Carl is to get my share of the community property we split. It seems only fair." She was breathing more heavily, her throat dry from talking. "But for the rest, well, I'd planned to have about half-a-dozen kids I haven't gotten around to."

"What if something happens to you before you get around to the kids?"

"I don't know yet."

"You don't seem very concerned about it."

"I'm not." Kate slowed. "Hey, can we stop a minute? I need to breathe a little."

"Sure." They walked in the surf line, letting the swash break over their calves.

"Until this murder business," she said when her chest had stopped heaving, "I never thought much about dying so I haven't made many 'provisions.' I've always let Dolph and Miles just take care of things for me."

He looked surprised. "Miles handles your business?"

"He used to. Which reminds me," she brightened. "The family may have a bastard out there somewhere who would have an easier time establishing a claim on the estate if I were gone."

"Interesting," he said. "Any other ideas?"

"You might talk to Sy Ratcher. He's suggested he was involved in some sort of transaction with Mother."

Tejeda shook his head. "My work is so much easier when two drunks stab each other over a bottle of Ripple. I think I'll need a degree in finance before we're through here. You ready to run yet?"

"Okay." She filled her lungs and loped along beside him.

"Do you have a phone number for your ex? I haven't been able to reach him."

"Call him here. He'll probably be home for lunch."

"Here?" Tejeda missed a step. "You're divorced but he lives here?"

"Temporarily. Just while his mother is visiting."

He nodded his head, as if the gears inside had shifted, but he didn't say anything. They ran quietly for a while, the distance between them more a function of his silence than of space. A few times she risked a quick glance at his face, and found it closed, his mind following an unknown but serious course of its own. He lengthened his stride, automatically it seemed, and she had to push to keep up with him. She did her best, but after a quarter of a mile, she felt spent, her breath catching raggedly in her chest. She dropped back.

Immediately, he slowed. "Ready to turn back?"

"If you want to sprint," she gasped, "go on without me."

"Sorry." His breathing was still easy and regular. He untied his shirt and wiped down his face and torso.

"You'll never get that clean again," she said.

"For damn sure," he laughed, "since my wife got custody of the washer."

"Oh." Kate waded farther into the cold salty water. "I'm supposed to run in a ten K next week. I don't think I'll make it."

"You will, if you keep your own pace." Holding up his folded pants cuffs, he followed her into the surf.

She splashed her face. "Wish this stuff were drinkable."

"D.A. give him a few days off?" Tejeda asked.

"Who?" It took her a second to trace his train of reference. "You mean Carl? He resigned from the D.A. He's working with my Uncle Dolph now."

"When?" It was Tejeda's turn for a double take. "Why?"

"This week. The why has something to do with football."

"Football? He was working on the Hopner case, wasn't he? Hopner is a baby food company. Was some footfall friend involved?"

"I think it's more abstract than that. Come on." She turned back toward the house. "He should be home by now. You can ask him."

They kept a slower pace going back, stopping only once to walk and cool off.

Kate saw Carl first, standing on the bluff watching the beach. She could sense his tension from his posture, the angle he held his head. She raised her hand and waved until she caught his eye. He waved back and ran down to meet them. Carl took the beach steps two at a time, barely breaking his stride when he hit the soft sand.

Kate slowed a little more. She tapped Tejeda's arm, glancing at his sodden slacks. "He's going to wonder what you were doing down here."

He smiled, giving her something that was more a flex of the cheek than a wink. "We'll never tell him, will we?"

"Lieutenant Tejeda." Carl extended his big hand. "Visiting the scene of the crime?"

"Always poking around." Tejeda sounded at ease as they walked back toward the stairway. "I hear you left the D.A."

"Time for a career change. Nice to be on the other side for a while."

"What does it have to do with football?" Tejeda asked.

"Nothing." Carl looked at Kate and shrugged.

"Cole Wexworth," Kate said.

"Cole Wexworth?" Tejeda's interest piqued. "I played against Wexworth at UCLA. Is he involved in the Hopner case?"

"No," Carl said. "It was just a story I told Kate to explain why I was changing jobs."

"Teague. Carl Teague." Tejeda rolled the name over a few more times. He retrieved his shoes and wilted jacket and started up the stairs ahead of Kate and Carl. Abruptly he stopped, almost tripping Carl. "Defensive tackle at Stanford?"

"Guilty."

"I started this?" Kate groaned.

Tejeda was walking up the stairs backward so he could talk to Carl. "You're the guy who clipped Wexworth and put him out of contention for the Heisman."

"Hey," Carl protested. "There was no clipping."

"What happened?" Tejeda asked.

"I was in a stance, waiting for the play." Carl was warming to the story. "I looked up and diagonally in front of me was Cole Wexworth, eyeing the ball like his life depended on it."

"In a way," Tejeda interjected, "it did."

"Yeah," Carl agreed. "He had a lot on the line: last game of his college career, looking ahead to the pro draft, Heisman and a Rose Bowl bid hanging on the outcome of the game. Problem was, he had bad knees. Remember?"

Tejeda shook his head. "No."

Bringing up the rear, Kate listened to the story for the nth time, noting how the fine points changed a little with each telling. This is football allegory, she thought; the facts weren't all that important.

"Wex was going to have the knees worked on as soon as the season was over. He shouldn't have been in there, but his coach wanted the game and Wex was his best bet. So, I was standing there with my rump in the air, looking up at an end who was out of position. The whistle blew. I saw my play, came up under on a diagonal, and knocked Wex before he could make his move. They carried him off the field, expensive knees gone. No Heisman. No Rose Bowl. No pro draft."

Tejeda looked doubtful. "What does Wex have to do with you moving off the baby food case?"

"You see," Carl took a deep breath, "sometimes I thought about Cole Wexworth and I'd break out in a cold sweat because I knew I was going to be in his position someday and someone with nothing to lose would cut me down."

"The Hopner case?" Tejeda asked.

"Yes. Wex was playing high-stakes ball and I wasn't. I had nothing to lose. I had another year to play. I was no All-American; just good enough to get my tuition paid. I could have held back and let him be a hero, but why should I? The outcome either way was the same to me. The point is, on Hopner *I* was the guy playing high-stakes ball, and they weren't."

"The Hopner Company is accused of negligently selling tainted baby formula, right? There are, what, six or seven dead babies on the complaint. What did you have to lose?"

"Two or three of my most productive years. Working night and day and weekends, and pulling out of everything else. In the end their insurance company would settle with everyone. Some judge would fine the company a million bucks, give the board of directors a little lecture, and meet them at the club for lunch."

"So you're switching teams."

"Yep. I've always preferred the defense."

They reached the lawn and there was a regrouping, with Carl now firmly between Kate and Tejeda.

Tejeda spent a lot of time rolling his shirt, tie, jacket, and shoes together in a sandy ball, stalling, Kate thought, while he rolled his thoughts together as well. "There were no threats from Hopner, were there?"

"Lieutenant Tejeda." Carl gave him a hard, court-room glare. "If there were, I would still be with the D.A. There's no mystery about my leaving the D.A. Dolph and I have wanted to work together for a long time. It just wasn't practical while Kate's mother was around."

"Why?" Kate grabbed his elbow, forcing him to turn toward her. She felt a lump of hot bile descend to her stomach. "Why would Mother even care?"

"You know." Carl flushed blotches of red over his even tan. When he spoke, his voice was low, secretive. "Because of Nugie."

"That's ridiculous," Kate protested. "Mother didn't even know about you and Nugie."

"Wait a minute," Tejeda jumped into the fray. "Who's Nugie?"

"Nugent Kennerly," Kate snapped. "You met Reece? She was his sister. Everything that happened with Nugie is ancient history."

"I like history," Tejeda shrugged. "It's a lot like detective work."

Carl didn't seem to hear him. His eyes were fixed on Kate. "Your mother didn't *know*?"

"No," Kate said, remembering the awful death-bed promise Nugie had forced her to make. "No one knows."

"But all these years," he seemed incredulous, "why did she treat me so... treat me the way she did?"

"It wasn't just you. Mother treated everyone like dung, unless they had something she needed." Kate turned back to Tejeda, a little embarrassed by his scrutiny of family skeletons as they tumbled out of closets. "I don't think this is getting us anywhere. Nugie died fourteen years ago next month. Now, that's sadder than hell, but it can't have had any relevance to my mother's death, or what happened to me last night." She turned and started walking toward the house. "If you'll excuse me, I need a shower."

"My mom's waiting for us," Carl said sharply. "Thought I'd take you both to lunch."

Kate stopped and looked down at the knit shirt clinging damply to her skin. "I'm a wreck."

"We'll wait 'til you clean up."

"Another time, okay?" She touched her black eye. "Besides, you don't want people to think you beat me."

"That's ridiculous," Carl protested faintly. "If you don't want to go, just say so."

"I don't want to go."

"Okay." He offered his hand to Tejeda, scanning the detective's sandy feet and ruined slacks. "Keep us posted."

"Of course." He let Carl retreat out of earshot before he turned back to Kate. "Seems a little tense."

"He calls it creative energy." She brushed at the sand on her legs. "Come in for a drink?"

"Thanks, but." He checked his watch. "It's late. I have an appointment."

"I enjoyed our run." She held out her hand.

"Wait a minute." He took hold of her hand and impelled her with him in the direction of his car. "You're coming with me."

"I am? Why?"

"Someone's trying to kill you, remember?"

SIX

"I'LL STAY and take my chances with a killer," Kate said, picking at the bottom of her sweaty shirt. "I'm not going anywhere like this."

"Won't take long." Tejeda said. "And no one will see you. I've made some arrangements for your protection, but it'll be about a half hour before they're set up. Until they are, I want to keep an eye on you."

Kate held back for a minute, weighing what he said. Then she remembered it was Esperanza's day to clean Uncle Miles's house, and Carl and Helga would be gone to lunch, leaving her all alone. "All right, I'll come. But the condition this shirt is in, you might regret it."

Helga, dressed in a billowy pastel-pink dress, came out of the front door as Kate and Tejeda came around the corner of the house. Kate waved to her, then hurried to catch up with Tejeda.

"Who's Brunnhilde?" he asked, nodding toward Helga.

"My mother-in-law, Helga Adams."

"Adams?"

"Helga something Teague something Adams. Couple of marriages involved."

Tejeda pursed his lips and studied Helga from the distance. "I see where your husband got his height. But he's prettier."

Kate laughed. "You're right."

"You teach, don't you?" A statement more than a question. "Aren't you missing your first day of school?"

"The college starts next week." She took a look at his nondescript city-issue car. "That thing air-conditioned?"

"Mas o menos," he said, opening the car door for her. Her bare legs were already sticking to the gray vinyl seat in the few seconds it took him to get in and turn the key in the ignition. The engine sputtered to a start, then almost died when he switched on the air conditioner.

"Takes a minute to cool off," he said, draping his shirt over the seat behind him. Skillfully, he infused the car into the noon-hour traffic. Although traffic was heavy on the boulevard, the beach front was strangely quiet. Only a few toddlers and their mothers walked along the sidewalk past the ice cream store. The older children were back in school.

"Tell me something," Tejeda said, his eyes focused on the rearview mirror as they drove inland. "Where were you the night your mother died?"

"On a date. Why? Am I a suspect?"

"No. Sometimes women kill their husbands. Sometimes they kill their children. But unless they're seriously crazy, they don't kill their mothers." He gave her a sideways glance. "And I don't think you're seriously crazy."

"Thanks. I think."

"What do you think your mother was doing downtown?"

"Wish I knew." Kate settled down in the seat, closer to the meager draft from the air vent, and fanned her hair up off her neck. "Mother didn't like to go downtown. She had some friends in the old 'nice' part of town, but she didn't like driving through the ghetto to get there. And she did some volunteer work for the battered women's shelter over on First Street. Mostly she worked on fund raising, but sometimes they called her to pick up a woman in trouble and deliver her to the shelter."

"Did she go alone?"

"Uncle Miles usually rode along with her. It was one of the few things that would get him out of the house, especially at night."

He thought for a minute. "That's pretty tough work for a nice lady of means."

"Mother was no cream puff. You know who my grandfather was?"

"Sure. Every cop knew Archie Byrd."

"Well, he and Mother had a lot in common."

He laughed. "That tells me a lot. The first time I saw him in action he was pretty old and frail. I was a rookie on the force, just out of college, sure that in our system of justice the good guys always won. One of my first court appearances I testified against one of Mr. Byrd's less wholesome clients. He taught me more about the real world that day than I learned in six months patrolling the streets. I felt ... disemboweled. A person like Archie could collect some powerful enemies during a life-time.''

"Powerful enough to murder?'' she asked.

"What's going on here is strictly amateur hour,'' he said. "In Archie's league folks weren't so sloppy.''

"Sloppy, huh?'' She rubbed her sore shoulder gently. "I'm glad Mother never made it to the big league, then.''

Tejeda turned off the main street into a tract of neat, post-war stucco houses. He followed what seemed, to Kate, to be an impossible maze of nearly identical tree-shaded streets. It was a quiet, well-cared-for neighborhood, the sort of area where children could go outside to play or trick-or-treat on Hallow-een without their parents worrying much. Kate imagined mothers swapping offspring with each other for quick trips to the market or P.T.A. meetings. It gave her a nice feeling, a sense of safety, and she didn't know if there was something about the set of the houses and the big old trees that made her feel that way, or if it was just being with Tejeda.

Tejeda pulled to the curb and stopped in front of a beige house. She noticed the lawn was browner around the edges than any of its neighbors, and needed a good trimming.

He opened his car door. "I'll only be a second. Come on in.''

"You live here?''

"Yes.''

She glanced down at her sandy feet and baggy shirt. "You promised no one would see me.''

"It's okay. No one's home.'' He collected his wad of clothes and waited for her. She followed him into the house, her nat-ural reticence giving way to curiosity about Tejeda's private life.

Tejeda dumped his clothes in a heap in an overstuffed arm-chair and scooped the morning paper off its twin. "Have a seat. Back in a sec.''

He left the room through an adjoining dining room. She could hear him walking through another room, pausing, then coming back.

"Heads up,'' he said as he tossed her a cold can of Diet 7-Up.

"Diet, huh? You trying to tell me something?'' She moved away from the furniture to open the can, holding it at arm's length to avoid the explosion of spray after the can's flight across the room.

"Relax, put your feet up," he said, heading toward a hall door. "I need to change."

Careful not to brush her sandy legs against anything, Kate sat on the edge of a chair and looked around the room. The furniture, in tones of blue and beige, looked as if it had been lifted intact from a department store display and reassembled here to fill the space. She wondered if Tejeda had called Bullock's and said he had a fourteen-by-fourteen-foot room, please send something over. Everything was so carefully coordinated that the room would have had a shrinelike quality, she thought, if it weren't for the shoe polish kit and three shoes on the coffee table, the pyramid of diet-soda cans on the hearth, and the liberal salting of dust everywhere.

On the end table beside her, eight fat bullets filled a small brass ashtray. At first, they bothered her. She knew policemen carried guns, but the reality the bullets represented was unsettling. Being with Tejeda didn't seem as safe anymore.

Oddly fascinated, she picked up a bullet and weighed its cold heaviness in her palm. She remembered the neat, red hole the shell from Uncle Miles's hunting rifle had made between the eyes of a tall-antlered Colorado elk. The bullet in her hand was much smaller than the long rifle shells, but it seemed more dangerous, designed as it was for human prey. Using only thumb and index finger, like tweezers, she picked up the bullets one at a time and set them down on the table on their flat ends, until they were in a straight row aimed at the ceiling like a battery of missiles. Then she tapped the end one and they toppled like dominoes, pinwheeling as they rolled around on the tabletop.

Kate settled back in the chair and drank the rest of her soda. When the can was empty she got up and added it to the top of the pyramid on the hearth.

The telephone on a little table by the hall door jingled a few times, someone dialing on an extension. She could hear water running, cupboard doors slamming, but no conversation. If Tejeda was talking to someone, he was keeping his voice low.

Kate felt drawn toward the telephone, knowing that the conversation somehow concerned her. She was trying to resist the compulsion to pick up the receiver, when it rang. Once. Feeling like a burglar caught in the act, she sprinted back to her chair and sat there in guilty silence.

Tejeda must have been waiting for the call, she thought, he answered it so quickly. Whatever, it was a short conversation; in moments, he was back in the room with her.

The change in him made her sit up. She felt again the impact of his attractiveness, but the slightly cocky, flirty cant to his posture was gone. He seemed stern, a bit angry even.

She smiled at him. "You're fast."

"When I have to be." His freshly washed hair was combed up away from his face, sharpening the angles of his high cheekbones and lending him a certain air of Indian dignity. As he straightened the lapels of his well-tailored, summer-weight gray suit, she looked for some reminder of the man who had rolled up his trousers to run with her on the beach. She thought she had lost him, until she noticed that damp tendrils of hair on his neck darkened the crisp edge of his pale blue shirt collar, spoiling its perfection.

"You look nice," she said.

"Thank you."

She tried again to find her way through his stern facade. "I suppose that means we aren't going running."

He didn't return her smile. He watched her as he straightened his tie, his eyes narrowed. "I just can't figure you out. Sometimes you're so, well, accessible. But I think you're stonewalling. What I need to know about the people around you and your mother I think only you can tell me. But you hold back." His voice was soft, but she felt its cutting edge. "You tried to deflect me earlier, to send me off after an alleged bastard and after old Sy Ratcher. I know, the whole town knows, your mother was trying to have your Uncle Miles put away. A lot of people were madder than hell about it. Isn't that a more likely territory to explore?"

"Maybe." She looked down at her hand on the arm of the chair, noting how her tan almost matched the center of one of the flowers in the upholstery pattern. She traced the outline of the flower with her fingernail, a diversion to keep from meeting his eyes.

He sat down on the arm of the chair close to her hand, his legs interrupting her tracing. "Maybe?"

"Maybe it's something I'm not ready to face," she said, feeling angry at him for no good reason she could identify. "Anyone who might kill Mother to protect Miles has to be someone pretty close. I'm not sure I want to know who."

"Could be Miles himself."

"No way." She cocked her head to look up at him.

"Your mother was a big threat to his freedom."

"But I'm not."

"Were you helping her get conservatorship?"

"You mean does he need to kill me, too? No. I thought what Mother was doing stank, and he knows it. She tried to use me at first, said she was only acting to protect my inheritance. But I defused her by entrusting all my interests to Dolph, as, in practice, Miles had."

"That didn't stop her, though, did it?"

"No."

"What did she want?"

"Power. She had influence; she got a lot of people together so they could get business deals going. They'd thank her, sometimes give her presents, but she'd be shut out of the real decision making. It galled her. I think she might have been trying to put together something on her own. That's why I told you about Sy Ratcher. He might have been involved."

"Ratcher is a pipsqueak, operates in a muzzy area somewhere beyond the letter of the law. Your mother would work with him?"

"She might. He's sort of an old family friend."

"I'll check him out," Tejeda shrugged. "Since Dolph had charge of the whole pile, your mother was a bigger threat to him than anyone."

"I suppose. But he quietly blocked her at every turn. That's why she went to the press. She tried to pass herself off as a poor, dispossessed widow trying to protect her sick brother-in-law, but it backfired. People in this town have a lot of respect for Dolph. And for Miles."

"What about your mother? She must have had some support. Who were her close friends?"

"Close friends?" Kate paused to think. It was a sad business, trying to find anyone really close to Mother. "Mina, of course, because she was family. And me, I guess, though she was pretty mad at me. She spent a lot of time with Uncle Miles out of a sense of duty."

"No one outside the family?"

"Mother had a way of alienating people," Kate said. "She had a big social circle. But no one was really close."

"No one?" He seemed skeptical.

"A long time ago Mother, Mina and Susan Ratcher..."

"Sy Ratcher's wife?" he interrupted.

"No. His stepmother. Anyway, the three women spent a lot of time together. They were in school together, their fathers were partners in a stock brokerage, they married three brothers. Though they drifted apart over the years, I think there was still a bond between them, in spite of all their hardships."

"What hardships?" Tejeda asked.

"Besides the usual deaths, divorces, and squabbles, there was a big scandal in their fathers' stock brokerage. Happened about the time they finished school. A lot of money disappeared."

"Where'd it go?"

"The way the three families hung together, I suspect they all took a share. But, in the end, Mina's father got the worst of it."

"Why?"

"He was the only one who actually went to prison, died there a few years later. My mother's father committed suicide before they went to trial, and Susan's father made a deal, gave some evidence I think, and he got off with a fine."

"Their fathers shafted one another, but the girls stayed together?"

"Sure," Kate smiled grimly. "My other grandfather, Grandpa Archie, was the defense attorney. When he lost, he gave the girls each a consolation prize."

"What was it?"

"A son to marry when the scandal had destroyed their prospects."

"Just the same," he smiled, relaxing back toward the personality she was more familiar with, "you'd expect some resentment among the women."

"No." Kate shook her head. "They were all in the same boat, victims of the same crime."

"Dammit!" He hit his hand with a fist. "You did it again. Every time I try to get you to tell me why someone might want to get at your mother, you tell me why he or she wouldn't."

She looked at him. "I can't tell, are you really mad or what?"

"What do you think?"

"I don't know. I'm just trying to figure out what I'm doing here. You're certainly not what I expected from a detective. One minute we're running on the beach, the next we're sitting around your living room and I'm getting the third degree. I'm half-expecting six dancing dwarfs and seduction by a band of gypsies."

He looked at his watch. "We don't have time for seduction."

"*Ab*duction." She felt her cheeks redden. "I meant *ab*duction."

"Either way, we don't have time for it. You ready to go?"

She stood up. "Go where?"

"Your house, of course."

"With you, one never knows."

Tejeda held the front door open for Kate, then closed and carefully locked it after them. Twirling the key ring on his finger he walked beside her to the car. "Abduction? Freud said there are no mistakes."

"Freud was mistaken," she said, getting into the car.

"Could be." Tejeda went around to the back of the car and unlocked the trunk. In the crack between the car body and the open trunk lid she could see him, a strip of shirt, a flash of dark blue tie, but she couldn't see what he was doing. The trunk closed with a whoosh, bouncing the car. He came back to her side of the car cradling something behind the crook of one arm.

"Hold on a sec," he said, opening Kate's door. He squatted in the opening, the door shielding him while he opened his suit coat and tucked a revolver into his shoulder holster.

"Are we gunning for somebody?"

"No." He checked his watch again, covering some embarrassment, she thought. "It's my kid. First day of the new term they let them out early. I just want to make sure her first day went all right."

"Your kid? Is that what we're doing here?"

"Sure," he said, standing up. "What'd you think this was, an abduction?"

An electronic bell shattered the stillness. Kate looked around for its source, and noticed for the first time the school at the far end of the block. Almost immediately, young teenagers came swarming out of the school gates, making irregular progress toward the street, stopping to make contact with someone, then racing to catch up with someone else, like a wave hitting the pilings of a pier before rushing to the beach.

Tejeda adjusted his jacket over the holster and shut the door. Hands thrust deep in his pockets, he walked slowly around to the front of the car, watching the emerging children carefully. He straightened as a small cluster of girls came swinging out of the schoolyard.

Kate strained forward to watch them. All in new, first-day-of-school outfits, their little girl bodies were perched atop long gangly legs, and anchored to the sidewalk by woman-sized feet, as if they were growing from the ground up. Kate smiled to herself, remembering how she had hated private school uniforms and had longed for the freedom to dress like the girls in public school. Though they offered a rainbow splash of color, these girls seemed just as much alike as she remembered the girls in uniforms looking.

A small girl with long black hair spotted Tejeda and detached herself, amoebalike, from the group. She came down the sidewalk, hair swinging in syncopation with her quick step. As if straining to hold himself back, Tejeda began to walk slowly to meet her.

"Daddy, what are you doing here?" Kate heard her say in a voice that failed to disguise its pleasure.

Tejeda bent and kissed the top of her gleaming head. The girl made a quick glance around to see if anyone was watching, as if unsure whether she should be pleased or embarrassed by the presence of her father. Tejeda relieved her of an untidy stack of books and papers. He made a mock-serious face as he aligned the edges of her stack before handing it back. Hands thrust deep in his pockets again, he walked with her until they were abreast of Kate's car window.

"Theresa, this is Mrs. Teague."

Theresa gave Kate an open appraisal with big eyes, duplicates of her father's. "Hi."

"Hello." Kate smiled, imagining what the girl must be thinking, to see this grubby-looking woman with a black eye and assorted bruises and abrasions in her father's car.

Tejeda gave the child a gentle shove. "Get along. Remember, no TV till you get the algebra done."

"Yeah, Daddy." She hooked a new-looking gym bag over her shoulder, then gave Kate one last survey before turning toward a trim green house with a tricycle on its patch of lawn.

"Hey you," he called to her back. "No soda pop at Mrs. Murphy's."

"Aw, Dad."

"It gives you zits."

She flipped her hair and disappeared into the house. Tejeda watched the door for a few moments, a softness in his eyes before turning back to Kate.

"Great kid," he said, getting into the car.

"With this shiner, she probably thinks I'm a criminal on the way to the slammer."

He chuckled. "That, or something worse. She has a cinematic imagination."

"Is she your only child?"

"No. My boy's a freshman at UC Santa Barbara, majoring in marine biology and surfing."

"You have custody of Theresa?"

"Sure."

It intrigued Kate. "Is your ex-wife away working?"

"No." Tejeda pulled into the stream of station wagons flowing from in front of the school. "Oh, well, maybe. I don't know what she's doing right now. She divorced Theresa and me a year ago. Last I heard from her she was heavily *into* Hopi mysticism." He smiled grimly at Kate. "Adolescence is a piece of cake next to the forties."

Kate saw a shadow of pain in his smile, like a vein of ore, a bump on the surface that runs deep into the earth. There was something about his silence, as if he were waiting for her to make the next move, to continue the subject or drop it. She cleared her throat. "Adolescence is a hard time for a girl to be without a mother."

"Theresa's okay. In fact, I think she's handled it a whole lot better than I have. She's found a sort of mother-substitute next door. She goes to Mrs. Murphy's every day 'til I get home. Mrs. Murphy has a new baby and a two-year-old. Theresa helps out and Mrs. Murphy mothers her a little in return."

"Sounds like a good arrangement," Kate said.

"Yeah. You know what's been the hardest part?"

She hesitated a moment, expecting him to say something about the cold side of the bed at night. "What?"

"Food. Neither of us can cook." When Kate laughed, he smiled. "What was hardest for you?"

"Swallowing my pride and moving in with my mother."

"You didn't have to," he said. "You could have afforded a place of your own."

"Sure. But I wanted to keep an eye on her. And there was another problem."

"What?"

"I can't cook."

His laugh was a short bark. "Did he get custody of the cook?"

"He *was* the cook."

"Life's tough." Tejeda turned onto Ocean Boulevard, forcing his smog-controlled car to overtake a city bus. When the car had stopped pinging, he gave the seat beside Kate a tentative pat. "Thanks for coming along. You're a good sport. We could have played it by the book and waited at your place for the surveillance guy to show up. But lately, Theresa needs to know I'm there for her."

"I understand," Kate said. She admired the love he had for his daughter, but it also hit that sore spot in her that longed for a child. A siren wail, like a baby crying at first, broke into her thoughts and upset the quiet of the beach front.

Tejeda slowed around the last curve before her house. "Gate's open," he said. "I told Green to keep it closed."

Kate looked up. "The gates move slowly. Someone probably just came in or went out. Or they're expecting somebody."

The siren caught up to them. An ambulance, its bulk swaying precariously as it sped around the curve behind them, gave three sharp warning blasts on its horn.

Getting out of its way, Tejeda pulled through the open gates and into the courtyard with a sharp jerk of the wheel. The force knocked Kate's battered shoulder painfully against the door. But the panicky sound of the siren stuck with them, following dangerously close behind them as if to push through the gate.

Tejeda pulled to the curb directly in front of Kate's house, and the ambulance passed, braking to a stop in front of them. The sound of the siren wound down from a whine to flat groan, and that's when Kate heard Esperanza, crying as she ran frantically across the lawn toward them.

Tejeda was out of the car and sprinting toward Esperanza before the engine had stopped. He caught her by the arms and was talking to her while Kate, awkward in her terror, fumbled ineffectually with the door handle. Finally, she was out of the car, but she stood frozen on the shimmering hot bricks, not wanting, for an instant, to know what horrible thing had happened.

Two ambulance attendants brushed past Kate, nearly colliding with her. Following them, like a cyclist in a jet stream, she ran to Esperanza.

"It's Mr. Miles," Esperanza sobbed, dropping to her knees in anguish. "He is dying."

SEVEN

"HE WAS FINE this morning." Mina punctuated with a cardboard cup of vending machine coffee, her angst apparent with the ever-higher waves of tepid coffee sloshing over the rim. "We talked, had a nice gossip, a little reminiscing. He seemed just fine. I can't understand this. Damn!"

Taking advantage of a lull between gestures, Kate took the cup from her aunt's hand and put it down in its puddle on the cold hospital floor. "Last night he said he was a little dizzy. I wish I hadn't let him talk me out of calling the doctor."

"But this morning he was great," Mina said. "Not dopey like he is sometimes when he's on heavy medication. He was more like his old self than I've seen him for a long time. Then when Esperanza took his lunch to him as usual, there he was, dead to the world. God, he looked so awful." Mina looked a little ill herself. "I don't know how much more we can take, Kate. First your mother. Now this."

"Do you believe bad luck comes in threes?" Kate touched the bruise under her eye.

Mina put her face close to Kate's, all the pixie sweetness turned down in a frown as she gave a close examination. "Watch out, someone around here is likely to mistake you for a casualty case and find you a bed. Didn't the leeches work?"

"Not you, too?" Kate groaned. She leaned back against the slick plastic chair. "God, I hate this place. The 'dying place' I used to call it. I remember sitting here with Mother, day after day, waiting for Daddy to die."

"You were barely five years old." Mina took Kate's hand. "You remember that?"

"I wish I could forget. Miles and Mother took me in to see him, to say good-bye." She shivered involuntarily, thinking about it. He'd been unbelievably pale, ghostlike, yellow from the cancer eating his liver. In her mind's camera she had two pictures of him, one of the big, handsome, forever-sunburned sportsman, the other the wasted figure sunken in a high white bed. Somehow, his ocher-tinged face merged with Mother's as Kate had last seen her in the morgue downstairs. The dying place. Kate squirmed irritably in her chair. "What's keeping Dolph and Carl? They've been talking with the doctors a long time."

"We don't have to sit here," Mina said. "Let's go down to the cafeteria. The nurse can page us there."

"Give them five more minutes."

She leaned back and waited for what seemed like an eternity, watching the long, empty corridor beyond the intensive care waiting room, expecting every shadow to be Dolph and Carl with news about Miles. A succession of nurses and orderlies crossed her line of vision, and with each she tensed, then sat back, disappointed. Finally two vague shapes appeared outlined in front of the hot white window at the end of the corridor. They moved amorphously toward her, their reflections shimmering on the polished floor like a mirage. She wanted so much for it to be Carl and Dolph that she couldn't trust her eyes when they loomed out of the white background together. Only when she heard Carl's voice as he spoke quietly to Dolph could she believe he was more than a mirage.

Rising, she reached out for Carl to hurry his approach. The realness of his hot, rough tweed coat as he embraced her was beautifully comforting. Her gesture had been impulsive, something akin to muscle memory, but when he kissed her she knew he had misinterpreted it as an expression of affection. Then she felt slightly abashed, as if she had taken something from him under false pretenses. Nervously, she patted the front of his jacket. "What's the word?"

Carl held her hand against his chest. "Looks like a grand mal seizure, but he might have taken something. He's in a coma. We'll know more when he comes around."

"*When* he comes around?" Kate asked for reassurance.

"If." Carl shrugged. "It's too early to tell. May have some heart complications. Could be a long wait. Dolph, do you want to take Mina home? I have to be downtown before City Hall closes, but I can stay here with Kate for a while, just in case."

As if weighted with grief, Dolph sat down beside Mina, taking her tenderly in his arms. They looked so sweet together,

Kate thought, so much a part of each other. Before long she would come here to perform this death watch for one of them, and she had to swallow the tearful lump in her throat. Which one first, she wondered? But it was too hard to imagine Dolph or Mina living without the other.

"Shall we go, Mina dear?" Dolph asked.

"Not yet," Mina said. "I want to stay. I want to be here when he wakes up."

"Sweetheart," Dolph said, "it could be weeks."

"So?" She was firm. "If it's all the same to you, I'll wait. He'd be scared to death if he woke up alone in this place. He'd think we'd committed him again."

A warm hand gripped Kate's shoulder from behind. She turned, half-expecting it to be Lieutenant Tejeda, who had disappeared after he'd driven her to the hospital. Instead, Esperanza stood there, framed against the empty hall beyond.

"I will wait here tonight," Esperanza announced. "You all go home and eat the dinner I left for you."

Kate kissed her lightly, feeling relieved of a great burden. "Are you sure?"

"Of course. You see," she said, pulling a thermos and a book out of her large handbag. "I am prepared for the night. You go. I will call you if there is anything to tell you."

"You're an angel," Kate said gratefully.

"And you," Esperanza scolded Kate, "are in not so good shape yourself. You-know-what are in their jar under the kitchen sink, waiting for you."

"Who's under the sink?" Carl asked.

"Never mind," Kate said. "Let's go."

Kate walked out into the dull sunshine beside Carl. Whenever they stopped or turned a corner or stepped over a curb, he would hold her arm or touch her hand. He was being very solicitous and she went along with him, testing a little for the substance that bound Dolph and Mina together.

"Do you feel like eating something?" Carl asked, unlocking the door of his ancient sports car.

"It's too hot to think about food." Kate folded herself into the low-slung car. "It's those damned brush fires. Everything tastes like ash."

"I have to stop by City Hall to pick up some documents. Come with me. Maybe you'll be hungry by the time I finish."

"Can't you send a clerk in your place?"

"Next time," he said over the roar of the rebuilt engine. "It impresses hell out of some of those mid-level bureaucrats to have a personal visit. When they think we're good buddies, I can send a clerk."

"I thought you left the politics of law behind when you left the D.A."

"Politics is what makes law interesting."

"Ah," she sighed, the mood broken by the turn of the conversation. "Should we stop and get your mother before we eat?"

"She has plans for dinner."

"Oh?"

He looked uncomfortable. "She has a date."

"You're kidding. Who?"

"I don't know." He pulled into the public lot behind the Civic Center. "Trust my old ma. She can always turn up something." He slid out of the car. "I'll only be a minute."

"It's too hot to wait here. I'll walk up with you."

He hesitated just an instant too long, his eyes fixed on the blue smudge under her eye. "I'll only be ten minutes."

"That's too long in this heat. I'll wait in the library."

"Suit yourself."

They parted at the main entrance of Santa Angelica's pink-stucco, W.P.A.-era City Hall. Kate waved, then walked across the quad to the new pyramid-shaped main branch of the city library.

The main floor was nearly deserted. Kate descended the central stairway and walked slowly into the history section, waiting for the air-conditioning to cool her. She pulled a familiar old volume off a high shelf and took it to a table. She thumbed through the book, enjoying the earthy smell that was equal parts dust and decaying paper. A movement at her side made her look up.

Lieutenant Tejeda leaned against the table.

"I wondered where you'd got to," she said, not surprised to see him. She had sensed him nearby all afternoon. "Did you follow me here?"

"Of course," he smiled. "You're under protective surveillance, remember? Actually, I saw you leaving the hospital so I headed back to the station. You pulled in right in front of me. I thought you might be coming to see me."

"In the library?"

"The police station is next door, right?" His smile was crooked, teasing. "I told you, I followed you."

"And?" She closed the book and folded her hands on top of it.

"How's your uncle?"

"Comatose."

"How are you holding up?"

"Okay."

"You look okay," he said, settling one hip on the edge of the table. His face became serious. "I got back some reports I ordered. We need to talk about some things. I know this is rotten timing, but I can't wait around anymore."

"We can't talk here," she looked across the silent library.

Tejeda led the way outside, up out of the Civic Center into the neighboring park. The air was stifling after the cool library. Tejeda led her into a shady recess in a little Japanese garden.

"It's nice here," Kate said. "I didn't know there was such a place."

"Hardly anyone comes here. It's a good place to talk."

"What do you want to talk about?"

"I don't know if this has any connection with what has been going on," he said, "but I have to run it by you." He pulled out his notebook and opened it.

"On October third, nineteen seventy-two, Katherine Byrd, you," he looked up at Kate accusingly, "and Esperanza Ruiz y Garcia were charged with illegal transportation of a corpse across international boundaries."

"So?"

"The corpse was the remains of one Nugent Kennerly." He looked up at her again, watching for her reaction. "The charges were dropped but you were deprived of your passport for a period of five years. A hand slap. You going to tell me about it?"

"It doesn't concern you. It's been more than a dozen years."

"Your husband mentioned Kennerly only this morning. Let me decide if it's important."

"Leave it alone. Please."

"Hey, look. I can go downtown and get the details. But the press follows pretty close behind me. Do you want to risk that?"

"You're threatening me."

"Damn right. I don't want to drag up something that will embarrass you. So you can tell me about it yourself or I can dig it up from other sources."

She sat down hard on the dry grass. It scratched her bare legs. Might as well tell him the whole sordid story, she decided. Everything was a matter of record anyway.

"Nugie was Mina's niece." She looked up at him, squinting against the sun behind him. "You know Reece?"

Tejeda nodded.

"Nugie was his sister. They're related to us through Mina. Sort of shirttail relatives." She couldn't see his expression very well against the glare. "Nugie and I were sharing an apartment up in Westwood. She was doing student teaching and I was in graduate school at UCLA. She got pregnant and it was a real disaster. She didn't want to go through with the pregnancy. Abortion wasn't legal here yet, so she asked me to go to Mexico with her."

"And Esperanza went along?"

"More like we went with her. She knew about a clinic in Ensenada that did clean abortions. So we went. Esperanza was our guide and translator." Kate pulled out a tuft of dry grass and toyed with it, something to do with her hands.

"Nugie had the abortion," she continued. "We wanted her to stay in the clinic overnight, but she was frightened and ashamed. She wanted to go home. The doctor said she was fine. He gave her a sedative and we made her a bed in the back seat of the car and she went to sleep."

"When we got to the border at Tijuana, we stopped and Esperanza checked her. She raised the blanket," Kate stopped and tried to collect enough saliva in her dry mouth to swallow. "Blood," she said. "The seat was covered."

"We woke her up. She was so cold." It hurt so much to talk about it, to remember beautiful Nugie dying as Kate tried in vain to hurry, as ragged children clung at the car windows, trying to sell chewing gum and bright paper flowers. She looked down at the dry grass in her hand. "We told Nugie we were going to take her to a hospital in Tijuana and she got hysterical. We were already at the border so we decided it was just as fast to cross and find a place than to look for something there. We went to a hospital in National City. It took less than ten minutes. But," she swallowed, "she was dead when we got there."

"What did you do?" He sat down next to her on the grass, leaving a little space between them, but not much.

She was surprised how easy it was to tell him. As before, he listened with intensity, with acceptance. She had never been able to tell anyone about Nugie, relying on Esperanza and her uncle to deal with the authorities. It had been the worst situation she was ever involved in and she had put it away, or tried to. Talking about it now she realized how close to the surface the whole painful memory was. Lieutenant Tejeda was looking at her, the brown eyes soft. She remembered how he had looked at his daughter and she wanted to lean her head against his shoulder and be comforted.

A group of little old men all dressed in white walked past on their way to the lawn bowls green. They looked at Kate and Tejeda with rude interest. It embarrassed Kate, making her feel as if she had been caught kissing in the park by her grandfather's cronies.

She stood up, brushing off the grass. "Carl has probably finished his business. I'd better go find him. He doesn't like to be kept waiting."

Tejeda stood up and they walked back toward the library. "I asked you what you did when your friend died."

"The police were there right away," she said after taking a deep breath. "It wasn't the first Mexican abortion they had seen go sour. They were debating what charges to book us on. So I called my uncle and he flew down. He was there within the hour. He was great."

"Your Uncle Dolph came down and bailed you out?"

"No." She was surprised by his assumption. "It was always Uncle Miles who bailed me out."

"*Always* bailed you out?"

"Figuratively. You know, overdrawn at the bank, needed his secretary to type a late term paper."

"Jailed in an antiwar demonstration."

She caught her breath. "Either you're a good guesser or you've done some heavy-duty checking. Miles had that record expunged."

"I have my sources." He looked down at her, holding her eyes with his own. "You chalked that one up to the follies of youth, I suppose."

"Protesting Vietnam was no folly," she bristled. She couldn't understand why his remark made her so angry, unless it was because he had already stripped away a few layers of her defenses. Something about him made her feel exposed, naked of protective coloration. She met his steady gaze.

"Don't tell *me* about it."

Through the flash of anger she caught a glimpse of the passion of the inner man. He took a deep breath and looked down, chagrined, a rush of color on his cheeks. "Forget it. So. You were going to tell me what happened when your uncle got to National City."

His hands were in his pockets. She slipped one hand in behind his, her fingertips on the exposed wrist at the end of his cuff, where his pulse beat faintly. "Tough guy," she said, bending her head so she could see his face. "Just the facts, ma'am."

Keeping his chin down he looked up at her through his lashes. A shy smile rounded the corners of his mouth. "You going to tell me the story, or what?"

"Not much more to tell," she said, squeezing his wrist gently before taking her hand away. "The police down there wanted to book us for negligent homicide or involuntary manslaughter or being party to an illegal action, the abortion. They were being really hard-nosed. Uncle Miles persuaded them to charge us only with transporting Nugie's body, though I know she wasn't dead when we crossed the border."

"The judge was very understanding about us not wanting to get entangled in the Mexican legal system and wanting to bring Nugie's body back to her family."

"So he took your passport as a hand slap. What happened to Esperanza?"

"She was in my mother's employ. He assumed we had just dragged her along as the faithful retainer. He dismissed her charges."

"Carl was the father?"

"How did you know?" She wasn't surprised at anything he knew anymore.

"That's the message I got from him this morning. This was before you were married?"

"Of course," she said. "I introduced Carl to Nugie. We got together later more or less because of what happened in Mexico." As Kate walked she crumbled little bits of brown grass between her fingers and let them drop onto the pavement, leaving a trail behind her, as if she might want to retrace her steps later.

"Carl had offered to marry Nugie," she said. She brushed her hands together. "The abortion was her idea. Nugie didn't want to force him into something. She didn't tell anyone in the family that she was pregnant with his baby."

"And you don't want them to know."

"What's the point? Anyway, none of this has any bearing on Mother's death."

"We'll see." He put a stick of gum in his mouth. "Damn," he said, spitting the wad back into its wrapper and tossing it into a trash can. "I need a cigarette. Theresa made me quit."

"Kate!" Carl's voice close beside her made her jump. "I was wondering what happened to you." He acknowledged the detective. "Lieutenant Tejeda."

Kate wondered how long Carl had been watching them. She noticed that, all of a sudden, the space between her and Tejeda widened. She looked up at Carl. "Are you ready to go?"

"If Lieutenant Tejeda's finished with you."

Tejeda nodded. "I was grilling her about her criminal past, her record as a campus radical."

Carl looked between them. "Did she tell you that's how we met? Her uncle hired me to defend her after a Vietnam Day rally." He edited the part about Nugie.

"Interesting," Tejeda said. He walked on the other side of Kate, like three old friends out for a stroll. "Anything more about Mr. Byrd's condition? Have they decided what happened?"

"I called in just a minute ago. Looks like a grand mal seizure." Carl leaned slightly in front of Kate to answer, physically taking charge. "Maybe drug related. We won't know until the tests come back."

Kate's hands balled into involuntary fists. "They're not thinking suicide are they?"

"No. Maybe he just miscalculated his Dilantin. Or forgot to take it."

"He's epileptic?" Tejeda asked.

"Yes," Kate said. "Since his last series of shock treatments he's had a few seizures. Usually when he's under stress. He's never had one like this before, though."

"Rough going," Tejeda said. "Are you heading back to the hospital?"

"No." Kate said firmly. "I was promised dinner. If it's all right with you, Lieutenant, we'll go."

"Sure," Tejeda said easily. "I'll be in touch." He waved then turned and walked with his easy stride toward the turquoise-faced police building.

Carl's old car shimmered with heat. "Do you really want dinner?" he asked, opening the car door for her.

"No. Let's just go home." She groaned as she eased herself down on the scorching seat. "Why don't you sell this heap and buy something more civilized? Lord knows you can afford better."

Carl nosed into evening traffic. "This car is part of my image."

"Oh, bull, Carl. This car is fifteen years old and hardly a classic. Wouldn't your image be better fortified if you had something decent?"

"If I bought what I can afford," Carl said, smiling broadly, "anyone could peg my income and position. If I bought something better than I can afford, I might be accused of buying what *you* can afford. As it is, everyone knows I can afford something better than I have, but what that might be they can only speculate."

"You amaze me. Aren't you straightforward about anything?"

He just smiled. "So what did the lieutenant want this time?"

"He was asking about Nugie."

Carl made a quick, wild swerve to the right, straightening just before he hit the curb. "Oh?"

"Don't worry about it." She turned away and watched boats sailing coolly toward the downtown marina and wondered how they found enough breeze to move. For once, the heavy stand of eucalyptus offered no relief as they drove in through the gates.

With some screeching of worn disc-brakes, Carl stopped in the courtyard. Grim, white lines framed his mouth. "There's nothing like smog to make a beautiful sunset, is there?"

"Gorgeous," Kate said, watching the luminous red horizon. Almost as reflex, she glanced toward the window where Miles always kept watch over the courtyard.

"Carl. Look!" she gasped. As she watched, the heavy drapes drew to one side. Then swayed back into place.

EIGHT

"I KNOW SOMEONE was in here when we drove up." Kate said firmly. "Whoever it was has probably left by now."

"We'll check it out anyway." Carl unlocked Miles's door with a key from Kate's ring. "I'm glad you didn't want to go in by yourself."

"After last night I'm afraid to go to the john by myself."

Carl slowly pushed open the heavy oak door, peering around the edge of the door as he felt the wall for the light switch. "Wait here." He motioned her back with a wave of his hand. "I'll take a look around."

"I saw that movie," Kate said, brushing past him. "The heroine got axed while she waited. I'm coming with you." Propelled more by curiosity than fear, she crossed the foyer and preceded Carl into the musty living room where Miles spent most of his time. The room was as she had seen it last; formally furnished with old but good pieces waxed and polished to a rich glow. Like a museum set-piece, it was lacking in personality, without framed portraits or mementoes or little treasures to give clues about the man who lived here. Except for the crossed cricket bats over the mantel.

Carl went over to the window where Miles usually stood to look out on the courtyard. The edge of the drapes had a faint greasy grayness where Miles held them. "Is this where you saw something?"

"Yes."

"*If* someone was in here, I hope he's had the sense to vacate by now. We better take a look around anyway. Aha!" He reached up and unhooked one of the cricket bats, weighing it in his hands like a club. "This's what we need. Just in case. You coming with me, Sherlock?"

"Right. Shall we check the doors first?"

"Lead the way. I don't know my way around in here."

"Just stay close," she said.

"Would I let you down?"

"No comment. Back door's this way." She led him through the still, tomb-cold dining room. As they opened the swing door to the kitchen, they could feel a warm breeze coming from the butler's pantry. The back door stood halfway open. "I hope this means he left."

Carl raised the bat to his shoulder and peered cautiously around the door. "Paramedics probably left it open when they took Miles."

"No," Kate said. "Lieutenant Tejeda and I locked up before we went to the hospital. Let's call the police."

"We don't have anything to tell them, yet." Carl weighed the bat in his hands. "Who played cricket?"

"They all did." Kate tried the doors of the silver cabinet. They were locked. "Miles and Dolph and all their friends. They used to come and play on the bluff and drink pin gin all day."

He smirked. "I can't imagine Miles and Dolph moving around fast enough."

"It was a long time ago." She led Carl across the hall to Miles's study. Everything seemed orderly. "Dolph played only when they were a man short, but Miles was the crack batsman. A leftover from his years at Oxford."

"Civilized." He followed her down the hall towards Miles's bedroom. "Doesn't look like anyone's been in here. Maybe you saw the wind blow the curtains."

"Could be." She was looking over her shoulder at Carl as she opened the bedroom door.

"Oh, shit!" He grabbed her by the arm and pulled her back. The room was in chaos, every drawer pulled out and dumped, their paper liners ripped out and wadded. "Don't go in."

"Let go of me. I want to call Tejeda." Kate pulled her arm free and rubbed it where Carl's fingers had dug into the flesh. Dodging around the jumble on the floor she found the telephone and dialed 911 and left a message for Tejeda. Hands on hips, she surveyed the mess. She felt drained, defeated; it was such a frighteningly brutal intrusion into Miles's carefully guarded private world. She looked up at Carl. "What could they have been looking for?"

"Who knows? Don't touch anything else in here. We'd better give the rest of the house a quick look-see in case this spook is still around. You want to wait for your boyfriend down here?''

The remark cut, maybe because there was some emotional truth to it, made her feel a little like an unfaithful wife. She glared at Carl. "That was uncalled for."

"It was. Sorry." He took her hand. "Coming?"

"Damn right. I'm not staying in here alone." Kate led Carl through the massive house. "Most of the house is shut up. Miles will only let Esperanza in here to clean for him, so he moved downstairs into the maid's room to make it easier for her. I don't think he uses the upstairs at all."

"Great place to hide, then." Carl tried several switches on a wall panel before a dull light came on over the broad stairway.

Kate walked up the stairs one step ahead of him, scared, staying close enough to him to feel his breath on her neck. A combination of fear and his physical closeness, she felt deep inside, somewhere behind her breastbone, a stirring, like blowing on an ember banked for the night under cold ashes. She leaned back a little. His hand came to the back of her neck, warmth spreading beyond the span of his palm. It was confusing, her sudden need to be close to him again. She smiled at him, remembering the little gestures, overtures to lovemaking.

"You okay?" he squeezed her neck gently.

She nodded.

"Where do we begin?" He tried a few doorknobs. "Doors are locked."

"Shouldn't be a problem." Kate reached inside a tall cloisonne vase on a narrow table and groped around for the ring of old iron keys she knew was hidden there. She pulled them out and dusted them off on her skirt before she handed them to Carl. "Old family tradition, hiding the keys so everyone can find them."

Carl unlocked the doors leading into four completely bare rooms. "There's nothing up here for anyone to take," he said. "Looks like no one ever lived here."

"Let's check the master bedroom." Kate headed for the end of the hall and threw the double doors open. The enormous room was stuffed with heavy old furniture of a style popular forty years earlier. A choking layer of undisturbed dust blanketed tabletops, dimming the wedding photographs of Miles and Susan.

"Pretty spooky," Carl said. "Good place for a Halloween party."

"It's depressing."

Carl hugged her. "Looks like Miles closed off this part of his life."

"Or put it on hold. Remember the scene from *Great Expectations* when Pip sees the old lady's room with the decayed wedding feast? That's what this house looks like to me. It's as if Miles was waiting for someone. Or something."

"Like what?"

"I don't know."

"Well, no one's been lurking up here. No footprints in the dust." He closed the door behind them. "What happened to the rest of his furniture?"

"Maybe his marriage to Susan ended before there was any more than this." A soft thud from below stopped her. "What was that?"

Carl held her tight against him, raising the cricket bat. "Who's there?" he yelled.

"Mr. Teague? Mrs. Teague?" A voice from the direction of the stairs. "Police."

"We're upstairs. Be right down."

They hurried to the stairs, meeting a uniformed officer on the landing. His hand rested on the butt of his service revolver. "Back door's unlocked. Called to you but no one answered, so I came on in."

"You gave us a start." Carl led the way back down to Miles's room. "Take a look in here."

The officer surveyed the room, shaking his head. "You touch anything?"

"In here, just the telephone," Kate said. "We were waiting for you."

"Okay, Lieutenant's on his way over." This fact seemed to impress the young officer, and he paused a moment, waiting for their reaction before he continued. "Someplace else we can wait?"

"Come in the kitchen," Kate said. "You thirsty? I am. Maybe there's some Coke in the refrigerator. I'm hungry, too. Weren't we going to get some dinner?"

"Still talking about food?" Tejeda came through the back door just as they passed it. He wore an oversize T-shirt, white with black sleeves and "S.A.P.D." across the back, and baseball shoes with rubber cleats.

"Hello," Kate said. "Home team losing its star player?"

Tejeda laughed. "They won't even know I'm gone. What happened here?"

The uniformed officer straightened, snapping to military attention. "Looks like a four-o-eight, sir. Bedroom across the hall. I'll show you."

"Let's hold off a sec," Tejeda said. "Wait for the lab boys."

"You don't need us," Kate said. "Be okay if we scramble some eggs?"

Tejeda gave the kitchen a quick glance, then shrugged. "Doesn't look like anyone was in here. Go ahead."

"Can we get you something?" she asked as she opened the refrigerator.

The officer interrupted before he could answer. "Lab van's here."

Tejeda smiled at Kate. "We'll be in the other room."

Kate made eggs and toast for herself and Carl. They ate standing up at the kitchen counter, being very quiet so they could eavesdrop on the policemen working across the hall.

They could just hear snatches, as the lab men moved between the back door and the bedroom. A variety of voices, all apparently deferring to Tejeda.

"Good bolt, Lieutenant. No scratches on the lock."

"Had to be a key." Tejeda's voice. "Harvey?"

"Lots of prints. Lots of partials."

"It ain't here." A different voice boomed outside the door.

"Where is it?" Tejeda following.

Kate looked at Carl, his head cocked to one side, straining to hear. She laughed. "Don't break your neck. C'mon. You wash, I'll dry."

Tejeda came into the kitchen as she was putting the last plate away.

"Find anything?" Carl asked.

"Lost something," he said. "Did your uncle keep anything of particular value in his room?"

Kate thought for a moment. Miles was always so secretive, so insistent on his privacy. "I don't really know."

"From the looks of it, someone was looking for something specific. Left behind jewelry, a little cash, a TV."

"Sounds like Mother's purse," Kate said.

"Like that," he agreed, leaning against the counter and folding his arms. "Know what's missing."

"What?"

"A drawer from the nightstand."

"Full of loot, maybe?" Carl said.

"Could be. Either our burglar wanted everything in the drawer or he didn't have time to sort through it when you two came in, so he took the whole shebang." Tejeda sighed, looking tired. "Where does that get us? What do you keep in a nightstand drawer?"

"Books." Kate shrugged her shoulders. "Things you want during the night, or want to get in a hurry in case of emergency."

"Rubbers. Diaphragm," Carl said.

"Right," she elbowed him. "I was thinking of a flashlight, candles, the insurance man's card. What do you keep there, Lieutenant?"

He thought a minute. "My service revolver and the kids' christening pictures, you know, a little album. And the socks that don't have mates, just in case the washer kicks one back."

"We should go quiz the guys in the other room," Carl said. "This is fascinating. Probably broke in just to see what Miles kept there."

"Small things," Kate said, ignoring Carl. What Tejeda had said reminded her of something. "Small personal things like photographs. Did you find any photographs?"

Tejeda nodded. "A few."

"Show me." Kate felt excitement rising as Tejeda put a small carton on the kitchen table and carefully took out an old black leather album. She reached for it, then stopped. "What about fingerprints?"

"Go ahead," Tejeda said. "The paper's too old and porous to hold prints."

She leafed through the crumbly pages, looking for the rest of the woman and the boy with good postwar shoes. Miles had arranged the album chronologically, beginning with his year at Oxford, ending with a few baby pictures of Kate. The photographs were still firmly held in their black corners, but toward the back of the album, there were gaps. On the last page sixteen photo corners defined the spaces of four missing pictures. Lodged in one of the corners was the torn edge of a yellowed, black-and-white print. She flicked the tiny fragment loose and looked up at Carl.

"What do you think?" she asked. "About the same vintage as the one I found on the beach."

"How can you tell anything from that little bit?" he challenged.

"For one thing, I can come pretty close to its date; around nineteen fifty."

Tejeda leaned over her shoulder. "How can you know that?"

"Easy. That's when I was born. The empty page comes right after my first baby pictures. Look here," she said, carefully turning back to the middle of the album. "Here's the first gap. Beside it is Mina in her Ambulance Corps uniform, so it was taken before nineteen forty-five, during the war. There are two gaps on the next page and Dolph in his uniform hugging Mina. See the suitcases next to him? This is probably when he came back from Europe, about nineteen forty-six."

Kate turned two more pages. "Oh, my God! Look, it's Esperanza. Can you believe how skinny she was?"

"Esperanza?" Carl said. "I didn't know she'd worked here so long."

"She came when Mina and Dolph got married. I think she worked for Mina's family until Mina's father went to prison. But Grandpa somehow got her to switch, to come and work in his house to help take care of me when I was little."

"You're a pretty good detective, Mrs. Teague," Tejeda smiled. "What else can you tell us about the missing pictures?"

"I shouldn't tell you anything," Kate said, "after what you said today about our bastard. But, look here." She flipped the pages, showing that, until the end of the album, the gaps came in a fairly regular pattern. "My guess is that there's about a year between each lacuna, beginning in maybe nineteen forty-three or forty-four, about the time of our bastard's birth. My guess is they're birthday pictures of a little boy whose mother could afford good shoes."

Kate closed the album and handed it back to Tejeda. "Esperanza's still at the hospital. Why don't you ask her?"

"I will," he said, tucking the album under his arm. She noticed then the holster bulging under his loose shirt. He followed her gaze and patted the bulge almost fondly. "You get used to it," he said.

"Lieutenant?" An officer came into the kitchen. "We're through in here."

Kate stayed by the back door, seeing the lab crew out, while Carl and the officer checked the rest of the house to make sure all the doors and windows were locked.

Tejeda waited with Kate in the kitchen until the others left. She thought he had something to say to her, but he was quiet. His silence began to make her uncomfortable.

"Are you going to look for my bastard?" she asked.

"Sure." He put his hand on her shoulder, like a prelude to a good-night kiss. Reflexively, it seemed, she leaned toward him. She caught herself and backed up, faking a cough as a cover.

There was a flicker in his dark eyes as he reached out to shake her hand. "Take care of yourself."

"I will. Thanks." Embarrassed a little, she closed the door behind him, trying to fathom the quickening he set off inside her. It was all confusing, a mixing of old feelings for Carl with her attraction to Tejeda. The pleasure she felt when Tejeda was around was tinged with the sense that somehow Carl was betrayed. Hardly a mystery, these dangerous feelings, she thought. How long had it been since she'd last had sex? Three months? Four? Too long.

Carl came back through the kitchen. "How you doin', sweetheart?"

"Funny you should ask," she laughed softly. "Have any qualms about bedding a woman with a black eye?"

"Thought you'd never ask," he chuckled, wrapping her in his arms. "Let's go home and I'll tuck you into bed before you fall off those gorgeous gams."

Kate leaned against him as they walked home, her head barely reaching his chest. Comfortable with his arms around her, she closed her eyes against the approaching night. She matched her steps with his, as she would if they were dancing, trying to concentrate on the movements of Carl's body to keep her mind from racing over the events of the past few days. Through the dark came flashes: her mother's battered face in the morgue, four legs in the corner of a torn photograph, the beach stairs looming in front of her as she fell. The rush of frightening images made her shudder.

"Cold?" Carl tightened his arm around her.

"Just hold me," she said, burying her face against him. She reached her hand under his jacket and pulled out his shirttail so she could burrow her hand inside to feel the warmth of his bare skin, the assertiveness of the muscles underneath.

"I want you, Kate." His mouth covered hers.

A little alarm went off somewhere near the pit of her stomach. For a long time before their separation sex had hidden the deep chasm between them. But even now, every time she was near him, unless he said something to ruin it, she felt the tremendous pull his sex had on her.

Then he stroked her back and the memory of the sheer pleasure his body could give her overwhelmed any reservations, impelling her to press closer to him, just to feel again the trembling he could set off through her. It had been a long time. And what was the harm?

"My place or yours?" he said, a tremor in his voice.

She brushed her lips across his cheek. "More room in mine."

In her room he lifted her, bringing their faces on a level, pressing his mouth over hers in a long, familiar kiss. "It's all right," he said, nuzzling the sensitive place at the base of her neck.

"Yes."

They helped each other to undress, feeling the well-remembered flesh as it was exposed.

Kate locked her arms around him and he carried her onto the big antique bed. He stretched along beside her, caressing her body with long, firm strokes that ignited her like flint striking in dry grass. She rolled on top of him and lowered herself to bring him inside. But he grabbed her at the waist and held her away. He slid out from under her and rolled away.

"What?" She felt as if someone had sucked her breath away.

"Not yet."

"Okay." She lay on her side, tight against him, one leg draped across him to keep his warmth next to her. "You want to play a little?" Easily, up on one elbow, with her hand she traced the long sinews of his big thighs from his knees up to the tiny dimples in the small of his back, punctuation marks in a patch of soft blond hair. She kissed him there, running her tongue over the hard, twin mounds of buttocks. Her hand slid down between his legs. She closed her eyes, remembering every texture of him, the fresh-bread warmth of him. She wanted him, *now*, probing, filling her as the pleasant ache inside became insistence.

"Enough. All right?" The sharpness of his voice chilled her.

"Sorry." She pulled away. "I thought *you* wanted this."

He sat up against the carved mahogany headboard, covering his lap with a pillow. He looked straight ahead. "I'm not sure I can do this, Kate. It's been awhile for us and it's not as easy as I thought it would be."

"It was never that easy for us. Just relax, sweetheart. Let muscle-memory take over."

"Give me a minute."

"I'm not going anywhere," she said, twining her fingers in the coils of his chest hair, trying for a cool, detached tone when she felt anything but. "Let's talk." She concentrated on the carved edges of the headboard cutting sharply into her bare back so that she could begin breathing regularly again.

"I'm sorry." He tossed the pillow aside. "I've been planning this for three days now. It's been all I could do at night to keep from breaking your door down."

"It hasn't been locked." This part was familiar, too. The endless analysis of what had gone wrong between them. Right now she didn't want analysis. Her needs were more basic. She looked at him, concern etching lines on his face. He was manipulating her even now, and she would have been mad, except for that face. God, what a terrific face.

She smiled, challenged. "Listen, it's been a rough day. Relax." She pushed him gently forward, kneeling behind him to massage his taut neck and shoulders, rubbing out the impressed leaves and whorls from the headboard. "For that matter, it's been a helluva week. We'll do it later," reaching her arms around him to knead his flat belly. "Tomorrow. Or the next day." She nestled her face against the short hairs at the nape of his neck. "Mmm." She licked the pink rim of his ear with the tip of her tongue. "You smell so good," a low whisper. Smiling to herself, she felt his hips begin to move, sending a new flood of warmth through her own body. She pressed her erect nipples against him as she leaned around to find his parted lips with her own. She heard the catch in her voice, and liked it: "And you taste so good."

His tongue probed deeply, insistently. She caught the flutter of his eyelids that meant any hesitation was forgotten. Pulling her into his arms, Carl guided her over his lap. "You're a witch, you know," he said, with deep, relaxed pleasure on his face.

"I know."

NINE

KATE LAY IN CARL'S ARMS and fell into a deep oblivious sleep. She dreamt she was falling again through space, but softly this time, floating, weightless. She reached her hands out toward an amorphous figure retreating ahead of her down the beach stairs, always just out of her grasp. The figure turned toward her, but she couldn't focus her sleep-filled eyes. Then, just at the instant of recognition, she startled awake.

The dream left her with a vague, lingering feeling of disappointment. Just a few more seconds, she thought, closing her eyes against the bright morning sun, and I would have known. She stretched, drifting to another level of alertness. But known what, she wondered? As real as it seemed, it was only a dream.

Reaching out, she felt the empty space on the bed beside her. Carl was already gone. She rolled over onto his pillow and breathed in the faint, woodsy scent on the pillowcase and thought how nice it would be to wake up with someone there again, a little cuddling and conversation before the day began. The way it had been with Carl a long time ago, before their relationship fell apart and any conversation could lead to a blow up that might ruin a day, or a lifetime.

She got up and dressed quickly, pulling on a pair of shorts and a knit shirt, sliding her feet into comfortable old sandals. She went downstairs in a rush, a little apprehensive about Carl's expectations after last night gnawing in the corners of her mind.

Toneless humming came from behind the kitchen door. As she pushed open the swing door, too late to back out, Kate realized who it was.

Helga stood at the sink drying dishes.

"You don't need to do that," Kate said, planting what she hoped would pass for a cheerful smile on her face.

"Esperanza came in so late, I wanted to help out this morning. Let me fix you something to eat."

"I'm not very hungry." Kate was famished, but she didn't want to get stuck in the kitchen with her ex-mother-in-law. "Have you heard anything about Uncle Miles?"

"Carl talked to Esperanza when she came in. There was no change during the night." Helga went to the freezer for a bag of ice. "I was just taking some iced tea out to the terrace for Mina. Would you like some?"

"Sounds good," Kate said, leaning across the kitchen counter to look out the window at the first clear sky for almost a week. Sky that bright in the morning meant a hot day.

Helga fussed, preparing a small silver tray with tall iced glasses, a crystal pitcher of tea and lemon, a single pink rose in a slender vase. It looked very formal and elegant. "You want sugar? Mina doesn't. The only sugar bowl I can find is this blue thing."

"I don't want sugar. The blue bowl is Esperanza's. Takes about six teaspoons in her coffee."

"I know. Mexican coffee, she calls it. She made me some."

Kate watched Helga's graceful, athletic movements as she moved around the kitchen. "Carl told me you had a date last night. Did you have a nice time?"

"Oh, yes."

From her expression Kate suspected sex was less complicated for Helga than for her son. "Anyone I know?"

"Have you met Sergeant Green? He sometimes comes around with Lieutenant Tejeda."

"He seems like a nice person." Kate had to suck in her cheeks to keep herself from adding, "But he's thirty years younger than you."

"He is nice. He's so smart. He's working with the lieutenant over at Miles's house right now. I thought I would take them something cold to drink later on." She paused and looked down at the tray, moving her lips as she counted glasses and spoons. "Do you think that would be okay?"

"Sure thing." She'd have liked to take something over to them, herself, just to find out what they were doing.

Kate opened the big tin bread box and looked inside for the stiff, waxed bakery bag Esperanza often hid under the loaf of bread for her midmorning snack. It was part of a silent joke between them; Esperanza, always on a diet, never admitted losing her private stash on the rare occasions Kate looted it. This morning the bag held two flaky croissants.

"Esperanza brought that in this morning," Helga said. "Let me cook you some eggs to go with it."

"No, thanks. This is enough." Kate dropped the bag on the tea tray, offending its symmetry.

Helga winced, reaching for the tray.

Kate picked it up. "I'll carry it out for you."

"Thank you, honey. I'll come join you when I've finished up in here."

Kate crossed the lawn to the latticed gazebo at the edge of the bluff. Mina sat there facing the beach, elbows on the old glass-topped wicker table, head bowed low as she wrote something in her inhibited little scrawl. She looked so small and vulnerable outlined against the horizon that Kate felt a sudden rush of affection for her. Putting down the tray, she bent slightly to smooth Mina's collar, ruffled by the wind.

Mina reached up reflexively to pat Kate's arm. "How are you today, darling?"

"A bit slow. Too much sleep, I think," Kate said. She pulled up an old wicker rocker that creaked comfortably as she sat. Scooting the chair closer to the table she upset a pile of cards and letters on the table in front of Mina. "You look industrious. What are you up to?"

"F's and G's. I'm responding to some of the condolences people wrote about your mother. There are so many!" She snapped the lid on her thick old fountain pen and reached for a glass of tea. Holding up a silver spoon to dazzle in the bright light, she smiled at Kate. "My, my, aren't we being grand?"

"Helga is having fun with the silver service. Do we need to do all this letter writing now?"

"I need something to keep myself occupied. And you've been through enough, darling. I didn't want you burdened with it."

"Thanks. I'd make a hash of it anyway. I'm no good at that sort of thing."

"I'm not either, actually. I wish your mother were here." She stifled a nervous little giggle. "Save us a lot of bother. She was always so good at dumb little notes. She knew exactly what to say and when to say it."

"She did, didn't she?" Kate raised her glass and drank the strong, bitter tea. Mother was always so damned right about everything. Kate set her glass down too hard.

Careful as always to turn the liver spots so they weren't noticeable, Mina rested her chin on her hands. She sighed. "Look at those little ones down on the beach. We used to sit up here together, your mother and I, and watch you kids play down there, you and Reece and Nugie. It doesn't seem so long ago." Eyes misty, Mina looked over at Kate. "Do you ever think about Nugie?"

"All the time."

"She was such a sweet girl, wasn't she? Such a waste." Mina shook her head. "We've never talked about Nugie, you and I."

"No. I don't know why you're bringing it up now. Unless.... Has Lieutenant Tejeda been talking to you?"

"That dark policeman?"

"Mina, for chrissake."

"Yes, he was asking," Mina bristled. "But I would never say anything to him about my Nugie. If you two girls thought it was none of my business, it's certainly none of his." She smiled but it didn't cover the anger in her voice. Keeping her eyes averted, she said, "I only wish you two had come to me before you went to Mexico. Could a baby have been such a tragedy?"

"I don't know. I felt it was Nugie's decision to make."

"But you helped her once she made her decision."

"I'm sorry, Mina. I don't know what to say to you." Hot wind ruffled the stack of correspondence. For some reason, right now talking about Nugie was harder than talking about Mother. Maybe it always would be.

Kate went over to the rail at the edge of the bluff and opened the bag of croissants. She meant to eat only one because they were so rich, but when the first one was gone she began pulling bits off the second, until there was nothing in the bag but crumbs. She tossed the crumbs down the face of the deeply eroded bluff and let the pigeons and gulls battle over them.

"We'd better reseed the bank down here before it rains," she said. A nice, neutral topic. "This dry weather has killed off the ice plant we put in after those kids set it on fire last summer. There isn't enough to hold the bank if it rains."

Mina was beside her, leaning over the railing, examining the bank like a high-priced botanist. Thank God, Kate thought, I've defused her.

"How did you know where to take her?" Mina asked.

"I don't know," Kate said, annoyed. "Didn't Miles tell you everything?"

"He told me that your mother instructed Esperanza where to take Nugie."

Kate almost choked. "How would my mother know about an abortion clinic?"

"She just always seemed to know about those things," Mina said, her knuckles bloodless in their stranglehold on the rail. "She helped me find one once."

"You!"

"Don't sound so shocked. Your generation wasn't the first to need that particular service."

"I am shocked. I just can't imagine you and my mother..."

"It's not what you think. A friend, not a friend actually, but a girl who worked here, asked us to help her get an abortion. I helped her as I suppose you helped Nugie."

"Wait a minute," Kate moved closer. "Was this the girl pregnant with Miles's baby?"

"Well, if you know the story, there's no point in repeating it."

"I *don't* know the story," Kate protested. "Who was the father, Miles or Daddy?"

"Could have been either. Or neither." Mina relaxed a little against the rough rail, snagging the fine light weave of her skirt. "I'm only sure that it wasn't Dolphy's, because he'd been in Europe too long."

"But there actually was no baby because the girl had an abortion?"

Mina nodded. "Can you imagine not wanting a baby?"

"Not personally. But then, for me, the subject never came up." Kate remembered what Reece had said, "Can you trust what Mina tells you?" Was there no bastard after all? "The abortion, when was it, exactly?"

"Oh, golly." Mina scratched her head. "As I said, Dolph was gone. He was away, I think, from late nineteen forty-two until the spring of nineteen forty-six." She tapped her fingers against the rail, counting silently. "Fall of nineteen forty-three. Late fall."

"And there was only one pregnant girl, right?"

"Good heavens, Kate," Mina laughed. "You make us sound like orgiasts. There might have been dozens, but that's the only one I know about. Why?"

"Remember the photograph I found on the beach? The little boy and the woman? I wondered if it might be the bastard and his mother."

"Of all the crazy ideas!"

"What if it is him?" Kate persisted. "What if the girl didn't go through with the abortion?"

Mina gave her a long, cold look. "Are you all right, Kate?"

"Sure."

"I mean, you're not fixating on this other abortion because you feel responsible for what happened to Nugie, are you?"

"Fixated?" Kate laughed. "What have you been reading? Anyway, this has nothing to do with Nugie. And although I feel bad about Nugie, I wasn't responsible for her death, except in a peripheral way. If anyone is fixated on Nugie, it's you."

"That's cruel."

"I know. Sorry."

"Nugie was the closest I came to having a daughter of my own. Now there's only Reece." Mina sighed deeply. "And you, of course," she said, too late.

"Of course," Kate said evenly. She covered Mina's hand with her own, aching for her, seeing herself childless and alone at Mina's age.

"I didn't mean that the way it sounded, sweetheart. You always had so many people around to love you. Reece and Nugie had only my sister and me."

"They had fathers."

"Oh, yes, lots of fathers. Just like Carl. It's not the same as what you had. How many times was Helga married?"

"Three, I think. I'm not sure." Kate reached for her glass and took a long drink. She felt hot and prickly all over.

"Now he has Dolph," Mina said.

The comment caught the tea halfway down. "As a father?"

"Dolph says Carl has a mind like Miles and Archie, like he would hope his own son would've had, if there'd been one."

"And do you feel motherly toward Carl?"

"Hardly." Mina bent toward the table and gathered her correspondence into a neat pile. Then she patted her smooth, silver hair, a quick check for strays. In a voice that was little more than a conspiratorial whisper she said, "Don't look around. Your mother-in-law is coming. We'll talk later. One thing I must say about Helga, she has kept her figure."

"My *ex*-mother-in-law, you mean." Kate turned and watched Helga glide across the lawn, her cotton skirt playing gracefully around her legs. From the distance, Kate thought, she could be mistaken for a beautiful, younger woman. The illusion dissolved as Helga neared. The strong angularity of her face, even softened as it was now by a wispy aureole of hair that had escaped from her coronet of braids, made her whole body seem coarse.

"May I join you?" Helga asked with her practiced gentility, as she sat down in a low wicker chair. The sweet smile she gave Mina and Kate seemed so incongruous on her long face. "I have good news. The doctor called from the hospital. He said that Mr. Byrd is stirring. He might wake up."

"Terrific." Kate turned to Mina. "Do you want me to drive you to the hospital so you can be with him?"

"What, darling?" Mina turned her face to Kate, but her eyes were far away.

"I said, do you want me..."

"Oh yes, I heard you. I can drive myself." Mina stood and started picking up her things. "Someone has to be with Miles, of course, but waiting is so boring. I'll go now if you'll promise to come by later, bring some cards. We'll play some rummy. Or bluff poker."

"Okay. If you won't cheat this time." Kate put a hand on the pile of letters. "I'll take care of this stuff. You go ahead."

"I'm going, I'm going." Mina dropped her pen and box of stationery in Kate's lap.

"Give me a call if anything happens," Kate said to Mina's retreating back. Without turning around, Mina waved a hand in acknowledgement.

"Will she be all right alone?" Helga asked.

"For a while, anyway. I have to get some work done this morning. I'm so far behind." She stood up, filling her arms with Mina's correspondence. "I hate to go in, it's so nice out here."

"I'll walk in with you, dear," Helga said, picking up the tea tray. They walked slowly toward the house. "It will be a great relief for you all when your uncle comes home, won't it?"

"Comes home?" The idea stopped Kate in her tracks. "Where will he come home to? I know he'd never want to live with me or with Dolphy, he's such a private person. But he can hardly live alone again after this episode."

"Something to think about, isn't it?" Helga gazed off toward Miles's house. "Such a pretty place. Be a shame for it to lie empty."

"Poor Miles." Kate sighed.

"Kate, I know you have more important things on your mind," Helga said, her voice theatrically serious. "But I want to ask your advice about something."

"Sure."

"I brought some of Carl's old trophies and plaques in case he would like them for his new office. Do you think his new place is too sophisticated for them?"

"No office is ever too sophisticated for football trophies, Helga. I think he'll love them." Kate juggled the things in her hand so she could open the back door. She held it for Helga with her shoulder.

"Oh! I forgot." Helga slid past her, being careful not to upset the glasses of tea. "There's a man called Sy Ratcher in the living room with Reece. He said he has a buyer for your house. Reece thought you might want to avoid going in there."

"No," Kate said. "I think it's time for a little talk with Mr. Ratcher."

With her fingers, Kate combed through her windblown hair as she walked down the hall to the study.

"Kate." Sy rose and took her hand in both of his. His skin felt dry, lizardy, like his scuffed imitation-reptile shoes. The shoes didn't seem to go with the rest of his rig, a mortician-gray three-piece suit, a red polyester tie pompously done in a fat four-in-hand knot tucked up among his chins. He presented such a contrast to Reece, who slumped in the corner of a sofa, his bare, sandy legs stretched out in front of him, a look of long-suffering boredom on his face.

"Sorry you were kept waiting, Sy," Kate said as she sat down next to Reece. "What's on your mind?"

A fine sweat shone on Ratcher's close-shaven cheeks. "You look wonderful, Kate."

"Oh, come on." Reece rolled his eyes. "Let's cut the preliminaries and get to it. Kate, Sy says he was working on a little development with your mother."

Kate saw Sy wince. "What sort of development?" she asked.

"We hadn't put any signatures to anything yet, but." Sy reached beside the chair and brought up a thick briefcase. Balancing the case on his knees, he shuffled through a stack of legal-size manila folders and came up with a thick, time-yellowed document. "You know what this is, of course."

"Let me see." Kate took it from him. "It's the grant deed for Grandpa Archie's property."

"Six-point-seven-two beach-front acres." He looked at her as if this had some heavy significance she should understand.

"The lot is divided in three parts," Kate said. "And unless every one of us agrees on something, nothing can be done with the land."

"That's where you're wrong, Kate. Read the deed."

She turned the first few pages of the thick document. "Why don't you just tell me the good parts?"

"Well." He leaned forward, eyes glistening. "Actually, Archie kept title to the whole plot. Dolph and Miles have life-estates in their domiciles only. So you see, the *land* has a single owner."

"So as Archie's heir..."

"Right!" Ratcher clapped his hands together gleefully. "The land is all yours."

"I still can't do anything with it," she reminded him.

"But you're wrong." He brought out a roll of blueprints and passed it lovingly to her. "Just look and see what a few good minds working together can come up with."

"Here, architect." She handed the roll to Reece. "Be useful."

Reece cleared a space on the cocktail table in front of them and spread out the plans. The first sheet was a plot map showing an overview of the three existing houses and the compound. Reece groaned as he turned to the second sheet.

In soft blue ink, sketched along the contour of the bluff was a solid wall of condominiums, extending like a cuboid-fungus over the land now occupied by Miles and Kate's houses. Dolph's house and terrace were left as an island and marked "Phase 3."

Sweat now ran down the sides of Sy's face. "Think of it. Two hundred and eighty luxury, ocean-view condos with a marina below. Unit prices from four hundred and fifty to nine hundred thousand dollars, more for customizing. Boat slips at forty thousand dollars a crack."

Kate wrapped an arm around Reece and rested her chin on his shoulder as she looked at the plans, disbelieving what she saw. She was glad Reece had stayed around for this, and not only because of his expertise. "What do you think?"

"It's Fantasyland, Sy," Reece laughed harshly. "You can't believe you could ever pull it off. In the first place, you'd never get zoning variances."

"That's a problem, all right," Sy nodded, slightly crestfallen. "Mrs. Byrd thought she could manage it, though. She had so many contacts."

"That's not the only problem," Kate said, rolling up the plans. "Mother couldn't deliver the land. Even if she had managed to get Miles put away, I would never have agreed to this. And now, I'd laugh at the whole scheme if there weren't some possibility it had something to do with Mother's murder."

Sy visibly recoiled. "I would be the last person to want any harm to come to your mother. Like I said, we hadn't gotten around to signatures, so without her I'm nowhere. I thought you might feel honor bound to respect her agreements."

"Honor bound?" Kate said. "Funny words for you to use."

"Sy," Reece stood up and moved toward Ratcher. "I think it's time for you to leave."

"All I can ask is that you give it some thought," Sy said as he gathered his papers into his briefcase. He reached for the roll of plans, but Kate snatched it away.

"I'll hang on to this," she said. "Police evidence, you know."

"CARL, YOU BUM." Kate held the telephone receiver between her chin and shoulder while she picked at the scab on her left elbow. "After last night I thought this conversation would be more fun. Some romantic you are."

Carl laughed into the phone. "We'll talk about *that* later."

"Okay, so what did Dolph find out about Mother's nefarious financial dealings?"

"Not much," Carl said. "He's submitted her will for probate, but it doesn't give many details."

"I didn't even know Mother had a will. Does it say anything about Sy Ratcher?"

"Not a thing. Dolph is bringing you a copy. The trust fund she was living on expired. Some of the capital was earmarked by Archie as a contribution to the annuity he set up for Esperanza. The remainder, and everything else she had, is yours."

"Everything else is probably just her personal things, jewelry mostly."

"I don't think you understand, Kate," Carl spoke very slowly, as if to a dull-witted child. "When your mother died you fell heir to your grandfather's *entire* estate. You're, well, independent now. You can quit your job and do anything you want. For the rest of your life."

"I know all that. What I want to do is exactly what I am doing. Why would I want to quit my job? School starts Monday."

"Exactly," Carl replied in the controlled voice with the patronizing edge that always made her boil. "With everything that has happened I don't see how you can make it."

"I won't leave the department in the lurch."

"The department chair can cover the classes with staff and part-timers."

"No."

"Kate, be reasonable. You don't need the money, for God's sake."

"Money has nothing to do with it. If I were in this for money I wouldn't be teaching." But she knew he wasn't listening. As committed as he was to his career, he never understood that her work was more to her than a source of income, however meager. It was *who* she was: Professor Kate Teague. She looked around the room, her grandfather's study—wood and leather and brass all polished to a rich patina. There was comfort here, and a self-assurance that derived from the power of its original owner, not her. Her *place* was a grubby little cubicle with gray, state-issued furniture. And she wasn't ready to give it up.

"Will you think about it?" Carl was still arguing, trying to bend her to his will.

Kate heard the urgency in his voice, but the words slid right by her like so much water slapping against a dam. The issue wasn't important to Carl anymore, she knew. He just wanted to win the argument. It had always been so much easier to give in than to assert herself. But things were different now and she didn't have to listen anymore. For the first time she realized how complete their breakup was, how clean the cut. It left her feeling as if something had been ripped out of her core. But there was a new sense of peace sliding into the void.

"Ask Dolph to keep checking, please," she interrupted the flow of words. There was a steely edge on her voice. "Remind him to meet Mina at the hospital. Talk to you later."

"Kate! Wait."

Even holding the receiver at arm's length, she could hear Carl, sounding tinny like an old recording. She put the receiver back to her ear but said nothing.

"I love you," he said. "I only want what's best for you, for us."

It was a familiar refrain; she'd heard it a hundred times. She hung up, holding the receiver down for a while, as if it might leap up with the force of Carl's anger.

Feeling a strong surge of energy, born from her own anger, Kate went upstairs to her study. Half her files and books were still in big cartons, just as the moving company had left them when she moved in at the beginning of summer, when she'd left Carl. The cartons had been packed in a hurry, so their contents were in no particular order. Finding the materials she would need for the first two weeks of school meant hours of digging and sorting.

She turned on her tapedeck and, humming to Vivaldi, she started making three piles on the floor, one for each different preparation she would be teaching. Everything that didn't pertain to her class load was left to be dealt with later, when she had more time. Christmas vacation, she thought. With five

classes and three preparations to keep her busy, the week after
Christmas would be soon enough to sort through everything
else.

The remainder of the morning passed quickly. The work re-
freshed her because it was a diversion from Carl and Miles and
everything else.

Shuffling together the drafts for her course outlines she
swiveled her chair around in the oriel and looked out toward the
beach. A strong wind brushed the cypresses against the windows of "safe harbor" with a familiar dog-scratching sound.
It was a beautiful day, swept clean of the smoke and ash that
had soiled the sky for the past week. Pushing open the case-
ment windows she leaned against the sill, resting her chin in her
palms to let the crisp sea air rush against her face. Lazily, she
turned her wrist and looked at her watch.

"Two o'clock. Damn," she muttered. She had invited Helga
to lunch. She dialed downstairs on the house line. It was busy.
Esperanza had probably unplugged the phone to nap, she
thought. Putting her outlines on top of her word processor, she
got up and went quietly downstairs to see if Helga still needed
feeding. As she passed the kitchen, she heard Esperanza
speaking in a low voice.

"*Si.*" Esperanza faced away from the door, hunched low
over the counter to speak on the telephone.

Thinking the call might be from the hospital, Kate waited in
the doorway, watching the starched white back.

"*Si*, Mrs. Ratcher. Tell Sy thank you."

TEN

"HIJA!" Esperanza bumped the counter and spun around to face Kate. The telephone receiver bounced in its cradle. "You startled me."

"Sorry. Was that Susan Ratcher?"

"Yes, big ears. She wanted to know about Mr. Miles."

"How strange."

"No, it is not strange. She was his wife once, remember. Is it strange that she still cares for him?"

"Guess not," Kate shrugged. "Unless she was calling on behalf of her stepson. Were there any other calls? And where is Helga? I was going to feed her lunch."

"Three calls. Number one was Carl who invited his mother out to lunch. You were invited too but I told him you were indisposed." She folded her arms across her ample chest and smiled at Kate. "You are not the only one with big ears. I did not tell him you were here."

"I love you, you know."

"You should." Esperanza tried to make a cross face. "Number three call was that handsome policeman. He wants to talk to you. I told him you would be at the hospital with time on your hands at eight o'clock."

"How do you know that?"

"Because call number two was Mr. Dolph. He wants you to keep your aunt's seat warm while he takes her out for something to eat, maybe to sneak a tranquilizer in her soup so she will come home and go to bed."

"Did Dolph say anything about Uncle Miles?"

"He seems better. But he's still out of this world." Esperanza brushed her hands to show she was finished.

"That's it for the telephone," Kate said. "Now you go take a nap."

"I will after one more thing. You didn't eat the dinner I made you last night and Helga says you had no breakfast. I made you a nice quiche and you will come and eat it before you get sick and your aunt starts sitting outside your room at the hospital which would do her health no good." She drew a deep breath.

"Okay, okay." Kate smiled at Esperanza. "For Mina's sake I'll eat."

Kate sat down at the kitchen table and devoured the quiche as if she hadn't eaten in weeks. When she finished she stretched, lazily pulling out the muscles stiff from sitting all morning. "Esperanza, did Lieutenant Tejeda tell you about the burglary at Miles's last night?"

"*Si*. He asked what was in the drawer, but I don't know. Mr. Miles is a good boy. He does his own room."

"Unlike me, huh?" Kate laughed. "What do you keep by *your* bed?"

"Me?" Esperanza shrugged. "In one I keep stockings. In the other just things."

"Like what things?"

"Like your baby pictures," she smiled. "And the little things you used to make me, you know, the embroidered hankies and things."

"Hardly worth burglarizing."

"To me they are priceless." Esperanza snatched the plates off the table. "You going to work some more?"

"No. I think I'll go down for a swim. Get the kinks out." She kissed Esperanza on the cheek. "Thanks. Lunch was great. Now, go rest."

Upstairs in her dressing room, Kate pulled on a one-piece swimsuit, feeling her bony rib-section as she pulled it up. She looked at herself in the long mirror on the back of the door and shook her head. "Scrawny broad," she muttered, patting her narrow hips and flat belly. Poor Carl worked so hard to stay trim. She wouldn't mind having some of his voluptuousness. She hurried downstairs and out of the house.

Coming around the corner of the house, she caught a fleeting glimpse of the brown-suited Sergeant Green and wondered if he were pulling surveillance duty or looking for Helga. He was gone from view before she had a chance to ask him.

"Kate!" Lydia, the narrowest string bikini bisecting her hard, brown torso, jogged across the lawn from Dolph's house. "Going swimming?"

"Yes." Kate waited for her to catch up. "Come with me?"

"I was going to run, but, hell, why not? Be a lot cooler."

At the top of the beach stairs, Lydia stopped and looked around. "This the place, right?"

"Where I fell? Yes."

"Doesn't it spook you to be here?"

"A little," Kate nodded, leading the way down the stairs.

At the landing Lydia stopped and looked up toward the bluff. "Where was he standing?"

"I don't know. Because of the overhang, you can't see the top from here."

"But how would he get there? Anyone coming across the lawn would have been too exposed. Unless he was lying in wait under the oleander hedge." Lydia leaned forward over the banister to get a better view of the ledge. "Stuff's poisonous, oleander. Unhealthy place for a skulker to hide."

"Skulker? How could anyone be skulking for me? No one knew I would be down here." Kate looked up, her eyes following the eroded bank above. Lydia was right, the only possible cover for someone sneaking up on the stairs was the oleander hedge that grew along the edge of the bluff. Even then, there were long gaps where chunks of the eroded bluff had given way, taking railing and plants with it. But the biggest problem would be getting across the broad lawn undetected.

Hot sun bore into her bare back. She slung her towel over her shoulder and started down the rough wooden steps to the beach. "Are we swimming, or what?"

"The gazebo," Lydia shouted after her. "It had to be the gazebo."

Kate stopped at the bottom, digging her toes into the hot white sand as she looked up at the gazebo perched at the edge of the bluff, a thick strand of unbroken oleander hedge stretching from its doorway thirty feet to the stairs.

A little breathless, Lydia put a moist hand on her arm. "What if someone were in the gazebo and simply took advantage of the opportunity to get you."

"Me in particular," Kate said, "or would just any passerby have done?"

"Don't know."

"Very comforting," Kate said. Sergeant Green's head appeared by the gazebo, watching the women below. Kate wasn't sure how secure his watchfulness made her feel. She turned to Lydia. "Hey, my feet are burning up. Let's go."

With Lydia close beside her, Kate ran across the beach and plunged into the gentle surf. Chilling water sluiced over her as she swam with powerful strokes parallel to the surf line, quickly outdistancing Lydia. At first, the salt water stung her skinned knees and made her bruised muscles ache. But the cold, faintly oil-scented water sharpened her senses, drawing tension from her, she thought, like good sex.

Exhausted but exhilarated after twenty minutes, she pulled herself, shivering, onto the sand. A lovely cool, moist breeze blew in across the water, providing relief from the dry Santa Ana winds that gathered heat as they passed across the land. Chest still heaving, Kate luxuriated in the radiated heat from the sand, lifting her face to the breeze as she waited for Lydia.

"What do you think?" Reece dropped to the sand behind her. "She drowning out there?"

"Who, Lydia?" Kate panted.

"She's muscle-bound, you know. Tends to sink."

"You can go in after her if you want to. I couldn't make it. Where did you come from, anyway?"

"I saw you two come down here." He yawned and scratched his belly, salting the coiled red hair with sand. "Just watching you is enough exercise for me."

"You lazy bum." Kate leaned back, using him as a backrest.

Reece squinted off toward the water. "Great place for a marina, don't you think?"

"Shut up," she laughed.

Lydia emerged from the water a few yards down the beach. Kate's wave caught her eye, and she slogged tiredly through the swash toward them.

"'Lo," she said, shaking her dripping hands over Reece.

"Cut it out," he protested.

"Go ahead," Kate laughed. "He deserves worse."

She leaned back against her elbows. "The way I feel right now, I could stay right here forever. Do what old Carl says and quit the job. Be a beach bum."

"Great idea," Lydia smiled. "You quit and I'll have a shot at an honest-to-God, full-time tenured teaching position."

"Don't do it, Kate," Reece warned. "She earns a real salary and I'll have to think up a new excuse for not marrying her."

Lydia punched at his shoulder. "You watch it or I'll find myself someone with a little more meat on his bones. And a little less meat between his ears."

"Sounds like Carl." Reece rolled over until his face was close to Kate's, their noses almost touching. "Is he available?"

"Who's interested, you or her?"

"All right." Lydia bolted to her feet. "You two aren't funny anymore. I'm going. I have things to do."

"What are you, everyone's conscience?" Reece gripped her sandy ankle. "Sit down."

"Yeah. Sit," Kate said. "I want to ask you something."

"Better be important."

"It is."

Lydia sat back down. "Okay. Shoot."

"What do you keep in the drawers of your bedside table?"

Lydia rolled her eyes. "Weird."

"It is. Someone broke into Miles's house and stole the drawer from his nightstand. I'm trying to figure out what might have been in it."

"I don't have a nightstand," Lydia said. "I sleep on a futon and use the floor for a table."

"Reece?"

"I sleep on Lydia and use the futon for a table. How's that going to help, anyway? It could be anything of a certain size. Ask Esperanza, she cleans for him."

"She doesn't know. Miles took care of his own room."

"Could be a family thing," Lydia said. "You know, like what their mother put by their little beds at night. What did your mother keep in hers?"

"Don't know." Kate jumped to her feet, pulling Lydia with her. "Let's go see."

Reece lay back on the sand and looked up at Kate and Lydia as they brushed themselves off. He yawned. "Sounds too damned industrious. *I'm* not going to waste the end of summer indoors. Look at that sky. Gorgeous."

"Then don't look back," Kate said, nodding her head toward the row of hills prodding the skyline beyond the house. A fat plume of black smoke stained the impossibly blue sky.

"Shit." Lydia kicked at the sand. "Just when we could breathe again. Another fire."

"You coming with me?" Kate asked.

"Yeah. I love nosing through other people's stuff."

They tiptoed through the kitchen in case Esperanza was sleeping, and went upstairs to Mother's room. Kate drew the heavy drapes, spilling light across the rose-colored carpet.

"Fabulous!" Lydia said, scanning the room from the doorway. She looked down at her bikini and bare feet. "I can't come in like this."

"'Course you can. Besides, I need you. I haven't had the courage to go through Mother's things alone."

Lydia went directly to the painting that hung above the silk-covered bed. The soft pastel colors and flower patterns in the room seemed to flow from the painting, a mother, head bowed over the small girl in her lap. "Is that real?"

"It's real," Kate assured her. "Beautiful, isn't it? A Mary Cassatt. Miles gave it to Mother when I was born. You want to get the drawers from the nightstand on that side of the bed? I'll get these."

"I knew it," Lydia said as she put her second drawer on the floor beside the others. "I'm just realizing how filthy rich you are. Look at this stuff."

"What'd you find?" Kate sat cross-legged on the deep carpet. She reached in and pulled up a tangle of pearls and old gold chains from the jumble of jewelry in the drawer. "Mother didn't take very good care of this stuff. Got it all scratched up."

"It's like a pirate's trove." Lydia knelt beside her. "But it's costume stuff. It can't be real."

"It is. Look at this." Kate turned over a small platinum brooch, a delicate dragonfly with emerald eyes and lapis wings, and showed her the jeweler's mark. "My grandmother liked Tiffany. I think most of this was hers. Some of it is pretty, the art nouveau pieces, anyway."

"It's dazzling. So what's in the other drawers?"

"Junk. Sewing kit. Old pictures."

Lydia picked up a yellowed snapshot. "Is that you? God, can't even see your face, the way the sun reflects off your braces. Who are these skinny kids? Look like refugees from Dachau."

"That's your true love, Reece. And his sister, Nugie. Good lookin' group weren't we?"

"No comment. What else is in here?"

"Three lurid paperback novels. Aspirin. Few dozen monogrammed handkerchiefs and lavender sachet." Kate opened a book-sized black leather folder, its edges worn from frequent handling. "My dad."

"He's gorgeous. Looks like Tyrone Power."

"I always thought he was a giant." Kate held the portrait beside her face. "I look just like him, right?"

"Maybe." Brow creased, Lydia looked from the portrait to Kate and back again. "There's a resemblance. But ... I guess it's the eyes. They're too different."

"I'm supposed to have his eyes."

"Musta been some other guy."

Feeling slightly disappointed, Kate put the folder on the floor beside her. "Anyway, that's what Mother kept by her bed, just stuff."

"And a little jewelry."

"And that. I doubt if Miles had a stash like it."

"Now do you file a report with that Lieutenant Hunk?"

"Talk to him, anyway." Kate looked at the bedside clock. "I better get moving. I'm meeting him at eight and I need to take a shower and run some errands first."

"I have to be going, too." Lydia sprang to her feet. "Volleyball team tryouts tonight."

"I'll see you out."

"Don't bother. I was planning to abscond with a handful of that pogy bait."

"Was there anything you liked?" Kate looked down at the drawer of jewelry then picked up the dragonfly and pinned it to Lydia's bikini top.

"I was joking."

"I know you were. Don't misinterpret this. I don't know what to do with all this stuff. It has no emotional value for me.

Except this." She picked up the folder with her father's portrait. "Go open that box on Mother's vanity."

Lydia centered the big wooden casket on the mirrored surface and lifted the lid, freeing six velvet-covered trays to swing out from a center post. With her fingertips she outlined one heavy necklace, skipping across the dozen pea-sized rubies as if they were fire. Every tray had its own load of heavy jewelry. "Jesus H. Christ."

"Mother liked Bulgari. Almost obscene, isn't it? Little presents from her friends. What am I going to do with it, Lydia? I'm certainly not going to wear any of it. And I don't have any children to pass it down to."

"You could endow the women's volleyball team."

Kate laughed. "I could."

Lydia picked at the little dragonfly. "What if I said I liked something from here better?"

"Do you?"

"No. I'd be afraid of someone knocking me on the head if I wore any of that." Her face flushed crimson under the tan. "Wrong thing to say. Sorry. Your mother wasn't wearing any big baubles when she was killed, was she?"

"Just her everyday stuff. It was all found on her. Anyway, she wouldn't die for any of it. It's insured."

"Get rid of it, Kate. Put it in a vault somewhere." Lydia folded in the trays and slammed down the lid. Something apparently occurred to her and her head snapped up. "What if something happened to you, who would inherit this stuff?"

"Until I make a new will, probably Carl."

"I don't believe it. Your mother's murdered and you inherit a pile of loot. Meanwhile old Carl moves in here for better access to his next victim. Someone tries to kill you and everyone says 'Who can be doing this?'"

Kate laughed. "You think Carl tried to kill me?"

"After I evicted him I'd think about it."

"It couldn't have been Carl," Kate said. "He wouldn't have botched it."

ELEVEN

"MINA CALLED." The message was stuck to the refrigerator door with a magnet. "Pls. bring Mr. M.'s robe and slippers with you to hosp. Mother's car needs driving. XOXOXO, E."

Quietly, so she wouldn't waken Esperanza, Kate opened the broom closet. She shoved the assorted mop and broom handles to one side and groped through the jumble of dust cloths and vacuum attachments to find the hook at the back where Mother always kept her spare set of keys. The hook was empty.

She went to the foyer and reached into the big Ming vase on the table by the door and fished around for Miles's house key. But with it she found Mother's big brass key ring, the one she'd always carried in her purse. It was a disturbing discovery. Why weren't the keys in Mother's purse when the police found it?

She weighed the keys, an unknown quantity, as she went outside.

The brightness of the afternoon had been soiled by the brush fire growing along the horizon. The dark sky gave an illusion of coolness, but the air was hot and still, strangled by the smoke. As she unlocked Miles's front door, Kate looked around, hoping Sergeant Green was close by. Even though Tejeda had spent the morning in the house, exorcising the place, she didn't much want to go in alone.

Leaving the big door open to provide light, she crossed the foyer into the dim living room. Miles's absence seemed to fill the room, bouncing as empty echoes off the walls. It wasn't until she pressed the light switch that she saw the small figure huddled in a corner of the massive sofa.

"Reece!" she screamed, panic tangling her feet, making her stumble over a corner of the Aubusson rug. "What the hell are you doing here?"

"Shit!" He bolted upright, startled from sleep. He focused on Kate and let out a long breath. "Oh. It's you. You scared me half to death, waking me like that." He yawned. "All that sunshine made me sleepy."

"What are you doing in here?" she demanded.

"After that burglary business, Mina asked me to move in to look after this old morgue. Where's Lydia?"

"Went home hours ago. Mina's become quite the little organizer. Why didn't you say something earlier?"

"Didn't think about it. Don't worry. I won't steal the family silver."

"I wasn't worried."

"God, Kate, it's so weird in here. I don't even know where I'll sleep. There's a gross, filthy bedroom upstairs and there's Miles's hard little bed down here in the maid's room. The mattress must be a hundred years old."

"We can bring a bed over for you."

"I can sack out on the couch. I hope the plumbing upstairs works. I just feel too strange around Miles's personal things. I can't bring myself to use his commode."

"You don't have to stay. The police are roaming around outside. No one will get in here again."

"What are *you* doing here?"

"Getting some things for Miles." She headed toward the back of the house, Reece walking close behind her. "How does his room look?"

"Okay. Esperanza put it back together." He trailed a finger along the yellowed hall wall. "This place is a mess. It'll have to be gutted and done over before anyone will live here again. How could Miles let it get so bad?"

"I don't think he ever cared much about it." She saw the architect's passion in his eyes as he traced the stenciled ceiling molding. "Depending on when and if Miles comes home, would you be interested in redoing the place for us? If he approves that is."

"Thought you'd never ask," he grinned.

"Maybe you could use the time you're here to sketch out some plans. And, who knows, maybe along the way you'll discover the Big Clue."

"Like Nancy Drew?"

"Yeah. Look in the handles of the cricket bats. Might find a treasure map or something."

"Would you settle for the big hall clock? Tejeda took the bats with him."

"Curiouser and curiouser," she said, opening the bedroom door. Except for the gap in the night table, everything was in order. She opened the closet and rummaged through it. Finding the robe, she tossed it onto the sagging bed and looked around for slippers and pajamas.

Reece sat on a corner of the bed and bundled Miles's things together as Kate tossed them to him. "If you want me to fix up the old place, I suppose you won't be tearing it down to build condos."

"What everyone keeps forgetting is that it isn't mine to tear down. I still can't understand why Mother and Sy carried their plans so far. And why would she work with Sy in the first place?"

"A legit businesswoman wouldn't have touched that deal with a fork. But don't underestimate Sy. I have a feeling this was the biggest thing he ever worked on, and he isn't going to let go of it easily."

"What can he do, though?" Kate asked.

"I don't know. Spread around a little *baksheesh*. You have to admit, slimy as he is, he isn't without his charms."

"Charms?"

"The way Attila's mother looked at him, I thought she was going to eat him up."

She laughed. "By Attila, you mean Carl?"

"Yeah. Sorry. Anyway, if you ever need me, I'm here. Just like old times. Remember who saved you when you climbed out on the ledge of 'safe harbor'?"

"I remember who talked me into going out on the ledge in the first place." She reached out and gently thumped his thin chest. "But thanks. Look, I have to relieve Mina at the hospital. Do you want to come with me?"

"No, thanks. Miles would have a relapse if mine was the first face he saw when he woke up."

"You're probably right." As she gathered Miles's bundle of gear, she thought about Reece and Nugie and herself as children. "What this place needs is some little ones to liven it up. When are you going to give in to Lydia?"

"Never." He grabbed her and bent her back like an apache dancer, planting a wet, squeaky kiss on her nose. "You are the only woman I could ever love."

"You idiot," she said, laughing to cover a sinking feeling. "Can't you ever be serious?"

KATE MANEUVERED her mother's big black Chrysler through the toll gate at the entrance to the hospital parking lot, pulling into the first available space. The last movement of her favorite Copland symphony was playing on the radio and she wanted to stay and listen to the end. But with the air-conditioner off, even the tinted windows couldn't keep the heat from quickly invading the interior, and she was soon forced out. Conscientiously, only because it wasn't her car, she made sure the doors were locked.

Humming, to finish the music in her mind, she waited for a break in traffic so she could cross the drive. In the dusky light, she saw Lieutenant Tejeda sitting on a bench by the opposite curb. Eyes closed, hands folded across his slightly rounded stomach, long legs stretched out in front of him, he seemed to be listening to a symphony of his own.

The street lights along the drive began to glow, making little headway against the gathering night. Kate hardly cast a shadow as she stopped in front of Tejeda. "Sleeping on city time?"

"The mind is still working." He sat upright, moving over to make room for her on the concrete bench. "How you doing? Your eye looks better."

"Thanks." She sat beside him, putting Miles's bundle on the bench between them and handed Tejeda Sy Ratcher's condo plans. "I don't know if this will lead you anywhere, but this is something Mother was involved with when she died."

He unrolled the plans and looked at them quickly. "What is it?"

"A pipe dream."

"Sy Ratcher," he said knowingly. "Thanks. I'll look into it."

"What did you come here to talk about?" Kate asked.

"Your Uncle Miles." He leaned back against the bench. "If he wakes up there are some things I want to ask him. But the condition he's in, I doubt he'll talk to me."

"But he will talk to me?"

"More likely."

The sound of a car engine made her look up; there was something familiar about it. A big, dark car came backing down the parking aisle in front of her, going too fast.

"Look at that jerk," Tejeda said. "They see a parking space that will save them ten steps and they'll kill for it. At least he could turn on his lights so people could see him coming."

Just then a little pickup backed into the car's path, forcing it to swerve crazily. Listing to one side, the car bumped the curb bordering some landscaping, two wheels gouging a crooked furrow through the marigolds. Finally, the car found the pavement again, pausing a moment for its shocks to absorb the bounce.

Kate picked up some of the excitement of the crowd around her, trying to anticipate what this driver might do next. With no lights on, she thought, it was the blackness of the car that gave drama to the situation. Even the car's windows were tinted black. Then she looked again, disbelief clouding her perception. She edged forward for confirmation.

"It's not possible," she gasped. "That's my mother's car."

"Who's driving it?"

"I am." It seemed at the moment a more reasonable answer than the only alternative that occurred to her. Mother never was much of a driver.

The car gunned its powerful motor and aimed directly at Kate and Tejeda. All other traffic stopped, wary drivers not knowing which way to go to avoid the inevitable collision.

Kate moved a few steps forward, trying to see the driver. But all she could see was the orange reflection of street lights in the tinted back window.

"Are you crazy?" Tejeda grabbed her arm and pulled her to one side. But the car corrected its course and followed them. In the instants available, Tejeda feinted to the right like a bull-fighter, hands riveted around Kate's arms.

Just as it jumped the curb in front of them, the car swerved sharply to the left, trapping Kate and Tejeda between its forward rush and the bench.

Tejeda dove backward over the solid bench, dragging Kate with him. As her face hit the sidewalk, Kate heard the sickening crunch of concrete and metal as the car sideswiped the other

side of the bench. Vaguely aware of the pain, she peered between Tejeda's shoulder and the underside of the bench as the
car's crumpled bumper snagged Miles's bundle. Then there was
a grinding of gears as the car, still moving, shifted from reverse and popped into drive. It bounced back over the curb and
sped away, a sleeve of Miles's pajamas waving in the air as if
appealing desperately for help.

Kate disentangled herself from Tejeda in time to see the car
crash through the parking lot arms, tires squealing as it turned
onto the street and away from the hospital.

Then suddenly, as the car disappeared, Kate felt an unnatural silence descend around her.

Tejeda yanked her to her feet, bringing his ashen face only
inches from hers. "Did you see who it was?"

Without breath or composure to speak she could only shrug
her shoulders.

Tejeda looked at the crowd gathering around them. "Stay
here," he ordered. Hand on his service revolver, he ran toward
the street.

Murmuring like trees in the wind, the bystanders drew into
a circle around her, keeping at a small distance. Eyes bright,
they watched her, as if disaster still clung to her and might strike
again.

To get out from under the collective stare she stepped to the
curb to gather the remains of Miles's belongings scattered on
the pavement. The shaving kit was smashed, the robe soiled in
the gutter, bringing realization of her near-miss crashing down
in a heavy, nauseating wave. The car had come so close, closer
than the stones on the stairs. Even with Tejeda beside her.

She knelt by some shrubbery and vomited Esperanza's
quiche.

Police sirens wailed past the broken gates, disrupting traffic
on the busy street beyond the parking lot. The angry skidding,
braking, and honking merged with the buzzing in her head and
swelled in her ears to an almost overwhelming crescendo of
confusion.

Hugging the remains of Miles's bundle tight against her
chest, Kate pulled herself to her feet and looked around for
something solid to hold on to, to steady herself.

It seemed like a long time before Tejeda came back. He wedged his way through the crowd and wrapped a protective arm around her. Chest heaving from running, his breath came in short gasps. "Missed him. Do you have any idea who it was?"

"No. It was so black."

"Did you leave your keys in the car?"

She looked around the pavement until she located her handbag. With shaking hands she opened it and pulled out her mother's key ring.

"Doesn't matter. Anyway, he wasn't after the car. Left it in back of the hospital in a delivery bay."

"He got away?"

"Only for the moment." He patted her back absently while he spoke.

"Ouch." She recoiled as he hit a tender spot.

"You okay?" He held her by the shoulders and looked into her face, concern etching deep lines in his forehead. His face relaxed into a crooked smile. "Hate to tell you this, but you're going to have a beautiful new shiner."

TWELVE

"SUICIDAL MANIAC." Kate shifted the ice-filled towel away from her swelling cheek and used it to push the mug of bitter hospital coffee away from her. Some coffee sloshed onto the police reports littering the formica table, and the sight of it made her gag back the sharp taste of the quiche she had left in the landscaping. "Why me, for God's sake? I liked being beaten up by the police better. Damned kamikaze."

Tejeda let her vent off steam for a while before he said anything. "Why do you say this character is suicidal?"

"Why else would he-she come after me with a goddam car?" She leaned closer to him. "This person was ready to risk capture, or, better yet, death, to get rid of me. Know what I think?"

"What?"

"I think that, in a twisted way, this is a very generous person. If he'll risk getting caught himself, he must be doing this to benefit someone else."

"Interesting idea." He dropped a stack of napkins on the spilled coffee and started wiping it up, a reflexive gesture, she thought, of a man accustomed to keeping house for himself. "Fortunately, our culprit doesn't know beans about how to commit a nice, clean murder. What a bungler."

"Don't sound so disappointed," she said.

"There's hope," he smiled. "Maybe he's a quick study."

"He's had lots of practice, anyway. Three assaults."

"Three?"

"Counting the attack on Mother."

"He was a lot more effective on that one." Tejeda reached across the table and gently turned Kate's face to the light. "Put the ice back on. You got quite a bump."

Kate put the frigid, sopping towel against the right side of her face. "Reece told me you confiscated Miles's cricket bats. Find anything?"

"Yeah," he nodded. "All the lab tests aren't in, but the pre-lims match it with your mother's wounds."

"Oh, damn." Feeling defeated, she slid back against the plastic seat. The news about the bats was only confirmation of what she already suspected. So far, every step of the investigation had brought this thing closer to the family circle. But who? Reece, Carl, Mina, Dolph, Esperanza, Helga? At least Miles was out of it. She tried to fathom what any of them had to gain in sufficient measure to exterminate her. She discounted money as the motive; it just wasn't that important to any of them. Not as important as her right to influence the decision made over Grandpa Archie's estate, including the law firm, investments, and the seven juicy acres. After seeing Mother's plan to build condos on the bluff, she could understand why someone would passionately want to get rid of Mother. But why get rid of Kate? Other than some painting and cleanup of her own house, she had no intention of interfering with the status quo. Unless that was the problem.

Tejeda nervously drummed the table with his fingertips, drawing Kate from her ruminations and making her aware she had been staring at his face, focused on the deep ebony eyes set in honey. Embarrassed, she turned away, catching the people at the next table staring at her. She smiled as they snapped their faces frontward. They had seen the incident in the parking lot and were probably curious, Kate thought, about the couple who had come so close to mayhem. Maybe they still felt a little excited to have danger so near.

The ice was beginning to give her a headache. She put it down amid the clutter in front of her and leaned closer to Tejeda, close enough to smell the coffee on his breath, close enough for some privacy from the other people. "Did you see my mother in the morgue?"

He nodded, swallowing hard.

She understood the reflex, having the same wad of bile in her throat every time she thought about the morgue. "Someone close, close enough to get the bat and return it later, bashed her head to Jell-O. The same person then, had easy access to keys: Mother's car keys today, Miles's back door key last night. And he has easy access to me. What's going to keep him from trying again? Where was your surveillance team this afternoon?"

"What makes you think they were watching *you*?"

"Then what am I? Bait?"

He thought about it. "In a way."

"Wonderful." She sat back, folding her arms across her chest. "I thought they were hanging around trying to prevent my untimely demise."

"We're detectives." He reached out and gripped her shoulder, a crooked smile teasing the corner of his mouth. "We don't prevent crimes. We solve them."

"That isn't comforting."

A tall, very young, uniformed policeman came into the cafeteria and looked around, searching for someone. Tejeda waved to him and he came over, bobbing and weaving around the irregularly placed tables and chairs. When he stopped next to Tejeda's chair Kate noticed his adolescent acne wasn't quite healed yet.

"Officer Frank Little," Tejeda said, "this is Kate Teague."

"Nice to meet you." He gave Kate a quick nod and appraisal before he turned his attention back to Tejeda. "Everything's cleaned up outside, sir. Car's in the impound lot."

"Thanks."

Little looked doubtfully at the soiled papers on the table. "If Mrs. Teague has signed the releases, I'll take them in with me."

"What releases?" Kate asked him.

"Standard release forms absolving the city of responsibility for your injuries."

"The city didn't injure me."

Little aimed a finger at Tejeda. "He's the city."

The lieutenant's color deepened from gold to red-bronze. "I threw you to the ground, remember?"

"And landed on top of me." She massaged her sore elbow. "I was in such a snit, I didn't even ask if you were hurt."

He gently touched the thick shiny hair on the crown of his head. "Just a little bump."

"Sorry." Kate offered her dripping towel full of ice. "Want a turn?"

"No, thanks."

A young busboy in an oversized white jacket appeared immediately at Tejeda's elbow. *"Quieres mas hielo?"*

"No, gracias." Tejeda slipped a coin into the boy's palm and waved him away. "No more ice. I don't know why people always assume I speak Spanish. My folks grew up right here in Santa Angelica, for chrissake. I had to take Spanish in school so I would know what people are all the time saying to me."

Little chuckled. "You need me anymore, Lieutenant?"

"Yeah. What time is your shift over?"

"Ten."

"Good." Tejeda turned to Kate. "Where are you going now?"

"Upstairs," she said. "It's my turn to sit with Miles."

"Okay, Little," he said, glancing around at the wall clock. "For the next hour and a half, I want you to stay close to Mrs. Teague. Stick with her until a replacement shows, okay?"

"Fine with me." Little gave Kate a more comprehensive appraisal when she stood up. "Since we're spending the night together, you might as well call me Frank."

"Thanks, Frank," she laughed.

"Uh, Lieutenant," Little began, "Sergeant Green said to tell you, you were right. He said you'd know what that meant."

Kate looked at Tejeda. "What *does* it mean?"

"A line of inquiry panned out." He drained his coffee cup as he stood up.

"Why don't you just tell me the whole story?" she asked. "I'm a big girl."

"Sorry." He shook his head. "I only have bits and pieces right now. They seem to be heading in one direction, but we could be wrong. As it is, it's a pretty thin trail, and I can't risk having it wiped out by a premature tip-off."

"So what do I do in the meantime?"

"For starters, stay close to Little here." Tejeda gripped her bruised shoulder and bent his head close to hers. "Had any acting training?"

"A little," she shrugged. "In college."

"Good. You're going to need it." He looked at his watch. "It's late. I better call Theresa. She's taking a survival for singles class in school and tonight she's cooking me something called cowboy casserole for dinner. I don't want her to burn it until I get there."

"You're leaving?" Kate had a flash of dread, thinking about facing her family upstairs and making everything seem normal.

"I'll be back." He put an arm lightly around her and walked her toward the bank of elevators. "I'll bring you some cowboy casserole, if it's edible."

Kate nestled against him a little, enjoying the closeness, wishing it would last longer. And go farther.

"If you get a chance," he said, "ask your aunt again about the maid's abortion."

"Does that mean I don't have to abandon my bastard?"

"Maybe." He traced the swelling on her cheek. "Then again, maybe not."

Officer Little walked on the other side of her, watching Tejeda out of the side of his eye, perplexity clouding his face. Kate smiled, realizing the young officer was a bit scandalized by Tejeda's familiarity with her. She wondered if it was Tejeda's rank or age that bothered him.

Little pushed the call button and the chrome elevator doors slid open. He got into the car and held the doors open, keeping his eyes averted from Kate and Tejeda. Kate was tempted to engage Tejeda in a long, passionate embrace, partly for the discomfort of Little but mostly because she thought she would like it.

Instead, Tejeda gave her back a reassuring pat. "Stay close to Little. I'll see you later."

Alone with her in the elevator, Little relaxed. "So, how long have you known the lieutenant?"

"Three days," she said.

"I thought you must be old friends, the amount of time he's spending on this case."

"Oh?" She smiled noncommittally, cautioned by his interest. "Is it unusual?"

"I've never known him to give a case so much personal attention. Most of the time, he's in his office at the station, doing administrative stuff. Normally, he only goes into the field to see what *we're* doing." He stood at the front of the elevator, watching the floor numbers flashing above the doors. "Guess there's something different about this case."

"Guess so." She looked at the dewy-soft skin under his chin, and decided he couldn't be more than twenty-two or twenty-three. He seemed too young to be so serious, to have the life-or-death responsibilities of a policeman. Then it occurred to her that she and Nugie had been just about his age when they'd made the life-or-death decisions about Nugie and her baby. It was just before her twenty-third birthday when she and Carl decided to put their shared grief over Nugie behind them and get married. Kate closed her eyes and leaned against the cold metal wall. For some decisions, maybe you're never old enough.

They reached the intensive care floor. Kate moved to the front of the car and waited for the doors to open. But Little motioned for her to wait. He stepped partway out into the corridor and looked around before he let Kate walk out past him. He did it all very casually, without any melodramatics, so she relaxed a bit about having to spend the evening under his watch.

They found Dolph and Mina playing gin rummy in the hall outside Miles's private room. Mina was running her fingers nervously through her hair so that it stood up in funny, ragged peaks. In contrast, her beautifully tailored summer dress hung perfectly on her ninety-two pound frame, so that, to Kate, she looked like someone's old, best-loved doll dressed up in a new frock. Her tired face looked pale and puffy under the cruel fluorescent light.

Officer Little hung back, then detoured to the nurses' station as if he had come up on separate business. Kate felt relieved; explaining why he was there would have been difficult.

"Kate, at last. Thank God." Mina slapped her cards down on the white formica table. "I'm down eighty-five cents to this shyster I'm playing. Either lend me some money or take his place."

"You going to stand for that from her, Kate? She thinks she can beat you." Dolph laughed but Kate noticed the bright red spots, like clown makeup, glowing on his cheeks. An overdose of adrenaline or fatigue.

"Mina always beats me at gin." Kate bent to kiss them in turn. "But she cheats."

"Where's Carl?" Dolph put his reading glasses in his breast pocket, then came to stand beside her. "I thought he would be right along."

"I haven't seen him."

"Probably stuck in that traffic snarl outside," Dolph said. "Some sort of accident. Is that what kept you, dear?"

"Yes. I got tied up in traffic." Kate resisted touching her throbbing cheek. With sad resignation she accepted the fact that Dolph and Mina were both suspects, maybe a terrible threat to her. She looped her arm through Dolph's and held on tight. "How's Miles?"

"I haven't seen him yet." He looked down at Mina and grinned. "I've been here only long enough to win three gin hands. But Mina has some good news."

"Indeed I do." She paused for dramatic affect. "Miles spoke to me."

"Terrific," Kate said. "Anything profound?"

An impish look crossed Mina's face. "He said, 'wa-a-a-ter.'" A natural mimic, she dragged the word out in a low gargle.

"It's something, anyway," Dolph said.

"He's ga-ga, but he's not comatose anymore." Mina's eyes were bright with fatigue. "He's sleeping now."

"We don't all have to hang around here," Kate said. "You two go on home. If you hear from Carl, tell him not to come. I'm okay here by myself. I'll let you know if anything happens."

With her brow furrowed, Mina peered up into Kate's face, squinting myopically. Without changing her line of focus she got up and came over to Kate, and putting a hand on either side of her face, brought her down so she could see her better. "Kate, darling, that shiner isn't looking any better. You should have it seen to before you leave the building. Take a look, Dolph."

"She's right, Kate." Dolph perched his reading glasses back on his nose. "That close to the eye, you should be careful."

Kate almost laughed aloud. If only they knew. Or did they?

"MRS. TEAGUE." Officer Little was waiting by Miles's room when Kate returned from seeing Dolph and Mina to the elevator. "The lieutenant wants me inconspicuous. So you might not always see me, but I'm here."

"Thanks, Frank. Hope this doesn't get too boring."

"Nah." He looked at his watch. "New shift of nurses comes on in half an hour. I'll find something to do."

"Go ahead. I'll check on my uncle."

The intensive care room looked like a cross between a video arcade and a morgue. Resembling a corpse prepared for burial, Miles lay in a high bed surrounded by video screens that recorded his body functions in wavy lines of green. I.V. tubes and computer cable held him in a tangled web. Over the blipping of the monitors Kate could hear his soft snoring, a reassuring and human sound among all the hardware.

She tucked the thin white blanket under his chin and touched his cheek, the taut skin as smooth and thin as tissue paper. And about as lively to the touch. Seeing him brought back memories of her mother and father, and how they had looked in death. Sadly, she accepted it as a certainty that he would never leave this place and come home.

After her father's funeral, Miles had come into Kate's room and held her, encouraging the tears her mother had ordered turned off.

"Sometimes bad things happen," he'd said, "and it takes a while to get used to them. So go ahead and cry." For many reasons, losing Miles would be harder than losing Mother.

Leaving the door ajar so she could hear him, she went back to the hall. Sometimes sitting on a slick, plastic-covered chair, sometimes pacing the dozen feet between his door and the nurse's desk, she waited.

Every time the elevator door opened, Officer Little appeared. If no one came out, he waved to her and disappeared again. Occasionally Kate heard soft female laughter from the direction he disappeared toward.

The vigil seemed interminable. Nurses bustled around her, checking the tubes and cables attached to Miles, adjusting his position, resetting the bank of monitors. She envied their activity.

Sometime after they had finished evening medication rounds, she stopped at the nurses' station. "Have anything I might borrow to read?"

The duty-nurse looked under the counter. "*Nursing Today* and *True Confessions*. Take your pick."

Kate laughed. "Which do you recommend?"

The nurse handed her *Nursing Today*. "Great article on PMS. You know, premenstrual syndrome."

"Thanks." Kate sat by Miles's door, trying to listen for him and concentrate on the long, technical article. Feeling sleepy, she laid the open magazine on her lap and closed her eyes.

"Queen Victoria had PMS." Lieutenant Tejeda seemed to come from nowhere. "She used to abuse her poor husband."

"The things you know. What brings you here?"

"Just checking on you."

"It's late. Where's Theresa?"

"She's sleeping at Mrs. Murphy's. Here." He handed her a bright orange Tupperware container. "Theresa sent you something."

Kate opened the container and looked at the shimmering brownish-gray mass inside. "What is it?"

"Cowboy casserole, as promised." He took a plastic fork out of his pocket. "Theresa hopes you like it. She said since it was you, I could stay as late as I want. She took her jammies over to Mrs. Murphy's."

"Precocious kid, that Theresa." Kate looked at the mass again. "Can't do it."

"C'mon, be a sport, try it. Just so I can say you did."

She took a bite, not chewing, the way you do with raw oysters. "Mmm," she smiled at him. "It's terrible."

"It is, isn't it? She didn't have any hamburger so she substituted browned tofu."

"Didn't know you could brown tofu."

"With steak sauce." He put the open container on the table. "How's your uncle?"

"Semiconscious. He asked Mina for some water. Mostly he just moans and snores."

"If he wakes up and he seems coherent, will you ask him some questions for me?"

"For instance?" she asked.

"See if he knows anything about the keys and the cricket bats?"

"That's all?"

"If you think he's up to it," he hesitated for a moment, flinching as if waiting for a blow, "ask him if he killed your mother."

"You're kidding, right?"

"It's nothing to kid about."

"Miles?"

"You think that's not possible?"

"I don't know." What was possible anymore? She rubbed her eyes, but everything was the same when she opened them, but not exactly the same; like looking through the backside of a mirror. "There's a sort of divine justice if Miles killed Mother, when you think of what she was trying to do to him. Then again, it makes things a lot neater."

"Neater?" He rolled the word over. He didn't seem to like the taste of it.

"I love my Uncle Miles very much and I don't want to believe he killed Mother. But he's dying, and I'd rather see this whole mess die with him than have my family dragged through an investigation and trial."

"Won't work." He shook his head. "Even if we get a deathbed confession from Miles, it isn't going to neaten up things. He sure as hell wasn't driving your mother's car tonight."

"I know." Kate had to hang on to the belief that Miles would never hurt her, no matter what he might have done to Mother. Then she thought for a minute and decided it was crazy to think that sweet, gentle Miles could have killed anyone. Even Mother. She felt disloyal to the whole family to have considered the idea, and was vexed with Tejeda for broaching the subject. She turned to him and asked, "Why don't you just ask him yourself?"

"Because the nurses won't let me wake him up, and I don't know how long I can wait around here."

"Then I hope he wakes up before you leave." She crossed her arms across her chest. "Because I won't ask him if he killed my mother."

"Suit yourself." A conspiratorial grin spread across his face. "But you want to know the answer, right?"

"Maybe," she sighed. "Maybe not. But I'm glad to have some company while I decide." She tried to get comfortable in the hard, molded seat. She sat sideways, facing Tejeda, with one leg tucked under her until it went to sleep, then she shifted forward and rubbed her tingling foot.

Tejeda yawned and leaned back, stretching his arm along the back of Kate's seat. "Besides the food, do you know what I miss about being married?"

"I can think of a few things," she laughed.

He smiled. "There's no one to wait around with. Like last summer, I took my son to have his wisdom teeth out. I spent half a day alone in a waiting room, thinking about all the crazy things that could go wrong. After a while I'd persuaded myself he'd never come out of the anesthesia, or they'd zap a facial nerve and he'd spend the rest of his life looking like Quasimodo. Then last week I drove him up to college and moved him into the dorm. All the way home I listed to myself all the ways he could destroy his life before he finishes his freshman year."

"I didn't know you were such a worrier."

"Normally, I'm not. Before last year, before my wife moved out, we would have been waiting there together, arguing about where we were going on vacation or why the checkbook didn't balance or why Congress should spend more on schools and less on bombs. It was a diversion. Now I have to be bored all by myself."

"How long were you married?"

"Nineteen years."

"That's a long time." She leaned back, his arm on the back of her chair cushioning her head. "What happened?"

"Not sure," he said, drumming a distracted tattoo on her shoulder. "Success, maybe. Cassy is a brainy, good-looking woman. I always wanted things to be perfect for her, but we had a pretty rough beginning. First I was in Vietnam, then I became a cop. And all that time she never knew if suddenly she'd be left a widow with little kids, half-expecting it all the time. I've been shot at more times than I can remember, hit a couple of times. She was a brick. Didn't say much about it, ever. Just fed me chicken soup and kissed the boo-boo.

"'Course, there was never much money. But she made do, found ways to economize so we had a comfortable life."

Kate couldn't imagine herself filling the shoes of the long-suffering Cassy. Or if she'd want to. She turned her head on his arm and looked up at his strong profile and thought it might be worth a try. "So what happened?"

He took a deep breath and let it out slowly. "Two years ago I made Lieutenant. I was safer, I didn't have to dodge bullets anymore. The pay was great, relatively speaking. I told Cassy to relax, do more for herself. The kids were old enough to take care of themselves, so she had time to do what she wanted. She could go back to college, finish her degree. She could do anything she wanted to."

"So what did she do?"

"First she bought some furniture, but she hated it, said she liked the old junk better. We went on a cruise, but she liked roughing it in the woods better. When we got home she cried for a week. Then she read about some Indians in New Mexico who were living in dire poverty. So she packed a bag and went to help them. She said we didn't need her anymore."

"Do you hear from her?"

"Rarely." He shook his head. "Sent the kids birthday cards and me a copy of the final divorce decree."

"How sad for you," she said. "Must be lonely."

"Lonely?" He gave her a startled look, then laughed. "Who says I'm lonely? Did you ever try living with a saint? I think she's just found her natural calling. Should have been a nun to start with."

She turned in her seat so she could look squarely at him. "A nun?"

"Some people are natural celibates," he said, running a finger along her chin. He kissed her lightly on the forehead, leaving a tracing of static electricity. "I'm not one of them."

"Lieutenant?" Officer Little came up silently. "Sorry to, uh, interrupt, but there's a call for you. Sergeant Green."

"Thanks." He squeezed Kate's arm. "Gotta go. Remember what I asked you to do. And Little, stay close."

Kate handed him the Tupperware, a way to delay him, if only for a moment. "Don't forget this."

"Right." He dumped it in a flat ceramic ashtray. "You loved it?"

"I loved it," she laughed, though she felt keen disappointment that he was going. She wanted him to turn around and ask her to come with him.

"Nice guy, the lieutenant," Little said as Tejeda disappeared into the elevator.

"Yes. Very nice." Kate stood up and stretched, putting her hand on the back of her neck where Tejeda's arm had warmed it. She smiled to herself; the warmth she felt extended far beyond her neck, a delicious voluptuousness for all its innocence. Yawning lazily, she asked, "What time is it?"

"Eleven."

"Seems later. I'm going to my uncle's room. Take a little nap. Where will you be?"

"I'll be right here." He sat down in her vacated seat and pushed the full ashtray and its smelly contents to the far side of the table. "I like earning overtime this way."

Kate went inside and quickly checked Miles, tucking his cold hands under the blanket. She pulled the room's only chair into the corner by the window and leaned her head against the sharp edge of the windowsill, closing her eyes. The heavy, morgue-like odor brought strong images of her mother, eddying in dizzy pools, drowning other thoughts.

"Margaret." A gritty voice. From somewhere in the room, or was it a dream? Kate sat up, not sure if she had dozed. The room was almost dark, the only light coming from the green video screens and the city lights outside. She rolled her head to stretch tight muscles.

"Margaret." The white blanket moved slightly.

Leaning forward, Kate could see narrow glints of light under Miles's eyelids. "It's not Margaret, Uncle Miles. It me, Kate."

The eyes closed and he coughed, sounding feeble and dry.

"Do you want some water?" She shook the pitcher of water on the bedside table. Hearing the rattle of ice, she half-filled a Styrofoam cup, put in a straw and offered it to him, supporting his neck in the crook of her arm.

His fingers, like a dry claw, wrapped around her hand on the cup. He drank, dribbling water and spittle down his chin.

"Can I get something else for you?" Alone with him, she felt a rising panic. He was so frail. As much as she loved him, she didn't want to be here alone if he died.

"Too late." Like gravel deep in his lungs.

"Let me get the nurse."

She pushed the call button and waited as Miles breathed in increasingly shallow gasps.

Finally, a female voice crackled through the speaker at the head of the bed. "May I help you? Just speak and I can hear you."

"My uncle is awake now."

"Yes, I can see on my monitor. Does he need anything?"

"I don't know." Kate looked at his stonelike face.

"We're watching him. Just call if he asks for something."

Miles had closed his eyes again. He was so still Kate went nearer to make sure he was breathing. She leaned her face over him.

His eyes popped round and bright. "How many babies did you take?"

Kate stumbled back, horrified. His voice was so clear she looked around quickly to see if someone else had slipped into the room and spoken.

How many babies? It made no sense to her. She couldn't be sure that he was really awake. Or that he would ever be more coherent than he was now. She stepped close to him again. But how could she ask him what Tejeda wanted? "Uncle Miles, can you hear me?"

"You won't do it again." He shook his crabbed hand at her. "Twice you took my baby. You won't take my baby away again."

"Tell me about your baby. Where is your baby?"

"Hah!" he cackled. "Safe at home. You can't get him now."

"Safe where?"

But he only shook his head, grinning. "I won't tell."

She looked at him, searching for the man she loved. But he seemed so changed, something that went beyond the gravity of his condition. Then things started to connect, like little keys in rusty old locks.

Mother had helped Miles's mistress find an abortionist, according to Mina. Miles loved children, but his only child had been lost to him because of the machinations of her mother. Although she knew that Mina and Susan had taken part, intuitively Kate knew it was her mother who had done the planning. And the persuading. Had the maid wanted to keep her baby?

Maybe he wasn't as incoherent as he seemed. She decided there was no harm in trying to get some answers from him. "Uncle Miles, Mother's keys are missing."

"I put your keys back," he contradicted.

Kate saw Little watching her from the doorway. "Call Lieutenant Tejeda, quickly, please. I need him. Now."

He nodded and closed the door.

Groping in the half-dark, Kate found a light switch. White light filled the room, dazzling her for a moment.

Miles didn't flinch.

"Uncle Miles, look at me." She leaned over him again. "It's not Margaret. It's Kate. Look at me." She held his shoulders gently in her hands, surprised by the firmness of the muscles under the hospital gown.

He gave her a moronic grin, like a drunk the instant before he passes out, long past sensibility.

"When did you have the keys?"

"It wasn't cricket, what you did," he said stupidly. "But it was damn good cricket what I did. Always a crack batsman." He started to giggle. *"Crack."* The giggling became hiccups. He arched his back, gripped by a violent spasm, his body rigid and trembling.

Kate held him firmly, to keep him from falling off the bed. Or from sliding into oblivion.

He looked up at her, eyes rolling back in their sockets.

"Did you hit Mother?" she demanded, trying to control the anger and frustration in her voice. There was so little time left. "Tell me what you know. Help me."

The spasm released him, and he relaxed in her arms, lying very still. The white face turned toward her. "Kate?" His voice was very faint.

"Thank God. Yes." She kept her face in his line of vision. "I'm frightened, Uncle Miles. I need to know what happened to Mother. I need to save myself."

"I can't help you anymore. I tried. Trust hope."

"I don't understand."

"Trust hope," he said through clenched teeth. He arched in rigid spasm again, grimacing as if something were pulling on him from the inside.

The door burst all the way open and a mass of green-gowned nurses filled the room. "Coronary," one of them yelled over her shoulder, elbowing past Kate to lean over Miles. "Where's the doc? Damn! Where's the doc? We have a grand mal seizure and he's in arrest."

"STAT," the P.A. in the hall crackled. "ICU. STAT. STAT."

A second wave of green pushed into the room, rolling ahead of them huge carts of emergency equipment.

Kate stood there, frozen, unwilling to let Miles slip away from her. Bony hands grabbed her arm and impelled her toward the door. "You have to get out."

Under the noise she heard the small blips on the video screens race frantically, then flatten into a steady tone.

THIRTEEN

"TEJEDA THINKS MILES killed Mother with his cricket bat."
Kate stopped when she heard the light tap at Dolph's study
door. Mina's maid came quietly into the room carrying a
breakfast tray. Kate waited for the maid to put the tray down
on Dolph's desk and then leave the room before she said anything more. "Do you think it's possible that Miles would kill
anyone?"

"It's possible." Dolph filled a small crystal glass with freshly
squeezed orange juice from a silver pitcher and drank it down.

"You're awfully calm about it."

"I'm also not persuaded. I only agree it is *possible*. Maybe
Miles thought the only way he could stop her from dumping
him in an institution so she could turn his place into condos was
to eliminate her. God knows more conventional means failed."
Dolph studied the buttered toast in his hand. "But if he wanted
to kill her, why didn't he haul out his deer rifle and make a
tidier job of it?"

"Oh, Dolph, please." The suggestion recalled a strong, vivid
image of her mother's battered head, adding a neat hole between her eyes. Then she remembered the eyes of the elk Miles
had shot in Colorado and she knew why he wouldn't have shot
Mother.

"Sorry, sweetheart." Dolph put the uneaten toast down
again. "What exactly did Miles say to you?"

"He said, 'It wasn't cricket.' "

"Cricket again. Miles sank back into a coma last night after
the docs revived him. What do you think the chances are we'll
be able to talk to him again?"

"None." Last night, after the doctors had stabilized Miles,
she had stayed for a few minutes, just to be with him one last
time. She remembered the emptiness in the air around Miles as
she pressed her cheek to his to say good-bye, as if the electricity in his body had been shut off.

"I thought not." Dolph shook his head, seemingly lost in deep thought. Then he turned to the tray and piled a plate with eggs and sausage and fruit. But he held his empty fork poised over his plate, his eyes locked on a point in the space in front of him.

All morning Kate had felt edgy, expectant. It was equal parts lack of sleep and waiting for the inevitable call from the hospital. The final call.

Carrying her cup of coffee, she got up and paced the sea of pale green carpet, noticing how the ocean shimmering dully beyond the French doors seemed merely an artful part of the room's decor. She looked around at the deliberate casualness, the way Dolph's law journals heaped in the whitewashed willow basket by his big reading chair were stacked just a little crookedly, as if they'd been carelessly tossed there. But even though the journals changed regularly, the angles of the stack were always the same. She began to feel that, like the carefully arranged vase of silk flowers on the corner of the desk, nothing here was quite genuine, or ever changed, and she wondered why she hadn't noticed it before. The comfort the place offered was artifice.

"You told Mina earlier that Miles babbled on for a while." Dolph dabbed at the corners of his mouth, as if he had eaten. "Besides the cricket thing, what did he say?"

"He said his baby is safe now. And to trust hope."

"Well, that's always good advice."

"What is?"

"Trust Hope. Hope is English for Esperanza, you know."

"Is that what he meant?"

"Sure. Esperanza anglicized her name when she came up from Mexico, asked us to call her Hope. And we did, until she went to work for your mother. Your mother thought Esperanza was more highbrow." He sipped his coffee. "Did you talk to Esperanza at all this morning?"

Kate shook her head. "Her day off. She took the bus to her sister's last night and won't be back till after dinner tonight. I don't know what she could tell me anyway."

"Ask her about the housekeeper's baby. Esperanza knows everything about anything that ever happened here. The problem is getting her to talk about it."

"Know who I think I might call?"

"Who?"

"Susan Ratcher."

"Don't do that. And quit pacing. I'm getting a crick in my neck watching you. Pour yourself some more coffee and land somewhere."

She pushed aside a stack of legal-size manila folders piled on the corner of the desk to make room for her empty coffee cup. The stack tipped over and spilled across the polished surface before she could catch it, folders and their contents cascading onto the carpet.

"Sorry." Kate knelt to gather it all together. "You'll have to sort these out yourself. I don't know what goes where."

"Don't worry about it." He poured himself a third cup of coffee. As Kate put the papers back on the desk, her own name typed in boldface across the middle of the top sheet, caught her eye.

"What is all this?"

"No reason not to tell you." He joined her behind the desk and put his reading glasses on, ready for work. "I'm writing a new will."

"Which reminds me. You said you'd send one of your staff over to redo mine."

"I will," he said, sitting down and sorting through the pile. "But I want you to hold off a few more days."

"Hold off for what?"

"Wait until we get a look at Miles's will."

"Oh, jeez." She rubbed at the dull thumping in her temples. "Miles isn't even dead. Yet."

"Hold on there. I'm no ghoul. Miles and I talked about this weeks ago. He said he would have old Tom Bodge send over a copy."

"Tom Bodge?" Kate asked, incredulous. She remembered Old Tom, all 280 asthmatic pounds of him. "He can't still be around."

"He is," Dolph laughed. "Very round. He isn't practicing law anymore, though. Miles entrusted his will to Tom because he said, Tom could be depended on to keep his mouth shut. Even with a snootful of pink gin. Anyway, I don't actually need to see the document. I'm sure you're Miles's sole legatee."

Kate thought of all the people he knew before his illness, all the charities he'd been involved with. "Why?"

"Because of conversations we had when we drew up our wills, before Dad died. You kids, you and Reece and Nugie, were still in school and we wanted to make sure you all had enough to get through in case something happened. Since Reece and Nugie were part of my wife's family, and I was paying the tuition for their preparation, I covered them and Miles was to make provisions for you."

"Sounds fair enough."

"At the time it was. But things have changed since then. Reece is self-supporting now, and Nugie, God love her, is beyond need."

The tempo of the pounding in her head increased. "You're not dispossessing Reece are you?"

"Dispossessing? No. He's well taken care of by Mina. But what I plan to do is put all three shares of Dad's estate back together. You, Miles, and I are all equal partners right now. In the not so distant future..."

"I'll be all alone up here."

"As it were," he nodded.

"I don't like it," Kate protested. "I suspect I know how you're going to take care of Mina. She'll get the interest from a trust during the remainder of her life, just like Mother did. Then the capital will revert to me. Right?"

"Essentially."

"There won't be anything for Reece except a few trinkets in a bottom drawer."

"What drawer?"

"Doesn't matter. It's not fair." She pounded the desk with her fist. "There's no need to cut Reece out."

"You sound like Mina," Dolph said wearily. "I've already done what I thought was appropriate for Reece. He's educated, self-sufficient. Moving beyond that, what I want to do is rejoin the three shares of the family estates. You notice I said *family*. It has nothing to do with Reece."

"All this," she swept her arms wide, taking in the expanse of bluff outside the window, "is a tremendous responsibility. It would be nice to have someone to share the burden with."

"I have faith in you, Kate, you'll manage. Anyway, once it's yours, you can do anything you want with it."

"Hadn't thought of that." She ruffled his sparse white hair. "Why don't you just live forever and save me a lot of bother?"

"I don't want to live forever." He pushed all the papers into one folder and dumped the mess into a bottom drawer. "I'm getting tired."

"I don't know why." Kate glanced out at the expanse of cool lawn. "Business seems to be slow down at the family store. All the hired help seems to have time off."

"Slow?" Dolph took off his glasses and rubbed his eyes. "We're swamped. But Carl's doing such a great job riding herd down there, I thought I'd stay home for a few days."

"I wasn't talking about you," she said, realizing that something was very wrong. She watched Carl striding across the lawn from the direction of her house. From his heavy posture she knew why he had come, and she steeled herself in preparation. "I meant Carl."

"What now?" Color drained from Dolph's face as he saw Carl through the window. He stood up and took Kate's arm, and together they went over to the open French doors and waited.

Carl stopped just inside the threshold, with his hands clasped in front of him like a mortician at a fifty-dollar funeral.

"The hospital called the office," he said. "I thought I'd better come personally."

"Miles?" Kate's voice sounded hollow against the silence. "He's dead?"

"Yes." Carl unclasped his hands in a gesture of helplessness as tears formed in Dolph's eyes and spilled down the valleys of his bloodless face. Dolph reached out and drew Kate close.

"Poor Miles," she sighed, wiping away her tears with the back of her hand. She buried her head against Dolph's chest and tried to imagine Miles gone forever. When her father died and she felt he'd abandoned her and left her stuck in the emotional morass between her mother and grandfather, Miles had rescued her time after time. By just loving her he had saved her from disappearing into a fantasy world where life seemed safer and she could live again with her magical father. Miles had stayed close by through the years, reassuring her even after his illness had locked him inside its lonely cocoon. He always watched over her from his window.

Kate took a deep breath and looked up at Dolph, saw the grief on his face, the anguish for the brother lost and everything they'd shared, and for all the vanished possibilities. "What happens now?"

"Well." Struggling for composure, Dolph's voice boomed too loud. Kate saw the effort it took him to square his shoulders. "We'll have a look at his will, see if he left us any funeral instructions. I'll call Old Tom Bodge and set up a meeting for tomorrow. If that's okay with you."

"Whatever you arrange will be fine." Kate kissed him lightly on his pale cheek. "Mina has to be told. Shall I do it?"

"Dear God." Dolph put his hands over his face and wept.

KATE HUNG UP the telephone in Dolph's kitchen. The bland efficiency of the hospital clerk made it easier for Kate to deal with the business of Miles's death. "The mortuary is removing the body from the hospital sometime today."

Carl nervously tapped a spoon against the edge of a can of drain cleaner by the sink. He seemed unusually jittery and upset, moved perhaps, Kate thought, by Dolph's grief, and unsure about what his role here was, business partner or member of the family. He thumped the can with the spoon; an exclamation point. "I'll go with you to the mortuary."

"Why? It's awful there."

"Just to be with you. We always seem to pull together in a tragedy." He dropped his gaze almost shyly and watched the tapping spoon while he spoke. "I need to make it up to you for bugging you yesterday about your job. Esperanza and my mother gave me hell for it." A self-deprecating grin lit his face, making him very appealing.

"Wish I'd been there," she smiled, envisioning the scene. "Anyway, we won't do anything about funeral plans until we've seen the will."

"If he didn't leave instructions you'll probably just do something like your mother's, won't you? Bury him up there with her and your father."

"No way." She put her hand over the spoon to stop its annoying rat-a-tat. "We could never bury Miles near Mother."

"Why?" he asked sharply.

"Carl, we think Miles killed Mother."

"That's insane."

"Maybe not."

"I just . . . Oh hell." Carl threw the spoon into the sink a jarring clatter. It matched the angry, exasperated tone of his voice. "I'm trying Kate. I really am. But . . . never mind. You going home?"

"No." She backed away from him, physically and emotionally, to make space for herself. Her handbag was open on the tile counter by the telephone. She capped her pen and tossed it in with the jumble of notes and gum wrappers. "I have an errand to run."

"Now?" He took a deep breath and wiped his forehead. "I was hoping we could spend some time together."

"I'm going to see Susan Ratcher."

"Why on earth?"

"She should be told about Miles. After all, they were married once." Kate reached past him to open the door. "And there are a few things I want to ask her about."

"Can't you just call her, for God's sake?"

"I need to talk to her, Carl. I'm going to see her."

"No." His face was red. "That's dumb."

"Dumb?"

Chagrined, he tried to soften his anger. "You shouldn't be alone."

"You're right. I'll take someone along." Kate lifted the keys to Dolph's Mercedes from a hook by the back door. "Tell Dolph I'm taking his car. There might be a bomb in mine."

"Kate, please don't go." He was begging now, almost desperate.

"Why not? What are you afraid I'll find out?"

"Nothing."

"You didn't have something to do with that deal between Sy and Mother did you?"

"Shit. No." The heat had drained from his voice, and ice filled the void.

"Then what can she tell me? Maybe I was adopted or something? Right now that might be good news." She left him standing in the kitchen looking glum and defeated.

Angry energy left over from the argument surged through her as she started Dolph's car with a roar. She was angry at Carl for making her mad, and angry with herself for letting him get to her so easily. It's time for him to move out, she decided, with or without his mother.

She screeched to a stop in front of Miles's house and jumped out of the car. Sprinting up the walk she yelled, "Reece! If you're in there, open up." She banged on the door. "Reece!"

"What is it?" He gave her a molelike squint from the door-way, shielding his eyes from the bright sunlight. He had a flat draftsman's pencil over each ear. "What's going on?"

"Come with me." She grabbed him by the hand and pulled him along. "I have an errand to run and I need a bodyguard."

"Okay, okay. But let me get some shoes on." He disappeared into the dark house and came right back, hopping on one foot then the other as he slipped on his battered, stringless sneakers. "Where're we going?"

"To see Susan Ratcher."

"Lucky us." Reece settled down in his seat and crossed his arms over his chest. "Why are you being so fierce?"

"Argument with Carl."

"That explains a lot. Now you need a real macho man, like me, to push around."

She glanced at him and smiled. "Am I pushing you around?"

"No more than usual. So, what inspires this visit to Mrs. Ratcher, the fight with Carl?"

"No, no." Breath caught in her throat as she remembered. She slowed down. "Reece, Miles died."

"Good God." He sat up and draped an arm around her. "I'm sorry, kid. Poor old guy. I don't know what to say."

She reached out and patted his hairy knee, glad he was there, as always.

"Wait a minute. I'm slow but I just got it. Susan's his ex-wife and our mission is to tell her about Miles?"

"That, too. But mostly I want to ask her about the bastard. It's something I need to do for both Miles and me. To save his baby and my neck." She glanced at Reece. "Mother took me to her house a couple of times. But I'm not sure I can find it again, can you?"

"I think so. Go up by the country club." He waved his hand in the general direction they would follow. "Is this visit what you and Attila were fighting about?"

"Yeah. Carl thinks it's 'dumb.'"

"Then it has my blessing. Drive on, Macduff."

They drove north, away from the beach, passing through older neighborhoods caught somewhere between decaying and historic. Once past the freeway and an old, once-posh business district, Reece strained forward, trying to read street signs. He pointed to the left. "There. Miramar Drive."

Kate turned onto a broad street shaded with massive elms. It was a neighborhood of large and graceful houses built during the 1920s when the first orange groves had been subdivided for wealthy midwesterners who could afford to escape to the milder winters of California. They brought their architecture with them; the immense old houses, set back from the street on high, smooth lawns, were built in the style dubbed "Iowa farmhouse" by local historians.

Kate looked down the street of similar, shingle-sided houses. "Now where?"

"Somewhere in the middle of the block," Reece said. "On the left. Just park here. We'll find it."

They got out of the car and walked down the street, looking for something that would identify the Ratchers' house. Under the canopy of old trees the still air was pleasantly cool.

Reece nodded toward a white house. "I think that's the Ratchers'."

"Yeah, looks like it." Kate was beginning to feel that maybe this wasn't such a good idea after all.

Reece held her hand, probably sensing her hesitation, maybe feeling some of his own. "We could skip this. Go get a pizza instead."

"No. We're here," she said with firm resolution. "Let's get on with it."

The lawn on either side of the front walkway looked as if it hadn't had water since the last spring rainfall. From the condition of the house, once a fine specimen of its kind, Kate knew that the Ratchers had fallen on hard times. She couldn't remember, had old Mr. Ratcher, Sy's father, died?

Reece scanned across the wide front. "What the place needs is a quick infusion of cash." He looked down at Kate. "But I guess we all should know that by now."

"Yeah." A dry chip of paint scuttled across the toe of her shoe as she crossed the porch to ring the doorbell.

Reece leaned close to her. "Last chance. Double mushrooms, hold the anchovies."

"Too late," she said as a crack of dark appeared at the edge of the door. Then the door was flung wide.

"Kate? Reece?" Susan Ratcher raised long, graceful fingers to check the perfection of her hair. "This is a surprise." She looked like Mother and Mina, Kate thought—trim, poised, impeccable. Except that her dress was more than a few seasons old.

"Hello, Mrs. Ratcher," Kate said. "We'd like to talk to you."

Susan Ratcher hesitated, a hopeful sort of flicker slipping across her face. "Please come in."

Kate tried to ignore the damp, disused smell of the place as Susan led them into what had been called a sun-parlor at the time the house was built. Heavy drapes now shut out all but a faint glimmer of light.

"Did you want to see Sy?" Susan stood in the middle of the room, the fingers of her clasped hands fluttering nervous arpeggios. "He's at his office right now. But I'll call him and he can be here in five minutes. Or they'll page him if he's out somewhere. You don't mind waiting, do you?"

Kate heard the desperation in Susan's voice and felt uneasy about having raised false hopes just by coming here. "Actually, it's you we want to speak with."

Obviously struggling to contain her disappointment, Susan turned away to open the drapes, using the time to regain her composure. She came and sat across from Kate in an old wicker rocker. "I thought maybe you had reconsidered Sy's proposal."

"Uh, Mrs. Ratcher." Kate shot Reece a quick sidelong glance, hoping for sudden inspiration to make this easier. After turning down Sy, how much help could they expect from Susan? "Right now, I don't think Sy's condo development is feasible."

"Maybe not," Susan conceded, "with Miles so sick and all."

"Mrs. Ratcher." Reece gripped Kate's hand tighter. "I'm sorry to be the bearer of bad news, but Miles passed away this morning."

"Oh dear." Susan pulled a tissue from under her cuff and dabbed where a tear might be expected to course. "Probably for the best, the poor soul."

The phrase made Kate cringe. It was like something Mother would have said.

Susan made a dry sniffle. "I appreciate your coming, Kate. After what you said to Sy, I didn't expect such consideration."

"I'm sorry. I think my mother gave Sy false expectations."

"It's partly my fault," Susan sighed. "I apologize for speaking this way about your mother, but I should have warned Sy not to get involved with her."

"No apology needed," Kate said, seeing her opening wedge. "You knew my mother for a long time, probably had a lot of experience with her little schemes over the years."

"Indeed I had." Susan tucked her tissue back under her cuff, no longer needed. "How she got away with half of what she did, I'll never know."

"Right." Kate leaned forward, closer to Susan. "I wondered if maybe this thing with Sy, about the condos, got started because Mother still owed you a big favor."

"Did she?" Susan seemed to probe the question for fruit-bearing possibilities. "Why?"

"Because of what happened between you and Miles."

"That was all very unpleasant. But it didn't concern your mother."

Kate hoped she could turn the conversation down the right path, and keep Susan interested until she had what she needed. "I understood Mother helped conceal your housekeeper's pregnancy from you."

"Everyone did, but that was Archie's idea, I think. They all wanted to make the girl go away before I suspected anything. But your mother's part in the scheme was small. None of us, Mina, me, your mother, wanted any more scandal—you know what happened to our fathers and their business—so we three would do just about anything to avoid bringing attention to our names."

"So they all lied to you?" Reece asked.

"Maybe they were trying to protect me."

"I know it's an uncomfortable subject, but could you tell us what happened?"

Susan picked at some lint on her skirt with the tips of her long nails, her lower lip thrust out thoughtfully. Then, decision made, she took a deep breath and settled back in her chair.

"It started with Mina," she began, her voice low, confidential. "She said she needed to get away for a vacation. She'd been doing some defense work, driving an ambulance I think, and she was worn out. She looked absolutely wretched, as I remember. There weren't many places you could get away to during the war because of gas rationing. So Esperanza said she had a cousin who worked in a resort in Mexico, somewhere around Ensenada. The border's only seventy miles south of here and Mina could get enough gas for the trip; there was no rationing in Mexico. As the story was originally told to me, Mina didn't want to go down there alone and Esperanza couldn't go because she was an illegal then and might have trouble getting back across the border."

Reece raised his eyebrows. "Esperanza was here illegally?"

"Oh, sure. Archie got papers for her later sometime."

Kate wanted to direct the conversation back to the trip. "I take it your housekeeper went with Mina."

"That was the plan all along. The girl was pregnant and Miles was the father, and she wanted to be taken care of. Archie paid her a lot of money to get rid of the baby. So this whole Mexico trip was just a cover for the girl's abortion. Archie got Mina to take her down to make sure she went through with it."

"And did she?"

"That's how I found out. Mina, your mother, and Archie all conspired to keep it a secret. Then, some months later, a bill came to our house from this clinic in Mexico and when I asked Miles what it was about he explained the whole thing."

"And that's when you left him?" Kate asked.

"No." She looked up at Kate with big mournful eyes. "I never wanted the divorce. I was willing to forget the whole thing. But Miles couldn't. He said he was in love with the girl, and he wanted the baby. I thought he was going to crack up over it."

"Did he know about the abortion beforehand?"

"Never." Susan exhaled a disdainful puff of air. "He would have stopped them."

"After you divorced him," Reece edged forward, enrapt, "why didn't he marry the girl?"

"She was long gone by then and I think she was pretty fed up with the whole Byrd tribe."

"Who was she?" Kate asked softly.

"Nobody." Susan finally sounded scandalized. "We didn't know her people at all. She was just a big girl from the Midwest. I think she was only about seventeen or eighteen, though she said she was older. Like a lot of girls, she came to California during the war to get a job and get a man. She was too young for defense work so she took a domestic position." Susan looked up. "Good domestics were impossible to find during the war. Otherwise I would never have hired her."

"What was her name?" Kate persisted.

"Let me think." Susan made a brief show of effort, but she was watching Kate the way a bargainer eyes the merchandise, as if trying to decide if the asking price is too high. "I just can't remember. I think I called her Bridget."

"Bridget?" After all they'd been through, how could Susan possibly forget the girl's name? Kate stopped herself from challenging the obvious lie. She might need to come back to Susan later.

"I called her Bridget because I called all my girls Bridget," Susan dissembled. And Kate gave her credit, she was good at the game of bluffing. "I never thought of her as anything but Bridget. Why?"

The "why?" was the kicker. Kate knew it was the call for a bid.

But Reece answered first. "Just curious. We've listened to the family gossip all our lives, but the stories get all twisted around. We wanted to know the truth."

"Now that Miles is gone," Susan said, rising from her chair, "why drag it all up?"

"Good point." Kate understood that the conversation was over. She stood and Reece followed. "It's been nice chatting with you."

"Nice to see you again, dear. You will let me know about funeral arrangements?"

"Of course." Something occurred to Kate as she stepped outside. She caught Susan just before the door shut. "One more little thing. I know this sounds like nonsense, but what did Miles keep in the drawers of his nightstand?"

"The drawers of his nightstand?" Susan repeated, as if testing her hearing. "Good heavens, it's been more than forty years, but let me think." She thought for a minute, shaking her head the whole time, so that Kate expected another "Bridget" answer.

"Little things," Susan finally said, and there was such a long pause that Kate was afraid she had finished. Then Susan shrugged and took another breath. "He kept his cuff links and shirt studs in a little box. His checks. And pictures, photographs of his friends, his mother. He liked to look at them at night before he went to sleep. He wasn't much of a reader, you know, not like Dolph and your father. That's all."

"Thanks," Kate said. "That's a big help."

"I can't imagine why." They left Susan standing in the open doorway, still puzzling over the question.

"You hit paydirt, kid," Reece said when they were out of earshot.

"I think so." She got in the car and reached across to pop the button on Reece's door. "Like I've been telling everybody, the burglar in Miles's house was stealing pictures."

"Yeah. But you said they were pictures of the bastard. Susan just exploded the bastard theory."

"Did she?" Kate tried to hold her speed within a reasonable infraction of the limit as they drove away from the Ratchers'. "You know the bill from the clinic in Mexico? What if it was for the delivery of a baby, and not an abortion? Wouldn't Mina have paid for the girl's abortion on the spot? A bill for obstetrical services would have come a few months later. Right?"

"You're tenacious. Can we stop for a pizza on our way?"

"On our way where?"

"I assume we're headed now for a clinic in Ensenada."

"It's not necessary," she said. "I've already been there."

FOURTEEN

"WHAT IS ALL THIS?" Kate sat down on the foot of her bed and twirled the bottle of iced champagne in the massive silver bucket. Her suspicions were aroused when she saw the Dom Perignon label. It looked like a setup to her—the expensive wine, the armful of pink roses from the garden spilled across her pillows, like maybe Helga had gotten into the silver service again to help Carl out. But what was he up to? Delicious sex last night, arguments this morning. She didn't know what to expect next.

Among the roses she found a little velvet box, and glanced around, expecting Carl to come out from somewhere and kneel beside her like the hero in some corny old movie. When, to her great relief, he didn't show, she reluctantly opened the box.

A single pearl, the size of a marble, dropped to the end of a fine gold chain. It was pretty and simple, more to her taste than the jewelry she'd found in Mother's room. And it matched the earrings Carl had given her on their last wedding anniversary, just before she'd moved out. But the gift made her wary. And she had no idea what had become of the earrings.

Kate put the pearl and its box out of sight. Giving it back would be tricky, but not as tricky as keeping it. Quickly, she changed out of the dress she had worn to Susan Ratcher's and into her new red jogging shorts and a Nike T-shirt. It was time to run, to loosen the kinks, to clear her head. At the bedroom door she turned and looked again at the arrangement on her bed.

It was time to get out of here.

She glanced at the hall clock as she passed. Five-thirty; lots of time to run. Depending on which bus Esperanza took, she wouldn't be home for another hour or two. Kate began plotting how she'd get the information she wanted out of tight-lipped Esperanza.

She stretched her arms up high, feeling her back and shoulder muscles loosen. She nudged the kitchen door open with her hip, intending to slip a frozen dinner into the oven to eat when she got back.

"Hi," Carl stood at the kitchen counter slicing a loaf of French bread. "I wondered what happened to you."

She stopped in her tracks when she saw him and the swing door slammed into her back. Rubbing the impact spot, she took in the steaks marinating in a pan by the sink, draining salad greens, and the bowl of Carl's homemade Roquefort dressing. It all seemed to belong with the wine chilling by her bed upstairs and her suspicions were again aroused. "You knew where I was going. What're you up to?"

"I'm preparing a farewell dinner."

"Oh?" She took a step into the room. Any way she looked at it, this was good news. If his mother left, Carl would be easier to dislodge. "Is Helga ready to go home?"

"I put her on a plane an hour ago. This is *my* swan song."

"You're leaving, then?" She didn't believe him, not with the champagne and pearl business. He had to have a kicker up his sleeve. "When?"

"Tonight. I stopped by our house and aired things out today. You know how stale it gets, shut up in hot weather." He turned back to work on his bread. "I left you a little present upstairs."

"I saw it. It's very pretty, but . . ."

"Don't get excited. It's just a token. I bought it when I got the earrings, to give to you later. I think you should have it." He kept his back to her, and she knew he was having difficulty with whatever it was he wanted to say. "I know my being here has made things pretty tough for you, emotionally, I mean. I'd hoped you might get used to having me underfoot again." He tried a light chuckle that died somewhere in his throat. "But I guess not. We just seem to argue all the time. Maybe we still need some distance between us to sort things out."

"I think you're right." Kate took another step into the room.

He smiled at her. "Thought I'd fix you one last decent meal before I turned you back over to Esperanza."

"She's a great cook."

"She burns everything. You want garlic on your bread?"

"I was going to run on the beach."

"I know I should have asked you first." He looked at all the food on the counter.

"Okay." Kate decided to postpone the run. After all, his leaving was an occasion to celebrate. And she was famished. She would figure out how to give him back the pearl later. "Yes. Lots of garlic."

The smell of food reminded her that she and Reece had never gotten around to lunch. She sat down at the table and pushed aside Esperanza's big sugar bowl to reach the bread box. She searched around until she found the usual hidden bakery bag. She took out the two croissants and pinched off some flaky crust.

Carl tipped the knife in her direction. "Don't eat those."

"I'm hungry."

"You won't have room for dinner."

"Sure I will." She walked over to the sink. "They're stale anyway. Esperanza bought them before she left for her sister's yesterday. Let me help you do something. Salad maybe? It's hard to ruin a salad."

"Maybe you can find a way." He tossed her a head of lettuce.

Kate switched on Esperanza's radio and hummed along with the Latin American music as she made the salad, glancing frequently at Carl. Everything seemed so ordinary that she kept waiting for something bizarre to happen.

Carl seemed more relaxed than she had seen him for a long time. Swaying to the music, he dropped the thick steaks under the broiler. *"Aye, aye, aye, aye,"* he sang along with the radio. *"Cielito lindo."*

"Pretty good, *gringo*," she flicked water at him from her fingertips.

He flicked water back. "I thought you'd acquired a taste for Latin lovers."

"You're right, Carl," she said dryly as she carried the salad toward the dining room. "I think it's time to put some distance between us."

"Sorry. It just slipped out." Carl followed her, carrying a bouquet of knives and forks. He set two places at one end of the long mahogany table. "I don't like you being in this house all alone."

"I'm not alone. I have Esperanza. Remember what Miles said, 'Trust Hope.'"

"Trust Hope?" He sat down and smothered his lettuce with Roquefort dressing. "Oh yeah. Esperanza is Spanish for hope. Dolph told me that's what they used to call her."

"At least it was her own name." Kate forked some salad. "Susan Ratcher said she called all her housekeepers Bridget. Must've had quite a turnover."

"That stinks." Carl's lips curled in disgust. "Poor girls had enough indignities to live with. She should at least have had the class to call them by their own names."

"Why, Carl. I think you're a humanist a-borning."

"Don't hold your breath." He stabbed some lettuce. "What else did you learn from dear Susan?"

"Actually, in spite of herself, she was rather helpful." Kate heard the back door open and she froze. The door shut, sending a waft of cool outside air against the swing door. "Esperanza's back. I'd better go in and tell her about Miles."

"She doesn't know yet?"

"There's no telephone at her sister's." Kate listened to Esperanza moving around in the kitchen. "I had to tell her about Mother, too. I hate it. Well, won't be any easier later."

"Not yet." Carl caught her hand before she could push her chair back. "This is our farewell dinner, remember? Let the bad news wait."

"I don't know." Kate looked down at her bowl, her appetite gone.

"At least give her time to get her coffee made. She'll need some fortifying."

The swing door opened. *"Hola,"* Esperanza chirped, carrying two plates of steaming meat and a basket of garlic bread. "These look ready." She put the plates in front of Carl and Kate.

"Thanks." Kate touched Esperanza's arm as she reached in front of her. Maybe the bad news should wait a little. Kate had a lot to ask her about and she didn't want Carl around to interfere. She forced a smile and looked up at Esperanza.

"Have you eaten? There's plenty of steak here. Why don't you get a plate?"

"My sister, Rosa, she always feeds me too much at her house. I'll just make some coffee." Esperanza breezed back into the kitchen and made a clatter of coffee pot and cups, humming tonelessly along with the radio.

The swing door opened again, the stale croissants on a plate preceding Esperanza through. "Anyone eating these?"

"Go ahead," Carl said, slicing off a large piece of rare meat. As the door closed he turned to Kate. "Aren't you eating? This looks great."

"I thought you said Esperanza overcooked everything." She began to cut the steak. Thick, red juice ran from the gash. She pushed her chair back from the table. "I'm going to put this back under the broiler."

Juggling the juice-filled plate in one hand, she reached with the other to push the swing door, but stopped when she heard a violent crash on the other side. Something solid, a falling chair maybe, hit the kitchen side of the door.

"Esperanza!" Kate pushed the door, but whatever had fallen wedged it shut. Alarmed when there was no answer, she put the plate down on the floor and used both hands to push the door. "You okay? What happened?"

A low, gagging, animal sound was the only response.

"Esperanza!" Panicked now, using sheer will to bolster her strength, she forced the door enough so that she could reach in and push away the blocking chair. The door fell open, sending Kate in a headlong rush into the kitchen.

Kate dashed toward Esperanza, who stood in the middle of the kitchen floor, arms flailing helplessly in the air.

Kate gagged when she saw Esperanza's face. Pink, bloody foam bubbled out of her gaping mouth, consuming the flesh of her lips and chin as it sizzled down to the collar of her starched dress.

For an instant Kate, stunned, just looked at her, not knowing what to do. "What happened?"

But the only answer from Esperanza was a gurgle of bloody foam.

Kate looked around the kitchen, trying frantically to find what had done this. She thought of knives and broken glass, until she saw spilled coffee and half-eaten croissants on the table.

Immediately she thought of poison and, moving fast, she dodged Esperanza's swinging arms, grabbed her around the middle and dragged her to the sink. She turned on the cold tap, forcing Esperanza's head under the running water.

"Open your mouth!" she demanded. "Let the water run into your mouth." Kate retched as blood and bits of flesh mingled among the scraps of lettuce and meat trimmings in the sink.

"What is it?" Carl was behind her.

"Looks like she's eaten something caustic. Quick, get her in the car."

He picked Esperanza up and carried her to the back door.

Kate grabbed the car keys. The remains of the croissants lay on a plate on the table. She dumped them into the crumpled bakery bag, and holding it at arm's length as if it held explosives, she ran outside.

FIFTEEN

"DAMMIT!" Lieutenant Tejeda stormed out of Esperanza's tiny emergency room cubicle. "I told you to be careful."

"You should have warned Esperanza, too," Kate said, defensively.

Carl was close beside her. "What did Esperanza get in her mouth?"

"Lye," Tejeda said. "Drain cleaner."

An icy finger ran down Kate's spine. "Was it in the croissants?"

"No. The sugar bowl."

"Shit." Carl put his hand over his mouth as if a bit of the lye might have dropped there.

Kate knew how he felt; her own mouth suddenly felt raw inside. "It's my fault. Everyone knew that I wanted to talk to Esperanza. Now she can't talk at all. We're lucky she wasn't killed."

"There wasn't enough to kill her," Tejeda said. "You think the lye was intended for Esperanza?"

"Must have been. No one else ever used her sugar bowl." Kate looked toward Esperanza's curtained cubicle. "How is she?"

"Scared. Sore. Third-degree burns in her mouth and throat. You saw what happened to her face when she tried to spit the stuff out? Good thing she didn't swallow much of it." Tejeda's hand was warm on Kate's shoulder. "It would have been worse if you hadn't acted so fast, flushed the area."

Kate gazed up at Tejeda, both relieved and glad that he was here. Something about him softened the edges of the crisis for her.

"It's not your fault, Kate." Carl reached out his arms and reeled her in, pressing her against him. It looked like an affectionate gesture, but she knew he was trying to draw her attention away from Tejeda, maybe trying to warn Tejeda off.

Annoyed, Kate pushed away from him. Down the hall the double ambulance-ramp doors slid open with an electronic whoosh, announcing the hurried entrance of an orderly in hospital white. He ran toward them. "Your car's blocking the ramp. Move it. Now. Paramedic's on his way in."

Carl hesitated, his grip tightening around Kate. He obviously didn't want to leave her alone with Tejeda.

Fed up with Carl's dramatics, Kate held her hand out for the keys. "I'll go."

"S'okay." He slouched away down the hall with his hands in his pockets, the orderly running backward in front of him, urging him to hurry. Carl ignored him.

Tejeda watched Carl's back. "Something bothering him?"

"Yes," she smiled. "You are."

He laughed. Carl heard him and turned and glared before he went out the door.

"I called you this afternoon," Tejeda said. "But you were out. Carl didn't give you the message?"

"Guess he forgot," she said. "I was at Susan Ratcher's, snooping around."

"She tell you anything?"

"A little. First of all, I was right—Miles mostly kept pictures in his nightstand. And they might have been pictures of his baby. The housekeeper went to Mexico for an abortion, but I'm not sure she went through with it. Her medical bills didn't arrive until months after she'd left."

"I better watch out. You'll be after my job."

"Not a chance. Why did you call earlier?"

"Wait a sec." He glanced down the empty hall then moved with her a few steps farther away from Esperanza's cubicle. "Does the Clinico Miraloma mean anything to you?"

" 'Fraid so. That's where we took Nugie."

"Two pregnant American women were admitted there for treatment in November of nineteen forty-three. One was given a so-called therapeutic abortion, the other stayed three months and delivered an eight-and-a-half-pound baby boy."

"Who were they?"

"Joan and Jane Smith."

"Big help. You think one of them was Miles's housekeeper?"

"It's a good possibility. But which one? They both gave the same billing address."

"That's strange. What's the address?"

"Miles Byrd's."

"Two women?" She tried to figure out the time frame. "Mina took the housekeeper to Mexico. But she couldn't have been pregnant because Dolph went overseas around Christmas of nineteen forty-two. He'd been gone almost a year by then."

"Think about it."

"I suppose it's possible," she said sadly. "Susan Ratcher said they would do anything to avoid scandal, but an abortion for Mina? That's too cruel. She always wanted children so much."

"Records at Clinico Miraloma show some follow-up treatment for infection on the woman who had the abortion. Could have left her sterile," he said. "But at least she lived. Doctor Guenther Maderos ring any bells?"

"Maderos?" She only vaguely remembered what he looked like, but otherwise he was clear in her mind. Nugie had decided that he was Mexico's Mengele because of his impossible, German-accented Spanish. She joked that she was going to turn him over to Dolph; he had to be an escaped Nazi. They had laughed at him every time he left the room, a way to cover their fear both of him and what would happen to Nugie.

Kate looked up at Tejeda. "Maderos performed Nugie's abortion."

"I know. He did Mina's too, if she was the other woman." He shook his head. "Doesn't have much of a track record, does he?"

"Poor Mina." Did she ever know Nugie had gone to Maderos, Kate wondered? If he had botched an abortion on Mina, knowing Nugie had been taken to him would have made her death seem even more of a waste. Maybe that explained the change in Mina since Nugie's death; she rarely expressed interest in anything that happened beyond today. Before Nugie died she had loved planning what she called "little treats" for the girls, taking Kate and Nugie to lunch in Beverly Hills, shopping weekends in San Francisco, theater trips to New York. Just the three of them, just for the pleasure of being together. But Nugie died. And Kate got married. And somewhere in there the specialness between Kate and Mina faded, maybe because it felt wrong without Nugie.

"Are you Miss Ruiz's employer?" The cool hand of a starched, white-clad nurse on her arm startled her. For a moment, the question didn't register; she'd never thought of herself as Esperanza's employer.

"Yes. I'm her employer." Kate felt a moment of panic. "Is she okay?"

"Miss Ruiz would like to see you." The woman smiled professional reassurance. "She's dressing. We're releasing her to go home."

Tejeda folded his arms and leaned against the wall. "I'll wait for you out here."

"Esperanza?" Kate pulled the curtain aside. Esperanza was slipping her dress on over her head and Kate helped her keep it away from the injuries on her face as she pulled it down.

Kate handled her with extreme caution, afraid she might accidentally touch one of the burns. "How do you feel?"

Esperanza raised her right shoulder, she wasn't sure how she felt. Her round black eyes appealed to Kate for explanation.

"I'm so sorry." Kate put an arm around Esperanza, who seemed suddenly very small and young as she huddled close to Kate. She seemed frightened, and Kate realized that this was probably the first time she had ever been admitted to a hospital. "I feel so responsible for this mess."

Esperanza touched the fading bruise by Kate's eye and shook her head.

"You're right," Kate said. "It was probably the same guy who did this to me."

Esperanza turned around and Kate helped her with her back zipper. With shaky hands, Esperanza tried to smooth the front of her blood-stained dress. A shiny, bitter-smelling ointment covered the burns on her lips and chin. Gingerly, Esperanza touched the corner of her mouth, and winced, the pain tearing her eyes.

"Are you ready to go home?" Kate asked.

Esperanza firmly shook her head. She reached for a small stack of prescriptions on the examination table and made a gesture as if she were writing.

Kate dug a pen out of her handbag and gave it to her.

"My sister," Esperanza wrote on the back of a prescription.

"She lives somewhere in Wilmington, right? Take us about an hour. Let's get your prescriptions filled, then we'll go to Rosa's, if you can direct me with hand signals."

Esperanza reached for Kate's hand and held on like a scared child. Kate felt the irony of this role reversal, bossy Esperanza, who had nurtured her since infancy, now clinging to her. In spite of the circumstances, it was a nice feeling.

Holding hands, they went out together.

Carl and Tejeda waited in chilly silence on opposite sides of the doorway. Kate spoke to the neutral space between them. "I'm taking Esperanza to her sister's."

"Like hell you are," Carl exploded, taking a menacing step toward her. "After what's happened I'm taking you home and keeping you under lock and key."

"Wait a minute." Tejeda held up a hand. "It might not be a bad idea if Mrs. Teague stays away from home for the night." He turned to Esperanza. "Can she sleep at your sister's tonight?"

Esperanza gripped Kate with both hands and nodded vigorously.

"Okay?" he asked Carl, but it was more an announcement than a request for agreement. He turned to Kate. "I can send an escort with you. He'll follow you until he's sure you aren't being tailed. As long as no one but us," he gave Carl a piercing look, "knows where you are, you should be safe. Safer, at any rate, than you'd be at home."

"I'm going with them," Carl said.

"Sorry," Tejeda said firmly. "The best thing you can do is go home and make everything seem as normal as possible until we get to the bottom of this."

"Home?" Carl looked at Kate.

"Please stay for one more night," she said, emphasizing one. Why did this have to happen just when he was about to move out?

"If it's what you want." It wasn't at all what she wanted, but Esperanza seemed so tired and agreeing to it seemed to be the only way they would get away from the hospital without more argument, and without Carl. Kate sensed something triumphant in Carl's manner as he took Esperanza's other hand.

With Tejeda trailing, the threesome went upstairs to the pharmacy and waited while Kate had Esperanza's prescriptions filled. The silent parade walked out to the parking lot, tension crackling in the spaces between them.

Kate pulled Dolph's Mercedes into the driveway and waited for the patrol car to fall in behind her. The officer at the wheel, his face hidden by the dark, blinked his lights once, and they pulled out of the parking lot together. As she drove across town through the evening traffic, he stayed conspicuously close behind her, waving casually every few moments when she checked her rearview mirror for him. Other drivers gave them a wide berth.

Kate headed north, toward Wilmington. Shortly before they reached the Los Angeles County line, the light behind her blinked twice. She looked up and the officer pulled along beside her. He smiled and pointed his thumb over his shoulder as he shook his head. No one had followed. He waved a last time, then headed for the first off ramp.

Suddenly alone, Kate felt vulnerable. Could she protect both herself and Esperanza if someone had managed to follow them, despite the escort?

Tense and watchful, she stayed in the middle lane until they were past the residential part of Long Beach. Beyond the city, the lighted freeway cut through a long dark stretch of factories and harbor storage yards like an endless yellow cord. The farther away the lights of the city, the thinner the traffic became. Kate relaxed a little, having fewer cars to worry about.

As they neared Wilmington, Kate could see exhaust fires from the immense oil refineries shooting through the black sky, filling the air with a sulfurous, rotten egg smell. Esperanza, who had seemed to be dozing, sniffed the air then sat up and looked around to check her bearings.

Occasionally, the flat, barren landscape around them was interrupted by forty-foot mounds of skeletal, rusting automobiles waiting to be crushed into neat cubes of scrap metal. The auto graveyards were eerie, Kate thought, encroaching along the freeway as if waiting for fresh material to fall in.

Esperanza poked Kate's arm then pointed to an off ramp that bisected the mounds.

"We get off here?" Kate asked doubtfully, checking to make sure that the roadway to her right was clear.

Esperanza nodded.

Staying in the third lane of four, Kate waited until she had almost passed the ramp, then cut sharply across two lanes, neatly missing the cement end-barrier. Pausing quickly at the stop sign at the end of the ramp, she checked behind her, but no one had followed.

Esperanza clutched the dash with one hand for stability, and with the other she directed Kate to turn right at the first intersection. On the left was a broken line of factories and warehouses deserted for the night. On the right a vast, black, mist-shrouded field separated the road from the scrapyards.

Esperanza leaned forward, her eyes riveted on the dark field. She held up her hand for Kate to slow the car. Then she pointed to a driveway apron cut into the concrete curb. There was only dirt field beyond the curb. Unsure, Kate slowed, then drove past the apron. Esperanza poked her again and made a circle motion with her finger. "Turn back," it indicated.

"You're kidding," Kate said, her courage failing when Esperanza repeated the circle with her finger. Kate obeyed and made a broad U-turn. She stopped across from the apron. "There's nothing there," she protested.

Esperanza made a familiar shooing gesture that had always meant, "Do it and don't argue."

Kate bumped the car up over the apron and onto the field. "If it were anyone but you I wouldn't do this. Where are you leading me?"

Esperanza pointed straight ahead to a faint light glowing in the middle of the darkness. Kate forced the car over dirt that had been baked to adobe by the long, dry summer. Eventually she picked up a rutted track that seemed to head toward the light that, as she got closer, appeared to come from a small square window maybe a hundred yards ahead.

Against the dark, Kate could make out the vague, irregular shapes of small buildings and the carcasses of a dozen cars. For an instant, the headlights caught a crude sign, "Sanchez Auto Dismantellers," painted on a rusted bumper and nailed to a wooden post.

The rutted path ended in front of a corroded, fifteen-foot camp trailer, its middle window the source of the yellow light. Kate stopped, but kept her motor idling. "Now what?"

Esperanza leaned across her and gave the horn a long blast.

Almost instantly the trailer door flew open with a metallic bang, shooting a rectangle of light across a gravel walkway lined with up-ended hubcaps. The straggling ends of a summer flower garden spilled over the hubcaps and onto the gravel.

Kate heard Esperanza fumbling with her door handle. She turned off the motor, but with the keys clutched and ready in her hand, she got out and walked around the car to help her. Gravel rolled into her sandals and dug painfully at the soles of her feet.

In the open doorway, a small round man appeared holding a cylinder that glinted metallically in the soft light. "Who's there?" he shouted, shaking the object in his hand as it released a weak beam of light.

Kate raised an arm to shield her eyes as he aimed the light at her.

"Kate! Is that you?" he called into the night.

Hearing her name in this strange place made her jump. How could anyone know she was coming? Frightened, she edged back toward her side of the car, ready to hop in and leave.

"Rosa!" the man called back over his shoulder as he stepped down from the wooden crate that served as the trailer's front step. He ran toward the car in a funny half-skip, a man no longer used to physical exertion.

Esperanza opened her door and the dome light in the car snapped on. Sitting there in the only patch of brightness in the dark field, she looked like an angel at a Christmas pageant.

"Esperanza!" The man gave the "r" a rich roll. "Holy Mary, Mother of God." He crossed himself before reaching for her. "The crazy things been going on, I thought it was Kate come to tell us you was dead."

"She's been hurt," Kate said, put at ease by his tenderness toward Esperanza. "She wanted me to bring her here."

"Of course." He took Esperanza by the arm and guided her slowly toward the trailer. Over his shoulder he said, "Come inside, Kate."

She strained against the darkness to see him better, to force recognition. He looked like a small, aging Mexican cowboy, short even in his high-heeled boots. As he stood waiting for her in the pale light from the open doorway, she saw him clearly for the first time, and was sure she had never encountered him before.

The woman, Rosa, appeared beside him, tugging her too-snug dress in place over her round middle. Kate knew the dress, one her mother had worn a few years ago. Welts showed down the sides where the seams had been let out to accommodate this smaller, younger version of Esperanza.

Brusque and angry, Rosa took charge of Esperanza as soon as she was inside. "Oscar," she ordered, "bring Kate inside. She's going to catch cold in those short pants."

Inside, the trailer was warm and cheery, smelling of strong coffee and the kerosene lamps that gave the tiny place a soft pink glow. How strange, Kate thought, this homey little island among the wrecking yards. She had time to take in the entire trailer while Rosa bustled in the narrow space, scooping up the day's newspapers and clearing away the dinner dishes.

A double bed with a red-embroidered, fringed coverlet filled the end of the trailer beyond the door where Kate stood. The far end was partitioned by a curtain that had once hung in Grandpa Archie's bedroom. In the seven feet of space between the bed and curtain were jammed a small sink, ice box, and stove to one side, and what looked like a cast-off coffee shop banquette and linoleum table on the other. There wasn't space for anyone to move until Rosa finished her picking up and stepped to the far end by the curtain.

With Oscar holding her elbow, Esperanza slid in behind the table and rested her head on her hands. A crucified Jesus, body twisted in agony, looked down sadly from the curtain rod above her.

"What happened?" Rosa asked, accusation ripe in her whole posture.

"I'm sorry," Kate looked from Oscar to Rosa. "It's hurts Esperanza to talk. She has some lye burns in her mouth."

"How in the name of thunder..." Oscar began.

"Not now, Oscar. Sit down, Kate." Rosa thumped her on the back. "It's not your fault, I'm sure. I told my sister not to go back to that place." She shook an accusing finger at Esperanza. "But you don't listen to me and now here you are."

Esperanza smiled in response, sliding across the cracked plastic seat to make room for Kate. She wagged a scolding finger at Rosa's back and Kate laughed softly, understanding her joke. Listening to Rosa was like hearing a good mimic imitate Esperanza.

Rosa continued her tirade as she lit a fire under a cast-iron kettle. Once it was going, she turned and examined the burns on Esperanza's face. Then she kissed her loudly on the forehead. "I'll get your room ready, honey. You look tired."

Moving sideways in the cramped space, Rosa went to the curtain and drew it aside. The curtain made a sort of alcove across the end of the trailer. In the shadows Kate could see a narrow bunk and above it a shelf neatly stacked with boxes and folded clothes. All of the available wallspace was covered with framed photographs and mementoes. Kate realized with a little sadness that that tiny space was Esperanza's real home, rather than the large, immaculate apartment off the kitchen of Kate's house.

Squeezing past Rosa, Esperanza went back and sat on her bed. Oscar followed and opened a collapsible canvas camp stool next to her. He lit a small kerosene lamp hanging from a corner hook above the bed and gestured for Kate to come and sit on the stool.

"Cozy," Kate said, alone with Esperanza inside the alcove with the curtain drawn. Kate helped her to undress, taking care as she pulled the stained dress past Esperanza's burns. She folded the dress across the foot of the bed while Esperanza took a nightgown from under the pillow and slipped it on.

"Just like old times, isn't it?" Kate removed the hairpins from Esperanza's bun and brushed the gray hair until it was smooth. "Except it's in reverse. You always used to tuck *me* in."

Esperanza smiled, the soft light catching tears in her eyes. She pressed Kate's hand against her cheek, then she held it up to see it better, concern darkening her face. Lye burns tattooed Kate's fingers.

"De nada." Kate put the hand behind her. "It's nothing. Get some sleep, my little *hija*."

Esperanza touched Kate's cheek then reached up and touched a cracked frame that hung at the head of the bed.

"Oh, my God. Did you save that from the trash?"

Esperanza nodded, her eyes heavy from the sedative given to her at the hospital. Under the glass was the motto Kate had embroidered for her grandfather when she was a child: "Red sky at morning, sailors take warning. Red sky at night, sailors' delight." The border of crude little sailboats she had struggled so long to stitch now looked faded and tired and hardly seaworthy.

Kate's high school portrait hung next to the motto. She winced a little when she saw herself, lips closed resolutely over the bands on her teeth that were removed the following summer, before she went away to college. There was also a portrait of Nugie, cool and glamorous in black velvet. Kate peered through the soft, wavery light, studying each photograph on the wall. There were Reece, Kate, and Nugie on the beach. A younger, slimmer Esperanza wearing an improbably feathered hat.

A hand-tinted picture of Kate as a one-year-old headed a long row of baby pictures, most of which she didn't recognize. There was a sameness about them all because of the style of photography current at that time. All of them were tinted to a romantically healthy rosiness. The canvas stool creaked under her as she looked from one smooth baby face to the next.

The fourth portrait stood out from the others because of the artificially blue eyes. It was a little boy smiling to show his two front teeth. His sparse blond hair was so fine and so fair it seemed transparent. Kate moved closer to see the photographer's signature scrawled across one corner: "Fortunato. Mexico. D.F."

She was drawn back to the eyes. The tinter had had a heavy hand; no eyes could be that blue. But there was something else about them that didn't seem possible. She held up her hands to frame out everything but the eyes. Then she moved her hands until all she could see were the eyes in her own baby portrait. The stool almost fell out from under her as she straightened up.

"It's him, isn't it? Miles's son, my cousin?"

Esperanza smiled so sleepily, Kate wasn't sure whether she had heard.

"You knew all along," Kate challenged with disbelief. "Where is he now?"

But Esperanza closed her eyes and rolled over. Kate sat beside her, waiting, expecting something more, until the quiet breathing became a gentle snore. She felt betrayed and angry. How much easier everything would have been if only she had been told the truth when she needed it.

If Esperanza knew the truth, others did, too. She picked up the stained dress and went out through the curtain.

Oscar and Rosa sat close together at the table, like conspirators, drinking from steaming mugs. There was a wariness in their eyes when they looked up at her.

"May I have some cold water and soap so I can wash this?" Kate asked, holding out the dress.

"Let me do it." Rosa took the dress from her. "You sit here and have some coffee." She put a china cup and saucer on the table next to Oscar's chipped mug.

The coffee was thick and sweet and delicious, exactly like Esperanza's coffee. Kate finished it quickly and Rosa refilled her cup. She remembered how hungry she was but realized that the coffee would probably have to suffice until breakfast.

More than anything, she wanted to ask Rosa and Oscar about the boy with the blue eyes. But they seemed so suspicious of her, as if she had come to take something from them. And maybe she had.

Not sure yet how to approach the subject of the boy, she opened her purse and took out Esperanza's prescriptions and lined them up on the table. She held up the silver tube of antibiotic ointment.

"This is for Esperanza's face burns. There is a mouthwash here and some pain pills if she can swallow them. The doctor says she must have only water for twenty-four hours, then she can have Jell-O and ice cream until she feels like eating solid food. I'll take her to our family doctor day after tomorrow for a checkup."

"Don't worry." Oscar swept the prescriptions to his side of the table. "We'll take care of her."

Kate toyed with her cup, watching Rosa's back as she stood at the sink scrubbing the dress. Oscar kept his eyes focused on the contents of his mug. Kate felt more than ever like an intruder, shut out from the past as well as from the unexpressed emotions that filled the small trailer.

"When I was a little girl," she began cautiously, "I remember Esperanza going to visit you in Mexico City. She brought me some maracas. When did you move up here?"

Rosa gave Oscar a hard stare over her shoulder.

"Long time ago," he said.

"There's a picture of my cousin, my Uncle Miles's son, in there." She nodded toward the curtain, trying to sound as if she had known all along about the boy, as if they had no secret to keep from her. "The picture was taken in Mexico City. Did you know him?"

Tears filled Oscar's eyes. "We knew lots of little boys." Kate looked at the stubborn set of Rosa's back, so much like Esperanza's. "I want to talk to him. My uncle died this morning. I think his son should know."

The shoulders sagged a little.

"Rosa?" Oscar seemed to need permission.

Rosa didn't respond. She wrung out the dress and turned away from the sink. She shook it out and laid it on the table, stretching the wet bodice to display the holes eaten through the fabric.

"Don't worry about staying here with us," she said. "We always took care of the little *chico*, and we will take care of you."

SIXTEEN

"YOU LOOK LIKE HELL, KATE." Reece lounged on the lawn in front of her house, sunning his freckled chest. "Been out tom-catting?"

"I feel like it." Kate slammed the door of the Mercedes and stretched. "I slept on a camp stool last night, listening to Es-peranza snore."

He turned serious. "She okay?"

"I think she will be. She was still sleeping when I left. I'm going to change and pick up some things for her, then I'm going back. I have to talk to her. Alone."

"It'll be tough getting away from here." Reece inclined his head toward Miles's house. "The troops have gathered. They're talking about sending the cavalry after you. Carl's pissed that he went along with Tejeda and let you go with Esperanza."

"He *let* me go?" she repeated, rankled. She looked toward Miles's house and saw that all the drapes were open. "Carl's still here?"

"Yep." Reece yawned and scratched some peeling flesh on his shoulder. "So is Old Tom Bodge. Thought I'd wait out here to warn you."

"Damn! I forgot about Old Tom and the will." She started toward the house, then stopped. She needed a shower and a little time to sort things out before she could face any of them. "Tell them to go ahead without me, will you?"

"You're the pot at the end of the rainbow, sweetheart. They can't do anything without you."

"Then hold them off for a while, please," she begged him. "I need to get cleaned up."

"I'll do what I can." He rolled to his feet.

"Thanks." She twirled the car keys on her finger and headed for her house. "I won't be long."

"For God's sake," Reece called after her, "do something with your hair."

"Why?" She reached up and touched it. Sticky from the morning fog, it lay in thick clumps along her neck. "Tina Turner pays a fortune for hair like this."

"But *she* can carry a tune," he yelled after her as she ran inside.

Upstairs, Kate undressed quickly, throwing Dolph's car keys on her bed and making a mental note to remember to take them with her.

The shower felt wonderful. She shampooed her hair and let the hot water run over her face, washing away the smells of cooking and Esperanza's bitter ointment that hung thickly in the air of the tiny trailer.

Not taking time to blow dry her hair, she toweled it and caught the sides up in big tortoise shell combs. In her dressing room she picked out a soft, gray silk skirt and blouse. With some reluctance she checked the results in the mirror. Cheeks still rosy from the shower, eyes the color of her blouse, the effect wasn't bad, she decided . . . considering.

Breakfast would help, but there wasn't time. She had left before Rosa finished frying her eggs and chorizo because the pall of silence in the trailer had become unbearable, even threatening.

Kate slipped into some low-heeled pumps and hurried toward the door, thinking about questions she would ask Esperanza. She picked up Dolph's keys and dropped them into her pocket.

They hung heavily in the light fabric of her skirt, bouncing against her thigh like noisy punctuation to the confusion of thoughts coursing through her head as she walked across the courtyard to Miles's house. How many of the people waiting inside for her shared Esperanza's secrets?

Miles's front door stood ajar. Kate took a big gulp of the hazy, smoggy air before she pushed the door open and crossed the silent foyer. She appreciated how bright it was; the brass wall sconces had been polished and fitted with new bulbs. Good for Reece, she thought, as she stepped into the living room. That step was like raising the lid of a tinny music box; Dolph, Mina, and Carl all began talking to her at once.

Carl raised his hands. "Give her a chance," he said, the man in charge. She veered away when he came toward her with his arms out. He backed off, but she saw the deep worry lines etched across his forehead.

"After what happened last night," he said, "we're all a bit on edge. When you were late for our appointment with Mr. Bodge, we were concerned about you. We didn't know when to expect you back."

"I didn't have a watch." Kate hesitated while everyone found a seat. As she looked around, she wondered if she had any real allies here, or, failing that, if there was a neutral zone. Tejeda had warned her she would need to be a good actor, but this would be a brutal test. When Mina patted the empty cushion beside her, Kate sat there.

"How is Esperanza?" Mina asked.

"Uncomfortable, but okay."

"Ghastly thing," Mina clucked. "She's lucky she wasn't killed."

"Not much chance of that." Carl moved from across the room to sit on Kate's other side. "She wouldn't accidentally eat enough lye to kill her."

"No," Kate said, trying to look casually at each face in the room. "It was just enough to keep her quiet for a while."

"Did that lieutenant fellow warn the market?" Mina puckered her face with indignation. "It's awful the way we can't trust the food we buy, all these crazies putting poison in things. It's just like that Tylenol scare."

"Food? Who mentioned food?" Reece marched in, balancing a grease-smeared pizza box in one hand and a steaming pot of coffee in the other. "Kate said she was hungry so I thought I would cater this little conclave."

"Thanks, Jeeves," Kate said, relieved he had come. She took the box from him and opened it, finding half a cold pizza with all it's pepperoni picked off. "Are you going to be the sacrificial taster?"

"It's all tested. I ate the rest of it for dinner last night." He patted his flat middle. "So far, all systems are 'go.'"

"It looks gross." Kate disengaged a thick slab of pizza. "But I'm so hungry I think I can choke this down if you pour me about a quart of coffee." She smiled at him. "But no sugar, okay?"

"There isn't any sugar." He glanced at Carl. "Lieutenant Hunk took it all away."

"Whenever you're ready." Dolph sounded vexed.

"Yes." A loud, hacking cough from the far side of the room froze all conversation. "Shall we proceed?" Old Tom Bodge, forgotten in the furor over Kate's entry, turned on a table lamp at his side. The effect was theatrical.

Kate looked at him, sitting deep in a high-backed chair, thin legs dangling from his fat belly. A web of red veins in his face gave the illusion of rosy good health, like Esperanza's tinted baby portraits. Kate remembered him as a younger man, overweight, overbearing, always working hard to be funny. Dolph had told her that Bodge could hold his tongue after a few pink gins. Probably, she thought, because he'd had a lot of practice. At that moment, he looked like he needed a drink.

Bodge covered his face with an immense linen handkerchief and coughed again while everyone waited. He wiped his rheumy eyes with pudgy knuckles, then examined his manicure.

Kate put her half-eaten pizza slice back in the box and rested her elbows on her knees. "Whenever you're ready, Mr. Bodge."

Bodge looked up at her, shrugged slightly, and after a deep phlegmy breath, he pulled a long manila envelope from his inside coat pocket. Kate could see from the torn flap that the seal had already been broken, and by less than patient hands.

Slowly, Bodge withdrew the single sheet of thick, creamy paper. Kate recognized Miles's personal stationery. Bodge looked at Kate again, then slowly removed and polished his thick bifocals.

"Get on with it," she whispered aside to Carl as Bodge put the glasses back on and read the page over to himself.

Carl put his arm around her and pulled her closer. "Relax," he said, smoothing her still-damp hair.

Kate felt smothered in Carl's embrace. She leaned forward and refilled her cup to put space between them.

There was another spell of coughing, another wiping of bifocals. A long sigh. "I find no funeral instructions," Bodge said finally, folding the will along its creases. "Maybe the reading of the will should wait for another time."

"Kate?" Dolph said. "What do you want to do?"

She looked at Bodge, all tucked into the folds of his stomach. She couldn't stand another session like this one. "You might as well read the whole will, Mr. Bodge. Since we're all here."

"As you wish." Bodge shifted in his chair, stirring up his gelatinous middle. "It's very brief, as you can see. There is an annuity for Esperanza Ruiz y Garcia. It's very straightforward, and since she isn't here we needn't bother with the specifics. Miles writes it is given 'for tender services rendered to a desperate man.'"

"What can that mean?" Mina chirped. She looked ruffled and flushed and ready for battle.

Kate patted her hand. "I'll explain it to you later."

Bodge looked at them irritably over the top of his glasses. "Whenever *you're* ready."

"Please," Kate said. "Continue."

"Thank you." He was like a prim schoolmaster. "Other than Miss Ruiz there is a single benefactor. He cleared his throat and pulled out his handkerchief again and blew his nose.

Everyone in the room except Bodge was looking at Kate and she wondered what they all expected. The pot at the end of the rainbow, Reece had said. She looked at every face in turn. Dolph was beaming at her as if he had given her a marvelous gift and was waiting for her to open it. Mina looked saccharine, a tea-party smile fixed on her face. Reece, true to form, stuck out his tongue at her to cover his feelings, or to make her laugh. She did laugh, a small, nervous chuckle. She felt like the contestant in a fixed game show, "And the winner is . . ."

Carl, sitting so close beside her she could feel his heat through the fabric of her skirt, was staring at the floor between his knees, his face a pale mask. She didn't know why he was even here, except that he seemed to have become indispensable to Dolph.

Kate cleared her throat. "Please, Mr. Bodge."

Bodge put his handkerchief away. He didn't look up. "'All other property and interests, both real and personal,'" He started to cough then seemed to decide against it. "'I bequeath to my natural son, Carl Teague.'"

The first thing Kate was aware of was Mina crying wetly against her shoulder. With both hands, she held Mina away and tried to look into her face, but Mina avoided her eyes. Through the shock of what Bodge had revealed, Kate began to understand so many things. The rest she wanted to know right now. She lifted Mina's chin. "Did you know?"

"No," Mina sobbed. "Not until Helga came."

"Mina!" Dolph had a dangerously unhealthy-looking pallor. "What does this mean?"

"Shut up," Mina snapped. "It doesn't concern you."

"Then whom does it concern?" Kate got up and backed away from the sofa, her glance passing between Carl's face set in stone, and Mina's dissolving into puffy wrinkles. Reece came up behind her and tried to embrace her, but she shrugged him away.

"Kate." Carl edged away from his seat and came toward her. "Is it really so terrible? Cousins marry all the time."

"Cousin's marrying? Is it as simple to you as that?"

"If it's the money," he said, his arms reaching for her as he moved closer, "you can have my share."

"You bastard." Kate backed away from him, repulsed by the thought of him touching her, of ever having touched her. "When you married me, you knew Miles was your father?"

Dolph groaned behind her and distracted Carl.

"Did you know?" Kate demanded.

"Yes. I always knew."

Dolph stood behind her, his hands trembling with barely controlled fury as he faced Carl. "How could you marry Kate and not tell her?"

"I didn't want to marry her." Long ovals of perspiration stained Carl's starched shirt. "At first, I mean. Miles wanted me to marry Nugie, so I would be part of the family and we could be together more."

"Then why didn't you marry Nugie?" Kate challenged.

"She wouldn't. I told her the truth when she got pregnant and she didn't want any part of me."

"You?" Mina roared up to Carl and slapped his face. He flinched, but didn't back away as she raised her hand to hit him again. Reece caught her hand in midair. She sagged against him, saying, "He killed your sister."

"No, he didn't." Reece smoothed Mina's hair. "It was Nugie's decision."

Carl exhaled loudly. "Thanks, pal."

"Don't thank *me* for anything." Reece's voice was low, more threatening than Mina's fist.

Mina looked up pleadingly into Reece's face. "Take me home."

Reece shook his head. "I can't leave Kate here alone."

"I'll be okay," Kate said. She looked at all the stunned, angry faces around her. "Will you all leave us, please. I need to speak with Carl alone."

"No," Dolph said simply.

"Reece, Mr. Bodge," Kate pleaded. "Please, take Dolph and Mina home."

"Okay," Reece said. "But if you aren't out of here in five minutes, we'll be back."

Kate took Dolph's hand. "Five minutes?"

He nodded. Dolph didn't so much as look at Mina as he left, and Kate understood the depth of his feelings of betrayal. How much would Mina tell him in the end?

When they were alone, Carl took a step toward Kate, his arms reaching out to hold her.

"No," she said. "Just talk, and nothing else."

He slumped into Bodge's chair. "There's nothing more to say."

"Who broke into Miles's house? Sorry, your house now."

"Mom."

"I thought so," Kate said. "She was trying to protect you?"

He nodded sadly. "Now that you and I are divorced, she was afraid Miles would die and you would go through his things and find out about me. If it got out, my career would be over."

"Is that why you hung around so long after the funeral, to get access to Miles?"

"No, Kate. I'm here because I love you. You have to believe me."

"Why?"

"Because it's the truth."

"Do you know anymore what the truth is?"

"I don't deserve that." His anger, always just under the surface, bubbled through his pretence of hurt innocence. "Really, how were you harmed? We had a pretty good life together for a lot of years."

"Did we?" She thought about it for a moment, trying to remember the beginnings. All the images from that time seemed blurred by her grief for Nugie. Is that what they had shared? She looked at Carl. "Why didn't you tell me the truth in the beginning, before it was too late?"

"The truth cost me Nugie. I couldn't risk losing you, too." He leaned forward, the expression on his face intense, committed. "Maybe it wasn't fair, but I needed you. I missed Nugie as much as you did. You were so much alike, the way you talked about things, the people you knew. Sometimes, just sometimes, I could close my eyes and you *were* Nugie."

"Maybe that's where you made your mistake. I never was Nugie. Not for an instant." His words had cut deep, excising any feelings she had left toward him. He had invalidated all their years together and she needed an emotional toehold somewhere.

"Kate?" Carl came to her and held her rigid body.

The arms around her felt like home. But when she looked up into that handsome face he was like a stranger. Suddenly he seemed shabby, like the Ratcher house, as if his trim paint was chipped and faded. She backed out of his embrace.

"What about our children?" she asked. "Didn't you worry that it might be dangerous for them, our being cousins?"

"I guess we were lucky, then, that we never had kids."

"No," she said, feeling a hot rush of sadness. "That's the one thing I regret."

"Hey, look. I'm not completely without character. After Nugie died I vowed I was never going through anything like that again." He looked her right in the eye. "I had a vasectomy."

It came like a physical blow that left her gasping. To save herself, she had to get away from him. She headed for the open front door and fresh air.

He followed her. "Where are you going?"

"Your five minutes are up." No matter how fast she walked, she couldn't shake him. Dolph's keys bounced against her leg as she broke into a run. They were in her hand by the time she reached the Mercedes at the curb.

"Kate, wait." Carl jogged across the courtyard behind her.

Without turning to look at him, to see how close he was she slid in behind the steering wheel and started the engine.

"Come on, now." He was at the window, reaching for the door handle. "Running away isn't going to help."

"Neither is staying," she said as she held the window-up button.

"Please." His hot breath made foggy patches on the window as he gripped the door handle. She pressed the automatic door lock and it made a satisfying "thunk," sealing her in the car.

"We have to talk." His face was inches away from hers on the other side of the glass, getting redder and angrier as he pulled fruitlessly on the door handle. Out of frustration, he banged a fist against the window. He hit the window again and something inside the door popped. She had to get away before he broke the glass.

She put the car in gear, released the parking brake, and eased away from the curb.

Hanging on to the door handle, Carl jogged along beside her. "Stop it, Kate. You're acting like a child."

She accelerated until he was forced to let go. He tumbled away from the car, rolling just the way his football coach had taught him. In the rearview mirror she saw him sitting in the middle of the courtyard, his knee shining through torn slacks, his perfect hair mussed appealingly. He looked like one of the lost children who sit under the lifeguard station at the beach waiting for their mothers to retrieve them.

Kate turned sharply onto Ocean Boulevard, somehow getting through the Saturday morning beach traffic, turning, stopping, avoiding cars and pedestrians without making conscious decisions. Everything outside the car was a blur, every sound muted by the hot anger of betrayal that filled her. Esperanza, Mina, Carl. Who else kept secrets from her while she was being attacked, first with stones, then with her mother's car? And what was it all about, anyway?

Kate opened the windows and let fresh air blow across her face, trying to clear the fog in her brain. Who and why? If Carl had managed to eliminate Kate before she changed her will, assuming he knew that he was Miles's heir, he might have been able to claim two of the three pieces of the Byrd estate. No, she thought, it wouldn't work. If she died, as soon as Miles's will was read, Carl would be the chief suspect. Convicted or not, it would ruin his career, a fate Carl would never risk. Anyway, Carl didn't give a damn about money. In fact, inherited money would be an embarrassment to him.

Then again, she thought, dodging around a group of cyclists, maybe the attacks were meant only to scare her so that she'd beg him to stay, to protect her. It was possible; he had such an overinflated ego and such a low estimation of her ability to take care of herself.

She drove aimlessly for a while, taking the path of least resistance through traffic. Sometimes she turned only because the way was clear, or raced a yellow light rather than move her foot to brake for a red. It didn't matter; she wasn't going anywhere in particular.

Caught at the light behind an armored car, she drummed her fingers restlessly against the steering wheel, half-expecting an automatic to appear at the gun-hole and aim for her head. Stranger things had been happening.

The light changed and the armored car turned one way, Kate the other. If it wasn't Carl, she thought, bogged in traffic approaching a shopping mall, then maybe it was someone who knew about Miles's will and wanted to eliminate both Kate and Carl. If Kate were murdered and Carl was convicted of the deed, who would benefit? Dolph, and through him, Mina. Reece maybe, as the only member of the younger generation to survive. Or Esperanza, for services rendered. Kate shuddered. Whatever the answer, it meant years of treacherous betrayal by someone she loved and trusted.

Like an old stable mare, the car seemed to know where it was headed. Gradually, Kate became aware of familiar things outside; the sounds of Saturday activity in a neighborhood of neat, postwar stucco houses. She was on a short, tree-lined street with a school at the end of the block. Beside her there was a trim green house with a tricycle parked on its small patch of grass, and she stopped, realizing with a start where she was. But why had she come here? And where was Tejeda?

SEVENTEEN

KATE SLOUCHED DOWN in her seat, wishing she could be invisible for a few minutes, until she could sort some things out. Like, what was she doing here? And where else could she go? But a woman with a black eye parked in a Mercedes wouldn't go unnoticed on this street with Toyotas and station wagons in the driveways.

She wasn't sure how she had managed to find Tejeda's house again. But what now? It was Saturday. Tejeda's day off. Time to be with his daughter. Maybe he wasn't even home.

At least she was somewhere and there was no traffic to dodge. Kate closed her eyes and tried to think where to go next.

Then Tejeda was beside her, reaching through the open window to unlock the door. "What happened?" he was asking, but she didn't know why he was so excited.

Feeling light-headed, drugged almost, Kate looked at him dumbly. He wore nothing but a saggy pair of gray knit shorts stenciled "property of S.A.P.D." She wanted to laugh but he seemed so upset. In the back of her mind she recognized the symptoms of shock, and tried to shake them off.

Tejeda opened the car door and pulled her out. He hurt her arms because she couldn't cooperate. As he would a drunk, he stood her on the sidewalk, holding her to keep her from falling. All that time he kept nattering away, asking what happened and was she hurt.

She reacted slowly, trying to work around the fog in her head. "It's okay," she said, looking up at his unshaven face. "I found Miles's bastard." She tried to swallow. "It's Carl."

Tejeda held her tight against his bare chest while she tried to summon tears that weren't there. Bits of cut grass stuck to his sweaty skin and fell onto her shoulder. She put her arms around him, but the lines of his body against her felt strange, uncomfortable. She held him tighter, as if she could mold him into the right shape. His erection pressed against the thin fabric of her skirt and she looked up at him, surprised.

Embarrassed, he stepped back. Taking her arm like a Boy Scout, he walked her across the street to his house, past the idled mower in the middle of the lawn.

"Theresa," Tejeda called as he ushered Kate inside.

Theresa looked up from the table she was dusting.

"Theresa, this is Mrs. Teague."

"We've met." The twelve-year-old gave Kate a worldly grin. She spread her dustcloth over the undusted half of the table she was working on. "I'm all through, Dad. I'm going to Kirsten's, okay?"

"When will you be back?" he asked.

"Later." She looked at Kate again, eyes wide. "Much later."

"Kids think they know so much," he said as Theresa slammed the door behind her. "Are you okay?"

She nodded.

He was looking her over, as if taking inventory. "You aren't hurt anywhere?"

"Not physically."

"Will you be okay here for a minute? I need to clean up."

"Go ahead. I'm all right."

Tejeda took three neckties off a doorknob on his way out of the room.

In the quiet ordinariness of Tejeda's house, she began to feel calmer, though her mouth still felt wadded with cotton. She knew in which general direction to look for the kitchen, and went to find it. Breakfast dishes were draining in a rack by the sink. She filled one of the glasses with tap water and drank it, feeling it slide into a cold lump in the pit of her stomach. Then she wet her hands and put them over her face and at the back of her neck. Slowly, things around her began to come back into focus, including the ugly scene with Carl.

She found her way back into the living room and sat in the same big chair she had used the first time she was there. She stretched her legs out and began to relax, feeling that this place was really the safe harbor. No one had ever been here before, not Carl or Dolph or Mina or any of them. Then she realized why she had come; they would never find her here.

In a few minutes, Tejeda, looking scrubbed and damp, came back into the room. With one hand he carried white tennis shoes, with the other he tucked his knit shirt into his jeans. She again noticed the slight, comfortable-looking roundness around his middle that she found tremendously appealing.

"Okay." He sat on the edge of the sofa and bent over to put on his shoes. "Start at the beginning."

Kate told him about the portrait in Esperanza's alcove at Rosa's and about the reading of the will. He leaned back with his hands folded across his stomach and listened, his dark eyes focused somewhere left of her chin.

"I have to go back to Rosa's," she said finally. "I have to find out what Esperanza knows. It's the only way I can save myself."

"Good idea." He stood up and reached for her hand. "It's my day off. I'd like to pay a little unofficial visit to Esperanza myself. Can you find Rosa's again?"

"Yes." Kate held up Dolph's car keys. "If you'll drive."

In the car, Kate turned in her seat so she could see Tejeda while she talked to him. She was glad he wasn't carrying his police revolver.

Once they were on the freeway, Tejeda said, "One cricket bat tested out. It's now the murder weapon of record."

"Have you any doubts about Miles using it?"

"From what we've found, no. But I think he either had help or someone has carried on where he left off."

"I just left a houseful of candidates."

"Who's at the head of your list, Mrs. Teague?"

"Mrs. Teague? That sounds so strange." Kate drew her knees up and rested her chin on them, feeling jittery from postshock letdown. "I don't feel like I ever was Mrs. anything. Just Kate."

"Are you all right?" His hand covered hers. "You look pale."

"I'm fine." She watched his vaguely Indian profile for a moment. "I was just thinking, Miles did have two babies, his child with Helga and his grandchild, Nugie and Carl's baby. He said both his babies were safe. Is that what he meant?"

"But both his babies weren't safe," Tejeda reminded her. "Carl's baby was aborted."

"Did you know Miles had his first breakdown the day Carl and I got married?"

"Interesting."

"Of course I didn't associate the two things at the time. Do you think he recognized Helga? It just occurred to me that he had his last seizure the day after she arrived for her visit." She covered her eyes, holding the tears behind her lids. "Poor Miles. What he must have gone through over the years."

"Did your mother know about Carl?"

"No," Kate said. It was nice for a change to be sure about something. "She saw secrets as debts to be collected. She would have called that one in a long time ago."

Tejeda glanced at her. "As in blackmail?"

"Maybe in a refined form." The familiar Wilmington oil refinery stench made Kate look up.

"Where do we turn off?" he asked.

"Off ramp after this one. Go north."

"What occurred to me," he said, maneuvering to the right side of the freeway and then down the exit ramp, "is that one by one all the heirs except you have been eliminated."

"Except Carl." Kate pointed right at the first intersection. "Turn there." She directed him to the street that ran along the empty field, hoping she could find the driveway apron again.

"If Mother had managed to get Miles put away," she said as she watched the curb, "she could have frittered away the legacy he had planned for his son, for Carl. He had to stop her without revealing Carl's secret."

"But it still doesn't explain why you were attacked."

Kate spotted the driveway. "Turn here."

"You're kidding." He eyed the field skeptically. "You didn't bring me out here for an abduction did you?"

She laughed. "I thought about it."

The trailer and its outbuildings, a collection of lopsided metal sheds, shimmered in the distance like a cartoon-desert oasis. Twisted bits of automobiles littered the field like the carcasses of animals that had perished on the way to the watering-hole.

"People live here?" Tejeda asked.

As if to answer him, Oscar stepped out of the largest shed, wiping motor oil from his hands onto his overalls. The shed, made of sheets of corrugated metal nailed to a wood frame, was almost indistinguishable from the heaps of scrap around the trailer.

Tejeda stopped next to Oscar and got out of the car, holding his door open to Kate to follow out his side.

"Oscar," Kate said, "this is Lieutenant Tejeda."

"I know. I know." Oscar tucked a wrench into his pocket and unhappily offered a grimy hand. "We been expecting someone, after what happened. Come with me."

He led them behind the trailer to a small vegetable garden where Esperanza and Rosa knelt on carpet squares, weeding the crooked furrows. A basket between them contained a few ears of scrawny corn and some oversized zucchini.

Kate knelt down beside Esperanza and checked the scabs forming over the burns on her face. They still looked raw and painful. "How are you feeling?" Kate asked.

"It hurts her too much to talk." Kate heard the warning in Rosa's voice. Rosa got to her feet using Esperanza's shoulder for support.

"I know about Carl." Kate said directly to Esperanza, ignoring Rosa as much as possible. She saw tears moisten Esperanza's long black lashes and felt sorry about the pain she had to bring the injured woman, but it was unavoidable. "You can write notes if it's easier, but it's time for you to do some talking before anyone else gets hurt."

"I will tell you." Rosa stepped in front of Kate, blocking her view of Esperanza. "Come inside."

Kate balked and turned to Esperanza. Looking sad, Esperanza nodded, making her shooing gesture.

"Okay," Kate said, standing close to Rosa so that the smaller woman had to look up to her. "Let's go."

"I will show you some things." Rosa gripped Kate's arm tightly as if to prevent her from escaping, and walked her toward the trailer. She glanced back at Esperanza. "Who is to say? Maybe you have a right to know."

Kate heard Tejeda scuffing the gravel as he followed. He had to duck his head to get through the low trailer door.

Rosa seemed even more cross than she'd been the night before. As she poured coffee for Kate and Tejeda, her movements were tense and quick. She plunked mugs down on the table in front of them, sloshing some of the steaming liquid. When she muttered something in Spanish under her breath, Tejeda chuckled.

"Don't count on it, *señora*," he said.

Rosa didn't acknowledge him. She bustled into Esperanza's alcove and came out with a tattered shoebox. Squeezing in behind the table, she placed the box on the seat beside her, out of view of her guests. As if she were hiding state secrets, she bent over her box, rifling through its contents and selecting a dozen yellowed photographs.

Kate thought about the picture fragment she had found on the beach and wondered if the rest of it might be in that box. But how would she get it away from Rosa to find out?

Brushing away imaginary crumbs from the table top, Rosa arranged the photographs in a semicircle facing Kate. The beautiful blond boy in Esperanza's alcove portrait looked out at her from every photograph. In holiday clothes, at the zoo, carrying schoolbooks, playing with pets, he stood with Esperanza or Rosa or Oscar, sometimes alone, and once with a tall slender woman Kate barely recognized as Helga. Always, he looked like a happy, cherished child. Someone special.

Kate studied all the ankles, but the three pairs here were all thicker than the ankles in her fragment.

"He was our *chico*, our little boy." Rosa picked up one of the pictures and held it against her breast. "Your grandfather gave Helga money to get rid of her baby. But she was too far along. Mr. Miles asked my sister for help. So after Helga had the baby she came to us."

Kate reached for a picture with a torn corner, but Rosa snatched it away. "Did these come from my Uncle Miles's house?"

"A few," Rosa shrugged. "Helga brought some to me, but most of these were mine."

"You were pretty close to Helga, then?"

"Not so much as with Mr. Miles. We never understood why she wouldn't wait for Mr. Miles's divorce, so the baby could have a father. But he took too long and she found someone else." Rosa's lips turned up in a sneer. "She always liked men too much. She left the baby with us and got married to some fellow. It didn't work out, so she came back for the boy and took him *norte*, across the border. We followed her to be close to our *chico*."

Kate saw her smile for the first time, a wide, tender smile as she thought about Carl.

"You never saw a sweeter boy," Rosa continued. "He was so beautiful and so smart. There never was a boy like him."

"Did you see him often?" Kate asked.

"Sometimes yes. Sometimes no. It depended. His mother moved around a lot, married a few more times. She would leave him with us when it suited her. And always they came to us when things went bad." Rosa picked up the box and half raised the lid. Inside, Kate could see cards and letters, and bits of a child's handwriting. "Mr. Miles always sent them money, even when she had a husband. He was better off without Helga. But he never got over losing the boy."

"Did Miles ever come here to see Carl?"

"Of course. He came here all the time, until..." She spiraled her finger at the side of her head. "You know, *loco*. When we had the boy alone he would always come. But never when Helga was around. He always begged her to bring the boy and come live with him and she didn't like to hear him." Rosa gave Tejeda a piercing glare, as if he were a conspirator. "But she always took his money."

"Surely Miles could have claimed legal custody of Carl," Kate said.

"Maybe." Rosa sounded doubtful. "But Helga said the boy wasn't safe with your mother and grandfather around."

Rosa had told Kate plenty, but crucial parts of the story were still missing. What seemed so strange to Kate was that this had gone on all during her lifetime among people she shared her most private feelings with and she never knew any of it. She could understand Esperanza and Miles keeping a bastard child under wraps—society had stricter rules forty-some years ago—but how could they let Kate marry him without saying something?

Kate cleared her throat and looked at Rosa. "Why didn't Esperanza tell me this before I married Carl?"

"He is your cousin. You would not have married him. Like Nugie would not." Rosa's face came close and she jabbed at the air with a stubby finger. "Your family owed him something. We would not interfere when he took his rightful place."

"Did any of you think of me and my rights?" It wasn't a challenge. She just wanted to know.

Rosa carefully gathered up the photographs and returned them to their box. She held the box tightly, as if she knew Kate wanted to take it.

Tejeda held Kate's hand under the table as he glared at Rosa. "The lady asked you a question."

Rosa only shook her head in response and stood up with her box. She opened the trailer door and gestured with her thumb, like a hitchhiker, for Kate and Tejeda to leave.

When Kate tried to pass her to get out the door, Rosa moved into her path. She stood so close Kate could see the gold in her back teeth. "We thought he was too good for you."

EIGHTEEN

ALL KATE WANTED was to get out of the trailer and away from the woman's long-stored hatred, but Rosa seemed to take up all the space.

Tejeda shouldered his way past Rosa and caught Kate's arm as she faltered at the doorstep. She took his hand as they hurried back to the car. Kate looked for Esperanza on the way, hoping there was something to salvage between them.

Oscar came out of his shed and opened the car door, to hurry them away.

"I want to see Esperanza," Kate said.

Oscar glanced toward the trailer and Kate saw the fear in his eyes. But of what? Rosa?

"Please go now," he said, and ducked back into his shed.

"He's right," Tejeda said. "We should just go now. When they simmer down I'll come back."

Kate hesitated, expecting to see Esperanza rush out to her from somewhere in the wreckage-strewn field. But she seemed to have disappeared behind Rosa's protective wall.

Reluctantly, Kate got into the car. As Tejeda sped away she sat close beside him, hanging on to him as if he might otherwise suddenly vaporize like the mirage her life had been with Carl and Esperanza. She looked back once as the car bounced over the field, leaving Esperanza and little *chico* behind in a cloud of gray dust. Far behind.

Once he was out on the street again, Tejeda pulled to the far side and stopped. He turned in the seat so his back was against the door and held Kate in his arms.

"Crazy old woman," he said. "She didn't need to say that."

"Maybe she did." She looked up into his deep brown eyes, "cow eyes" Esperanza had called them.

He kissed her, tentatively at first, then with more insistence. After a few minutes he started to pull away.

"Sorry," he said, combing her hair away from her face with his fingers. "That wasn't fair. Not after what just happened."

"After what just happened," she said, "it's exactly what I needed." She touched his face, the crisp rasp of his whiskers roughing her skin, replacing her anger toward Rosa with a different, more pleasant tension. She reached up to him and lightly traced the space between his lips with the tip of her tongue.

His soft laugh as he teased her tongue with his own was like the beginning of a whole new language she was eager to learn. He kissed the side of her neck just above her collarbone and she shivered, a delighted giggle escaping where her lips touched his shoulder.

"You liked that?" he laughed.

"Try here." She pointed to a spot just below her ear. Then she turned and touched the back of her neck. "And especially here."

"And here." He tickled her ribs, gently jabbing as she laughed and tried to escape. "And everywhere."

She relaxed her head against his chest as his arms crossed in front of her, his hands lightly resting on her breasts. She nestled her cheek against his shoulder and with her hand caressed the muscled arm that held her. She wanted all of him. She wanted to see and touch and taste every inch of him. But not here. She had a strong feeling that what was to follow between them needed a proper beginning. And from the quiet that had settled over Tejeda, she sensed he agreed.

Kate brought his hand up and kissed it, then sat up.

"Ready to go home?" he asked.

She nodded, but home, her house at any rate, seemed an empty prospect.

Tejeda started the car. Kate stayed close to him with his right arm wrapped around her. Reaching through the steering wheel with his left hand to shift the car into gear, he said, "I don't know if I can drive like this anymore. 'Course I've had no practice in a Mercedes. Used to borrow my dad's Plymouth."

"What does your dad do?" she asked as she twined her fingers in his. It seemed suddenly important to know.

"He's the band director at Santa Angelica High."

"And your mother?"

"Teaches third grade at Archibald Byrd Elementary School."

"My grandpa's school," she said. Her uncles had donated land for the school as a memorial to their father, and Kate always thought that was strange. Her grandfather sent his boys, and Kate, to private schools because, he said, public schools were a hotbed of mediocrity. Kate smiled. Maybe the gift was a last little gesture of defiance. If it was, the whole family had conspired in it. "I came home from boarding school for the dedication of the school."

"I know. That was the first time I saw you. You had a mouth full of braces."

"How can you remember that?"

"My mom pointed you out. See, when I was a kid my folks used to take us to the beach below your house. My little sister called your house 'the castle' and she and Mom made up stories about the little princess who lived there."

"You're making this up."

"No," he grinned. "It's true. Every time your picture was on the society page, Terry, my sister, would show us the princess."

"I wish you'd told me this sooner," she said, laughing to cover her chagrin.

"You like being a princess?"

"No. It stinks," she said. "But knowing about your family would have spared me some grief. See, for a while I thought you might be Miles's bastard."

"Me?" The car lurched forward as he started. "Whatever gave you such an idea?"

"Remember Officer Little? The man you sent with me at the hospital?" When he nodded, she continued. "He thought it was strange you were spending so much time on Mother's case because normally you don't go out digging around hillsides for clues. He said mostly you supervise the lowlier detectives."

"Lowlier?"

"He says you're pretty big potatoes."

"Think I'll keep an eye on Little, recruit him into my department." Tejeda took his eyes off the road for an instant to look at Kate. "But how does that make me a bastard?"

"You're about the right age. For a while I wondered if Esperanza had been Miles's lover. They were always pretty close."

"Don't ever let my mother hear any of this."

"You do look more like Esperanza than like Helga."

"Glad to hear it."

"But what really made me wonder about you was that you were around all the time but Sergeant Green did all the dirty work."

"I'm good at delegating," he chuckled. "So how long did this suspicion last?"

"About an hour. At various times I also considered Reece, Sy Ratcher, Lydia, and myself."

He pulled her closer. "But not Carl?"

"No. Never Carl." It was still too outrageous to accept fully. She tried to imagine him living in the trailer with Rosa and Oscar, using the outhouse they had directed her to that morning. He was always so meticulous; everything around him had to be clean and orderly and top quality. Except his car, she thought. Then she wondered if Oscar kept the car running, and if maybe that was why Carl hung on to it.

Kate's hand was asleep so she disengaged her fingers from Tejeda's and shook them out. His arm was probably numb, too, she thought. He flexed it and rested it on the back of the seat. She moved away from him a little and tucked her left leg up under her so that she was turned in the seat facing his profile. The point of her bent knee just touched his thigh. He was awfully quiet.

"Come clean," she said. "Why did you come out of your office for this case?"

For a moment he didn't seem to hear. On the Central Santa Angelica off ramp ahead of them an ancient blue slat-truck with Tijuana license plates threatened to spill its load of salvaged tires at every curve. Tejeda, both hands on the wheel now, seemed to be calculating his best route of escape if the truck went over.

The blue truck rolled into a service station by the bottom of the ramp and Tejeda relaxed. He glanced at Kate. "You want the truth?"

"Yes."

He hesitated, braking for a red light. "I had orders from the mayor."

She was watching his face, just because it was nice to watch. When he mentioned the mayor she saw that something bothered him. "What did the mayor want you to do?"

"Media people had stirred up a lot of public interest in your mother's death because of who she was," he said. "Some planning commissioner put a bug in the mayor's ear about your mother and Sy Ratcher lobbying for zoning variances on land they had no tie to. He was worried about who might have been involved and what they might have done to your mother. So the mayor, being a public whatsis, didn't want to be caught with his pants down on network TV, in case there was more involved than a mugging. He and a lot of his friends have had business dealings with your mother."

"Did he want you to . . ."

"Cover up? No. He just wanted a head start on the six o'clock news teams. Does that bother you?"

"No," she reassured him, feeling that Tejeda had more qualms about the mayor's motives than she had. She knew the mayor. He'd been her grandfather's fair-haired boy on the city council many years ago. He was a decent man. But like most men who had risen as far as he had, he had buried a few bones along the way. Kate understood the power structure of Santa Angelica well enough to realize that if he fell from grace, some of her family interests might tumble with him. So he's less than perfect. Who isn't? she thought, remembering Nugie and a few other incidents in her own past.

They were in Northtown, the suburban, inland area of Santa Angelica. Tejeda turned left off the busy north-south boulevard that divided that part of the city into commercial and residential areas. Approaching the maze of short streets in Tejeda's neighborhood from this direction, Kate was completely lost until they were on his block.

He stopped the car and held out the keys to her. "Come in for a drink?"

"Yes." She pocketed the keys.

"Theresa," he called as he opened the front door. When there was no response, he smiled. "She's flown the coop."

"Where is she?" Kate asked. She thought he should seem more concerned; they'd been gone several hours.

"She's in the neighborhood." He led the way to the kitchen. "Since my wife left, Theresa never leaves the block without telling me. Her counselor says it's insurance so I'll know where to find her if I suddenly decide to leave, too."

"What'll it be?" He opened the refrigerator and looked at its meager contents. "Diet root beer, or..." He moved a wilted head of lettuce. "Or half a diet root beer?"

"Make it half a diet root beer."

He opened the can and divided it between two glasses, handing one to Kate.

"Dad!" The front door slammed. "Are we going to have lunch or what? I'm starved." Theresa stopped suddenly when she saw Kate.

"I haven't been to the market yet," he said. "If you're hungry, you'll just have to scout around and find something."

"That means hot dogs again." She sighed and looked up at Kate. "Did you guys eat already?"

"No," Kate said. "I'd love a hot dog."

"Daddy, couldn't we go to McDonald's?"

"I'll go to the market later." He took Kate by the hand and led her toward the living room. "Right now Mrs. Teague and I have some things to talk about."

From the living room Kate could hear Theresa banging cupboard doors and pots in the kitchen and she felt like an intruder. Tejeda had family things to take care of. She jangled the car keys in her pocket. "I should go."

"Where?"

She looked down at the keys in her hand, but they gave her no help. "I don't know."

He put his arms around her. His lips, cold from the drink, brushed across her cheek. "Stay here."

"Oops." Theresa stood in the doorway, holding a napkin-covered plate. Kate laughed, caught in the act by a twelve-year-old chaperon, but stopped when she saw the red rising under Tejeda's collar.

He covered his eyes. "What's up, squirt?"

"I've, uh, made some hot dogs in the microwave," Theresa said. "You wanna come and eat them or should I go back to Kirsten's?"

"You make it sound like I kick you out all the time so I can have women in here."

"Does he?" Kate asked, putting her hand in his.

"No. But I've sort of practiced in my mind what I would do if he ever did."

Tejeda walked over and bent his head close to his daughter's. "Maybe you should go see Kirsten."

"Right." Theresa wrapped a catsup-oozing hot dog in a paper napkin. "Anyway, I left my books at Kirsten's."

"You didn't take any books with you," Tejeda reminded her.

"Mmph," she said around a mouthful, banging the door behind her.

"Sorry," Tejeda was trying, unsuccessfully, to look stern. "How do kids know so much?"

"Their parents teach them," Kate said. He turned to her and she saw again that softness in his eyes. She put her hand on the back of his neck and brought his face down to hers. Lightly, she kissed him. "I can't stay very long."

"Might not be the Ritz around here, but you get round-the-clock police protection."

She burrowed her hand inside his shirt and kissed the corner of his impish grin. "Think I'm safe here, Lieutenant?"

"Only if you want to be." He held her close as they walked down the hall to his bedroom. With his hand on the doorknob he hesitated. She covered his hand and turned the knob.

Late afternoon sun filtered through his blue drapes, casting the room in a cool, gray light. Tejeda sat on the corner of the bed and held out his arms for her, inviting her into his private place. Kate moved into the circle he made and pulled his shirt over his head. Under her fingertips she could feel a slight trembling as she stroked the smooth, honey-colored skin of his back.

"Is that desire," she said, "or second thoughts?"

"Anticipation."

She pulled her blouse out of her skirt band.

"Let me." He unbuttoned her blouse, tasting the bare flesh as he exposed it. Drawing her blouse down over her shoulders, he traced the contours of her firm, round breasts with his tongue.

He reached behind her to unfasten her skirt. At that moment she remembered about Carl's vasectomy. All those years he had led her to believe she was sterile. But it was only part of his fraud. The realization was like an unexpected gift; there was no reason anymore she couldn't have a child. She held Tejeda's face in her hands and saw the gentle strength there. There was something they really needed to talk about later.

The skirt fell down around her ankles and she kicked it away. She wanted to get closer to him, to feel every part of him next to her. There was so much about him she still didn't know. But there was time.

With one hand she pulled his zipper down over the mound in his jeans, guiding them off his rump and onto the floor. "God, you're beautiful," she said, combing the hair on his long thighs with her fingers.

"Mmm," he sighed, burying his face between her breasts. He cupped her buttocks in his hands and brought her up to straddle his lap. "Something I meant to tell you that first time we met."

"What?" Her bare legs circled his waist. She tucked a foot under him and massaged him with her toes.

"You have a great caboose. Most thin women never get theirs out of the roundhouse. But you . . ."

She covered his mouth with her own, running her tongue along his even teeth, memorizing the taste and smell and texture of him, as if in that way she could always keep a part of him.

He drew her back across the bed and she stretched along the length of his body, sandwiching one leg between his to feel the dark bristles scratch the tender inside of her thigh. With their heads together, her toes barely reached past his knees.

"Something else I meant to tell you."

"I hadn't noticed you being so shy." Her fingers traced his spine from his neck to the hollow of his back.

He flinched in reflex. "No fair tickling." He caught her hand and brought it to his lips. "I meant to tell you I'd be back for you."

NINETEEN

KATE TURNED AROUND to let Tejeda button her skirt.

The room was awash in the cool, gray light of dusk.

Everywhere it was so quiet. The calm before the storm, Kate thought. Or was it the eye of the hurricane? She parted the bedroom drapes to look outside, to make sure they hadn't somehow been cut adrift. "It's getting foggy."

"Looks like it." He flicked on the overhead light so he could see what he was doing. Then, button finally fastened, he hugged her from behind, kissing the back of her neck. "Might be hazy out there, but I think things are pretty clear in here. At least I hope they are."

She turned in his arms and looked up into his smiling face. "I love you, Lieutenant."

His sudden bark of laughter made her back up, afraid she had asked for too much, or asked it too soon. "That bothers you?"

"Yes, it bothers me a *lot*." He was trying to control his mirth.

"Sorry." Crestfallen, she went over to the dresser and tried to plump her hair. Maybe she was just susceptible right now to any display of affection, she thought. And maybe out of her need to pump up her sagging self-esteem, she had read too much into what Tejeda had said. She looked into the mirror and saw him watching her, the softness still there, deep in the Indian-brown eyes. "I'm ready to go now."

"Kate, that's not what I meant." He stood behind her and talked to her reflection. "Say 'I love you, Roger,' not 'I love you Lieutenant.'"

"I love you, Roger."

The last syllable of his name was lost as he kissed her, lifting her up to him so that her feet left the floor. Seeming almost overcome by emotion, he sat back down on the edge of the bed, cradling her in his lap. He held her that way, her head against his chest, rocking her back and forth slowly, for what seemed a long time.

The pattern of his breathing, the rhythm of his heart became sounds so intimate they were excruciating. She wanted to keep this peaceful moment for as long as she could; the house ahead would be filled with confrontation as she tried to pick up the thread of her life among the ruins of her family.

"This might not be what you want to hear." He tangled his fingers in the hair at the nape of her neck. "This place has been awfully empty since my wife left. I was mad at her for going and hurt that I failed her somehow. I didn't want to let anyone get close enough to hurt me like that again."

She didn't dare to move.

"But you salved the wounds." She could feel the intensity of emotion in his voice echoing through his chest. "Don't go home."

"I have to. For a while, anyway." She smoothed the collar of his shirt to have something to do with her hands. It made her remember the texture of his bare flesh against hers and she wished she could stay. "There are too many things that need to be settled."

"I know you're right. But I don't like it. Let me drive you, make sure you're okay." They left the bedroom holding hands, not ready to break physical contact. "I need to make some phone calls first."

Tejeda called Mrs. Murphy and arranged for her to keep Theresa overnight. Then he called for a plainclothes unit to meet them at Kate's. She listened to him giving orders, playing the ranking policeman, and she couldn't help smiling.

He hung up the phone. "You look like the cat who caught the mouse. What's up?"

"What would they say down at headquarters if they could see you now?"

"Probably," he kissed the end of her nose. "You're fired. Listen a minute." His tone became very official, very serious. "Miles is dead now, and he isn't cover anymore for whoever has been harassing you. I expect that pretty soon now 'whoever' is either going to desist or get more serious about it.

I'm not sure that taking you home is a good idea. Except that you might flush the buzzard out by being there. Tonight we'll stay close, keep an eye on you. But after that," his fingers bit into her shoulders. "I don't know what I can slide past accounting."

Fog was rolling in from the beach as they drove, blurring lights and landmarks into a surreal diffusion. By the time Tejeda parked in the courtyard, the fog was so thick that visibility was less than ten yards. From the car, her house, even with its lights on, loomed like a vague shadow against the sea of whiteness.

"Come in," Kate said, pausing in the doorway.

"Just to check it out," he said, squeezing her hand. He looked around the broad foyer with its polished marble floor and antique appointments and shook his head. "Home sweet home?"

" 'Tis a humble place, but mine own," she said, laughing.

"But I hear the neighborhood's going." Carl, like a rigid martinet, slowly descended the long staircase toward them. It was an awful moment for her as the three of them stood frozen in an awkward tableau.

Kate wished she could spare Tejeda the embarrassment of a confrontation. From the sly tilt to his eyes, Kate knew Carl saw that something had happened between Kate and Tejeda and he wouldn't hesitate to use it as ammunition. Tejeda might be in a vulnerable position professionally because of her. She waited for Carl to reach the bottom step. "What are you doing here?"

"You asked me to stay, remember?"

"That was last night. Now you have a place of your own."

Carl looked at Tejeda, then at Kate; his pale gray eyes turned to ice. "I like it better here."

"Do you want him to leave?" Tejeda asked her.

"He's going," she said. "Aren't you, Carl?"

"If we can talk first. Alone." He glared at Tejeda. "Do we need your approval?"

"No. You need hers. Kate?"

"Where will you be?"

"Outside," Tejeda said. "The other unit's on its way. I'll go watch for them."

"Then it's okay," she said. "We do have some things to settle. Thanks for bringing me home, Roger." She took his hand and tried not to linger in his grasp. She didn't want to give Carl any more ammunition. Brushing past Carl without another word or glance she walked up the stairs to the bedroom.

"Damn," she groaned as she flipped on the light. The room was in a depressing state of decay because neither she nor Esperanza had been home to clean it. Pink roses, withered after two days without water, littered her bed and gave off a sickly, funereal scent. Brown petals trailed across the carpet like footprints to nowhere.

The unopened bottle of champagne was still in the ice bucket, its label floating on the tepid water. Leaving her shoes in the general clutter of dirty clothes and wet bath towels on the floor, she uncorked the wine and sipped it from the bottle as she walked into the bathroom. The first taste bit her throat. Resting her back against the sink, she took another drink and held it in her mouth a moment to smooth it before she swallowed it. She was still standing there, holding the bottle by its neck, when Carl walked in.

"Hello," she said, chin down, focusing on the floor. Dread and the wine hit her stomach at the same time. Seeing him hurt more than she had expected. It had been too easy when she was with Tejeda to put aside the twelve years with Carl. But Tejeda wasn't with her now, and the twelve years were.

He stood in the doorway and watched her. "How long has this been going on between you and Lieutenant Taco?"

"Ah, yes. The football ploy." Maybe it wouldn't be so hard after all, she thought. "The best defense is a good offense. Or is that backward?" She poured the wine into the sink.

"I know you're pretty mad at me right now, Kate." Carl took a step toward her but stopped when she turned away. "If you think about it, nothing actually has happened."

"You're going to give me your tits and ass courtroom routine, right? I think you'd better shut up before you make this worse than it already is."

"Okay, okay. I'm sorry. You have a right to be upset. But so have I. This has been the worst day of my life, not knowing where you were or what you might be doing."

She hadn't a clue about what he was up to. "Doing?"

"Are you going to tell?" There was an edge of panic in the way his voice slipped half an octave. "Are you going to take out a two-column ad and announce to the world that I'm . . ." The words died in his throat.

"No."

He exhaled in that peculiar way the accused at the bar have when they hear they've been acquitted. It's like they've held the same breath through the entire trial and can finally let go of it.

"I'm not going to lie for you, either."

"But the family."

"Of course, we should be concerned about the family." She walked into her closet and came out with a suitcase. "Like Uncle Miles. What do you think it did to him all those years, sitting at his window, watching you come and go without giving him the least acknowledgment?"

"That's the way he wanted it."

Kate carried the suitcase down the hall to the room Carl had been using, tossed it onto the rumpled bed, and opened it.

"And Helga?" she asked as he came into the room. "He wanted her here, too?"

"Yes." Carl reclined on the bed next to the bag, curling around it a little, as if to anchor it.

"How do you know this? Did you ever talk to him?"

"We talked on the telephone all the time, when I was at the office. Every month when he sent Mom her check he begged her to come. He wanted her here, where he felt she always belonged."

"But she wouldn't come until my mother was gone, right?"

"Do you blame her?"

"That's all it means to you?" She opened the top dresser drawer and looked at the neat rows of socks. Packing them would be an intimate contact she didn't want, so she pulled the whole drawer out and handed it to him. "Do you understand what Miles did for you and Helga?"

He held the drawer on his lap, making no move to unload it into the suitcase or to get up off the bed, "We don't know for sure he did anything."

"*I* know."

"Then you're safe now, right?" Angrily, he pushed the drawer aside and it spilled to the floor. Folded socks rolled eccentrically around his feet; navy, black, charcoal, the whole range of his spectrum. "If Miles killed your mother, what do you need with that Saint Bernard out there?"

"He's trying to make sure I'm not murdered in my sleep."

"You aren't afraid of me, are you, Kate?"

She listened for the emotional tremor in his voice, looked for the concerned crease in his brow. But it wasn't there. "I know one thing. It wasn't you who tried to kill me."

"Thank God for that."

"If it had been you, you would have succeeded." She pulled out another drawer and put it next to him. "Are you staying at Miles's house?"

He rolled over, put his hands behind his head and gazed at the ceiling. He was trying to seem nonchalant, Kate thought. But his skin had gone very pale, and tense white parentheses framed his mouth. "I'm not packing anything, not if you're really in danger."

"Suit yourself. But you're not staying here."

"I'll be at Miles's, then."

She watched how much time it took for him to get to his feet and knew that it wasn't all over yet. "I'll see you out."

Hoping to hurry him, Kate went down the stairs first, setting a fast pace. But she had time to call and make sure Reece had cleared out of Miles's house before Carl finally made an appearance at the bottom of the stairs.

"Went back for my toothbrush." He held it up in front of him like a candle. "We'll talk tomorrow, when you've had time to think."

"Good-night, Carl." She turned to open the front door as Carl leaned to kiss her cheek. It was an awkward, desperate gesture. Afraid he was going to say something more, or do something, she swung the door wide, using it like a shield.

Tejeda stood framed in the open door, making wide crescents in the fog with his swinging flashlight as he leaned easily against the wall.

Defeated, Carl sauntered out past Kate. "Evening, Lieutenant." His words were rich with sarcasm.

"Mr. Teague." Tejeda bowed in mock deference. He watched until Carl's back had disappeared into the fog before he turned to Kate. "He didn't pack his jammies."

"He doesn't wear any."

"Right." Tejeda whistled in some air. "Are you okay?"

"Surviving. It's safe to come in now."

"Not yet. If I go in there, I won't be coming out real fast." He gestured with his thumb toward the fog. "Until these guys finish setting up, I'm door monitor."

Kate peered into the white. "What guys?"

"We have you surrounded in case anyone tries something. Don't worry about it. Just go inside and bolt the doors. I'll see you later."

"Sure thing." A cold draft ran up her back as she looked out into the gloom, trying to find some warm, human shapes. It was eerie, imagining people out there in the fog watching the house, watching her. Standing in the light of the open door she felt strangely exposed and vulnerable.

"See you later." She retreated inside and shot the door bolt home with a firm and satisfying "chunk."

It was going to be a long night, all alone in the house for the first time, with who knew how many people outside watching, and she felt frightened. Wanting a little fortification, she went to the kitchen to make coffee.

She found the kitchen in worse shape than the bedroom. No one had cleaned it since Esperanza was rushed to the emergency room.

And the police investigators had been there to add to the mess. Every surface had round black smudges where they had looked for fingerprints. Packages of food lay open on the table and the countertops. Had they taken samples from everything she wondered.

Feeling a little squeamish about eating anything that had been opened and might still contain some lye, Kate went into the big pantry for a fresh can of coffee and something to eat.

Piling cans in one arm, she came out with virgin coffee, a few little paper-wrapped cans of deviled ham, and a Boston brown bread that was baked in its can. She opened a new jar of mayonnaise and could tell from the whoosh sound it made that it had never been opened before. It was hardly gourmet fare, but it would do.

While the coffee brewed, she began to scrub the kitchen. Closing her eyes, she rubbed out the blood stains in the sink, then fed the remains of the interrupted dinner into the garbage disposal. She went to the broom closet by the back door for a mop, and was startled to see a man standing outside. He smiled and waved, and she recognized him as the young officer who had come the night Helga burglarized Miles's house. He was still there a few minutes later when she put the mop away.

By the time the coffee was ready, the kitchen, while not up to Esperanza's standards, was presentable. Kate sliced the bread and made little round sandwiches spread with ham and mayonnaise. After sampling a few and deciding they were edible, she piled them on a plate and put them on a tray with half-a-dozen mugs.

She filled one of the mugs and carried it to the back door and handed it out to the policeman on duty there. "Hope you don't get cold out here tonight."

"Thanks." He took the cup. "Fog's a relief after all that heat, though, isn't it?"

"Guess it is," she shrugged, wishing she could see across the lawn. After bolting the door, she picked up the tray and carried it to the front door. She was a little disappointed to find Tejeda wasn't alone. He stood with his back to the door, head bent in conversation, laughing with another man in plainclothes. Still laughing, he came to her as she wrestled with the tray and the door handle.

"What's this?" He took the tray from her.

"Just some coffee." Because of the other man she didn't remind him that he hadn't had dinner. "I count three of you, but there are extra cups in case there are more of you out there in the fog someplace."

"Thanks. I thought you couldn't cook."

"Can't. But I can do wonders with a can opener." She nodded to the other officer. "Good-night."

"Wait a minute, Kate." Tejeda put the tray down on the steps and sprinted toward her. "Let me check the lock for you." He stepped inside with her and pushed the door shut.

"Alone at last," she laughed as he embraced her. The kiss he gave her was quick, but full of warmth and passion.

"Are you going to be all right in here tonight alone?"

"Is that an offer?" She smoothed the worried furrows on his forehead.

"No such luck. Look," he held her close, "I know, with everything that's going on, it'll be a rough night for you. But I'll be right here."

He kissed her again lightly before he opened the door. "Here," he paused on his way out and put something in her left hand.

She looked at the cluster of keys he put in her palm. "What are these?"

"My car keys. After my wife left, Theresa slept with them so she'd know I wasn't going anywhere without her. I thought they might make you feel better."

"Thanks." She clutched the keys close to her. "But we didn't come in your car."

"Doesn't matter," he said as he went back out into the fog. "I have another set. Get some sleep. I have a feeling you're going to need it."

Kate closed and locked the heavy front door. Turning on every light switch as she passed it, Kate made her way slowly through the house, checking doors and windows, and watching for faces in the fog. As she walked up the stairs, she memorized every creaking step, just in case.

"In case of what?" she said aloud, watching for any movement in the dark passage above. She couldn't see very much, like the night she was on the beach stairs. The stones had come so quietly out of the darkness then, slamming into her with no more fanfare than a sudden breeze. Shuddering, remembering the pain, she hurried down the hall to her bedroom.

"Go on. Scare yourself senseless," she chastised herself. A look at the state of the room stopped her short. The clutter was like an unfinished argument, bits and pieces lying around to be picked up later. She wasn't ready for it.

Stepping into the room only to get to her dressing room, Kate changed quickly into faded jeans and a pink pullover. From a hall linen closet she took a pillow and an afghan and retreated into her study, the room that had always been her "safe harbor." With some effort, she pushed her desk in front of the door, knowing it wouldn't stop anyone who was really determined to get in. But it would slow him.

Kate turned her big reading chair into the oriel and dropped the pillow and afghan on the seat. She opened the tall middle window and looked down into the fog, feeling the damp air smooth and cool on her cheeks. Standing there, the sea and the bluff hidden under the dense white blanket, the room seemed suspended on clouds. She was alone, isolated and safe. But she knew it was only an illusion.

Curled up in the chair, afghan tucked under her chin, Kate listened to the muffled "aah-ooh" of ships' foghorns out on the water. The sound was familiar and comforting, a constant after all the chaos.

Snatches of low, male conversation outside her grandfather's study door below reassured her that Tejeda was still there. Clutching his keys in her hand, she slipped into a light, fitful sleep full of harsh and confusing images too transitory to be dreams.

There was someone following her, but she couldn't see his face. She tried to get away but the fog dragged her down and he kept getting closer. She beat at him with a cricket bat, but with no effect. A crowd of people she should have recognized loomed out of the fog and pleaded for her help. There was something terribly wrong, and she heard them screaming. "The bluff! The bluff!"

Kate startled awake, shoving the afghan away from her. As the dream images faded, the voices grew louder.

TWENTY

KATE GOT TO HER FEET, pushed the desk away from the door, and peered out into the dark hall.

The silence in the house hung like a shroud around her. It seemed unnatural, as temporary as the pause between breaths. Someone was waiting for her. She could feel it.

Her back pressed flat against the wall, she made her way down the hall to the stairway. The cold, textured plaster snagged at her sweater, roughened the skin of her palms as she went down the steps, careful to put her weight only on the side of each riser to keep it from creaking. She didn't make a sound, a technique she'd perfected as a teenager sneaking in after her midnight curfew.

From the bottom step, the front door seemed to be acres away across the exposed foyer. To reach the door she had to pass a trio of tall arches, gaping like great deep holes—one that led to the living room, one on the other side that led to the study, and one behind her that led to the back hall past the kitchen.

Summoning her failing courage, Kate dashed across the polished floor. Feeling the blackness close in behind her, she fumbled with the dead bolts. Finally, she got the door open and dashed out into the white night.

"Roger!" Kate screamed into the misted abyss. Footsteps ran toward her across the bricks, and she recognized their rhythm before she could see anyone. She left the shelter of the house lights to meet him.

"Kate!" Tejeda materialized out of the fog. "What are you doing out here?"

"I heard people screaming." She put her arms around him, brushing her cheek against the damp front of his shirt, so familiar and normal. "What's happening?"

"Look there." He turned her toward the bluff. The sun was rising, turning the fog a blazing orange. Except that it was rising in the wrong direction. And hours too soon.

Then Kate smelled it. "Gasoline," she said.

"Come with me." Tejeda surrounded her with his arms. "And stay close."

She tried to keep up with his long strides as they hurried through the fog toward the source of the orange light. Finally, near the edge of the bluff, she saw it, and dropped back in dismay. The beach stairs were enveloped in sheets of fire that rose into the night like silk scarves billowing in the wind.

Three uniformed policemen aimed garden hoses at the stairs. Their slim jets of water shot into the swirling mist and fell short of the flames.

"Forget it, Ralph," Tejeda called to the nearest officer. "The stairs are gone and there's not much else here to burn." As he said it, an ember shot out from the side of the stairs and set off a line of flame that snaked rapidly across the dry ice plant on the bluff.

Frightening but beautiful, Kate thought, watching the play of light catch in the fog. She'd seen fire on the bluff many times, but it had never been this spectacular before. And it had never seemed dangerous. Except for the stairs, which were now beyond saving, there was little more than dry scrub and ice plant to burn.

The spreading line of flame lit the top of the bluff like a moving spotlight, picking up shapes in silhouette. Beside the gazebo Kate now saw Dolph, Lydia, and Mina's maid huddled together in their robes and slippers, watching the fire below them. Reece, shivering in his khaki shorts and bare feet, stood away from the group, closer to the fire, as if he were trying to get warm.

Kate looked along the bluff through the fog, but couldn't find Mina anywhere. Maybe she was still too humiliated by the secrets uncovered during the reading of Miles's will to face anyone. Kate ached for her, wondering if she would ever be able to confess to Dolph the whole story about Helga, and about her own abortion. Old secrets, old scars, she thought sadly.

Eventually, Kate hoped, some of the damage done to the family could be patched up. Enough at least so they could live together again comfortably. But what were they going to do about Carl?

"Kate!" Reece jogged toward her across the lawn.

"How did it start?" Kate asked, fascinated by the twisting thread of flame below.

"Someone torched the bluff. Kids with a campfire again, probably."

"Ice plant doesn't burn like that," Kate said, watching the thin line of fire define the arsonist's path. "Smell the gas?"

A branch of flame licked up the bluff and caught an olean-der ten feet below where they stood. The dry bush flared quickly, forcing them back a few steps. Through the fog, Kate felt its heat flash and die as it was almost instantly consumed.

"Damn kids," Reece said. "Don't they know what a pain it is to reseed the bluff?"

"Wasn't kids," Tejeda said. "Someone wanted us away from the house."

"Scary shit." Reece shook from the cold.

"Why don't you go put on some clothes?" Kate snapped, a cover for her growing panic. "You'll get sick."

"My things are still at Miles's." Reece blew on his hands to warm them. "Carl has barricaded himself inside there and I don't want to press him. Even to get my toothbrush."

Kate touched his shoulder. "Sorry I got you involved in this mess."

"Don't worry about it. Keeps my other problems in per-spective." Reece plunged his hands into his pockets, his nar-row frame bent in a depressed slouch. "Yesterday, Lydia and I got evicted. For cohabiting. Can you believe it? Damn philis-tine landlady. Anyway, we were going to stay with Dolph and Mina until we found something. But that's been pretty awful; Mina's been locked in her room all day, crying."

"Has Mina talked to Dolph?" Kate asked.

"She's not talking to anyone," Reece said. "Even Esper-anza."

Kate brightened. "Esperanza called?"

"She wanted to talk to you, but you weren't back yet. I couldn't understand her very well, but she said something like Rosa only speaks for herself."

Kate glanced up at Tejeda, who shook his head as if cautioning her not to hope. But she couldn't help it. "Does she want to come home?"

"She'll call again in the morning."

"Good." Kate looked at Reece, shivering in his shorts. She admired him, always so loyal when it got him so little. "Until you find a new place, you and Lydia can stay with me. I'd love some company. That house is too spooky to be in alone."

"Thanks. We'll be over tomorrow sometime." He flinched as a scrub oak incinerated below them. "Shouldn't someone call the fire department?"

"We have," Tejeda said. "All the units in the area are out on other calls."

Kate looked toward the hills, where brush fires had raged out of control earlier in the week. The feeling that someone was out there waiting flooded back as she saw only the white drape of cold fog. "All the big fires are out, aren't they?"

Tejeda held Kate close. "This is probably the only fire in Santa Angelica tonight."

"The spook's getting better," she said appreciatively, watching the policemen wet the bank with their hoses. "As a diversion, this is damned good. With no firemen available, your policemen would have to leave the house and come down here, wouldn't they?"

A loud snap cracked the air like a starter's pistol. An upper stair-support piling gave way and fell to the side. There was a pause, then the remains of the stairway swayed to one side, groaning an octave lower than the foghorns in the bay. All at once, as if some connective string had been jerked out, the whole stairway collapsed against the bluff, sending a shower of sparks into the fog like fireworks in slow motion.

When the ash and dust settled, Kate saw the embers of the stairs glowing in a line down the face of the scorched bluff. They looked like the skeleton of some monstrous beast. Now extinct.

TEJEDA OPENED the bedside drawer and put something in it.

"What's that?" Kate asked.

"My service revolver." He sat down beside her and folded his legs tailor-fashion in front of him, his back against the headboard.

Kate slid into the nest made by Tejeda's folded legs and snuggled against him. "Is it all over?"

"For a while. There's no one inside the house, and they're still watching outside." He wrapped his long arms around her and rested his cheek against the top of her head, naturally, as if he'd been with her just like this a hundred times before. He yawned. "What time is it?"

Kate glanced at the bedside clock. "Four-thirty. You tired?"

"Sleepy." They stretched out on the bed and he closed his eyes. "Lovin' makes me sleepy."

Kate watched him fall asleep. One of his hands rested on Kate's hip, the other under his cheek, pushing out his mouth like a pouty child. As he fell deeper into sleep he seemed to become totally vulnerable, and totally desirable. Must have been an adorable child, she thought, regretting that she had missed knowing him then.

She draped an arm around him and closed her eyes. But it took too much effort to keep them closed. She was tired, but after all the day's excitement and trauma she couldn't sleep. Slowly, so she wouldn't disturb him, she got up. She took a blanket from the cupboard and spread it over Tejeda, kissing him as she tucked it around him.

He smiled and sighed, but didn't move. She put on a short robe and went to the bathroom to run a hot bath. After soaking for half an hour she still didn't feel like sleeping.

She looked out the bedroom window. A long run on the beach would help, she thought. But it was still dark outside, and it was beginning to rain. Something glinted wetly near the beach stairs and she remembered sadly that they were gone. It would be a long, muddy scramble to run on the beach until the stairs were rebuilt.

The best alternative to a run, she decided, was the boring new book about Alexander Hamilton and the Federalists. She pulled her robe closer around her and went down the hall to her study, pausing first to listen to Tejeda's soft snoring.

The afghan was still draped over her chair on the oriel. Kate turned on the reading light and sat down with the new book. She opened it to the middle and studied the half-dozen pages of black-and-white pictures and reproduced documents. Then, sighing heavily, she found the dog-eared page where she had left off and started to read.

The dry, lifeless prose, accompanied by the steady patter of rain against the windows, lulled her into a contented sleepiness. She rested her head on her forearms and listened as the storm became more and more violent, whipping the cypresses against the window with a rhythmic scraping. A stray branch hit the window with a loud pop that made her jerk upright in her deep chair.

A bolt of lightning shot through the sky and the lights flickered.

Just the storm, Kate thought, enjoying its power. She closed her book and turned off the lamp to watch the storm blowing in off the Pacific, a sou'wester coming up from Mexico. It moved in rapidly, as if it could extinguish the sun just rising in the east.

Fat drops of rain pecked at the oriel windows, like birds trying to get in out of the storm. Below her, the spine of burned beach stairs was awash in a torrent of mud. With few plant roots to hold it after the fire, the sandy soil mixed with the rain and washed down to the beach in long shafts, like slices from a cake.

The burned stairway, parts of it still connected together, floated on a shifting base of mud, slithering down the face of the bluff. Kate watched the ruins until they were nothing more than a spill of burned lumber heaped on the sand. When they were gone, she felt cut off, as if some vital escape route had disappeared.

On the desk behind her the telephone rang. She yawned and reached for it.

"Hello?"

"Die, bitch."

"Shit." She slammed down the receiver, then picked it up again and listened. Someone was there, at least the other end was still off the hook. She could hear something on the line, a familiar hollow background fuzz. The call had been made on the house phone. Someone was inside the house.

Kate ran down the hall, trying to control her fear, trying to keep her steps quiet. She opened her bedroom door.

Tejeda was still tucked under the blanket as she'd left him, his back to the door.

"Roger." She gently shook his shoulder. "Wake up. Someone's here."

When he didn't respond, she shook him harder. "Wake up, dammit."

He fell onto his back and she gagged. The right side of his face was a mound of blue and red pulp, his eye lost in swollen pads of oozing flesh.

"Not you," she sobbed, ripping the blanket back to listen to his chest. Under the smooth skin the faint breath came in irregular gasps. She covered him again to keep him warm, then reached for the telephone.

The line was still open. As long as it was, she couldn't call out for help. She didn't want to leave him, but she had to get him help. Fast. She had to find an open telephone. She tried to count. There were six, maybe eight extensions in the house.

As she leaned over Tejeda to check him again before leaving, a hot hand gripped her throat from behind, another pressed something cold and sharp against the corner of her eye.

"Don't move." It was the raspy voice from the telephone.

Kate was caught in an awkward stance, half-leaning with nothing to support her. She knew that she couldn't stay that way for long. Though she didn't dare move even her eyes, the feet on the floor behind her were within her focus. The feet looked heavy in plastic rain shoes, but the ankles were trim. The ankles in the torn photograph.

"Let me stand up, Mina."

"Stay where you are. You can die here with your policeman."

"Why?" Kate tried to seem calm. "At least tell me why I have to die."

The line of cold metal moved to press the sinews of her throat. "All right. Stand up." The metal pressed harder. "But slowly. This is Dolph's straight razor, and it's very sharp. I stropped it myself."

"Is Dolph okay?" Kate felt her anguish growing as she thought of all the others who might be Mina's targets.

"Dolph can't die until you do. Otherwise, what's the point of it all?"

"Point of what?" Kate asked. It was so ludicrous to think of Mina as a desperate killer that Kate, out of nervousness and shock, kept waiting for her to say it was a big joke. "You don't want to kill me, Mina."

"Don't patronize me, young lady. You sound like Dolph. Always so superior." Mina was shorter than Kate, and although her grip was tight, her arms had to get tired sooner or later from reaching up. She shifted slightly and the blade of the razor nicked Kate's throat, no more than a slip while shaving. "I won't fail this time."

Kate felt a trickle of blood run behind the collar of her robe. Shrinking as far from the blade as she could, she tried to find some reason for what was happening. And to think of some way to disarm Mina without getting her throat slashed.

"This isn't necessary," Kate said, imagining the blade slicing through her vocal cords if she antagonized Mina. "I won't let Dolph disown Reece."

"Reece!" Mina cackled derisively. "You damned fool. Reece can take care of himself. It's *me. I'm* being dispossessed in your favor. Dolph is leaving me in *your* care."

"I can assign his estate to you."

"But it's mine. I earned it. After all those years, putting up with crap from your mother and everybody. No more." Her thin fingers dug into Kate's throat. "I'll be damned before I take any handouts from you or any other Byrd again. For the birds."

Kate felt Mina draw the razor back, ready to cut deep. She managed to twist in Mina's grasp, so that the blade missed her throat and glanced off her chin. Kate raised her shoulder to touch the insistent itch where the blade touched her, and felt hot, wet blood. The razor was so sharp she hadn't felt it cut.

"Mina, please," she said, hoping to buy time. Mina couldn't hold her in this insane grip much longer before her muscles gave out. Beside her, Tejeda's breath became a ragged whistle. Any way she looked at it, she didn't have much time.

"Your friend sounds bad," Mina said. Kate understood from the little giggle at the end that she was enjoying the slow torture. It gave her hope, letting Mina draw it out until Kate could find her opportunity.

"My mother's head looked worse than Tejeda's," Kate said. "Did you do it?"

"No. Miles did."

"But you helped him?"

"I just sort of urged him on. It was pretty easy. He hated Margaret almost as much as I did. I told him she was making you divorce Carl, to cut him out of any hope of inheritance. Then I said Margaret would dump Miles in an institution and tear down his house. That's all it really took. I faked a phone call from the women's shelter to lure her out. Then he took her downtown and bashed her head in."

Kate felt Mina relaxing. The blade still pressed into the side of her neck hard enough so that Kate felt her jugular pulsing against it. But the left hand was weakening.

"What did you do to Miles?" Kate asked, keeping Mina busy.

"Sooner or later he was going to talk, so I switched his Dilantin for sugarless mints. All the pressure he was under, it wouldn't take long.'

"You know the best part?" Mina sighed, almost trancelike. Her elbow dipped slightly, but she caught herself and pressed the razor harder against Kate's neck. "That last day, when I was sure he wasn't ever coming to his senses and I left the hospital. Before you or Dolph came. I was going home, but I couldn't remember where I parked my car. Then you drove up in your mother's black heap, and it gave me the idea. I'm sorry I missed, but it was a damned good try."

"So were the other tries, the stones on the beach stairs, the lye in the sugar."

"Yes, they were. The stones were inspiration. I was in the gazebo that night, trying to figure out how I was going to stop you from looking for the baby, when you came out and stood there. Like you were waiting for me."

Kate saw her advantage while Mina preened. She grabbed the arm with the blade and backed away from it, butting Mina's face with the back of her head. As they struggled, the razor sliced down Kate's cheek like a sliver of ice.

Once she was away from the razor, the advantage was Kate's. She threw Mina onto the bed, wedging the right hand with the blade underneath her. She twisted the thin wrist until she heard bones crack, and the right hand fell open.

Kate snatched up the razor and folded it into its handle and threw it across the room. Then she yanked Mina up off the bed, to keep her as far away from Tejeda as possible, and held her pinned against the wall.

"Why?" she demanded. "Was it all for money?"

Mina spat in her face and Kate shook her, letting her head bounce against the flowered wallpaper.

"Tell me why!" She raised a hand to slap Mina but, even in her fury, wasn't sure she could do it.

"All right." Mina shielded her face with her free hand. "I did it for my son. So you wouldn't spoil everything for my son."

"Your son?" Kate anticipated new tricks while thinking that maybe Mina truly was insane. "You have no son. You went to Mexico and had an abortion."

"You're wrong. Helga had an abortion. I had a son."

"Reece?"

"No, you idiot. Carl."

"That's crazy."

Mina began to shake and Kate was afraid she would faint. Or worse. She moved her to the closest chair and sat her down, holding her shoulders against the seat back. "If Carl is your son, why did Helga claim him?"

"I couldn't have taken a baby home. Dolph had been gone a year already. He would have divorced me. Alone I had nothing, no way to support a baby. So we made a deal, Helga and

I. She would claim that Carl was hers so that Miles would support her.''

"And what did you get?''

"My baby lived.''

"Mina.'' Kate knelt down in front of her, feeling terrible about the rough treatment she had given her aunt, no matter how necessary. "How did this start? Miles had taken care of Carl. We wouldn't let Mother get control of Miles's estate. Everything was safe.''

"No, it wasn't,'' Mina sobbed. "Your damned mother found a snapshot of me and Carl in Mexico when he was confirmed in the church. She knew when I was pregnant and she figured it all out. She was the most devious, ruthless woman on the face of this earth, and I hated her!

"Your mother blackmailed me. If I didn't help her get Miles put away she was going to tell. Then it would be all over for both Carl and me. Miles would change his will. Dolph would divorce me. And you would have everything Carl should have had.''

Tejeda groaned and, in reflex, Kate glanced toward him. Mina took advantage of the moment and brought her knee up under Kate's chin, sending her sprawling backward. Like a thing possessed, Mina sprang from the chair and across the room to where Kate had flung the razor.

Kate dashed after her, grabbing for her but missing. As Mina reached the razor, Kate rolled across the corner of the bed and landed on the floor on the far side of Tejeda. She yanked the drawer out of the bedside table and found his service revolver.

She cocked the hammer and aimed the heavy blue gun at Mina's midsection. "Put down the razor, Mina. Miles taught me how to use one of these things.''

"But you won't.'' Mina opened the razor and took a step toward her. "You sniveled for a week after Miles shot an elk. You won't shoot me.''

"Just come downstairs with me.'' Kate felt better with the big weapon in her hand. "I have to get help.''

"Did you ever notice?'' Mina turned her head to one side coquettishly, "that Carl has your father's eyes?''

Mina and her father? The revolver sagged in Kate's hands.

Mina leaped toward Tejeda, the point of her blade like the needle of a compass aimed at his neck.

The police special slug caught Mina in midair and flung her on her back before Kate even felt its heavy recoil.

TWENTY-ONE

TEJEDA OPENED HIS unbandaged eye and looked at Kate. "What time is it?"

"Tuesday." Kate closed the awful book about Alexander Hamilton and the Federalists and walked over to her bed and sat down beside him. She checked the gauze turban that circled his head before she bent to kiss him.

"Where's Theresa?"

"At school. Mrs. Murphy will bring her here at three."

"Does my head hurt?"

"It should. You have a fractured skull and about two dozen stitches."

He squinted his eye and looked at her again. "What's that thing on your face?"

"Combat ribbons." She touched the twin line of tiny sutures that vee'd from the corner of her mouth to her chin and back up along her jawline.

Color was coming back into his one visible cheek. "Are you okay?"

"I'm fine, Lieutenant. But you're going to have one hell of a shiner."

Worldwide Mysteries—keeping you in suspense with award-winning authors.

THE DEAD ROOM—Herbert Resnicow $3.50 ☐
When a murdered man is found in a dead room, an anechoic
chamber used to test stereo equipment, Ed Baer and his son
investigate the virtually impossible crime, and unravel an
ingenious mystery.

MADISON AVENUE MURDER—Gillian Hall $3.50 ☐
A young woman investigates the brutal murder of a successful
art director and comes to understand the chilling flip side of
passionate love . . . and the lowly places to which the highest
ambitions can fall.

LULLABY OF MURDER—Dorothy Salisbury Davis $3.50 ☐
A reporter investigates the murder of a famous New York gossip
columnist and finds herself caught up in a web of hate, deceit
and revenge.

IN REMEMBRANCE OF ROSE—M. R. D. Meek $3.50 ☐
An elderly woman is found dead, victim of an apparent robbery
attempt. But lawyer Lennox Kemp is suspicious and discovers
that facts are scarce and bizarre, leading him to believe that
there is something sinister at play.

Not available in Canada.

Total Amount	$ _____
Plus 75¢ Postage	_____.75
Payment enclosed	$ _____

Please send a check or money order payable to Worldwide Mysteries.

In the U.S.A.	In Canada
Worldwide Mysteries	Worldwide Mysteries
901 Fuhrmann Blvd.	P.O. Box 609
Box 1325	Fort Erie, Ontario
Buffalo, NY 14269-1325	L2A 5X3

Please Print

Name: _____

Address: _____

City: _____

State/Prov: _____

Zip/Postal Code: _____

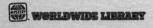 **WORLDWIDE LIBRARY**

Return to the scene of the crime with Worldwide Mysteries!

REMEMBER TO KILL ME—Hugh Pentecost $3.50 ☐
Pierre Chambrun, manager of the Hotel Beaumont in New York, must cope with the shooting of a close friend, a hostage situation and a gang of hoods terrorizing guests.

DEADLY INNOCENTS—Mark Sadler $3.50 ☐
A brutal murder leads private investigator Paul Shaw to a man who will pay quite handsomely if Shaw will forget the case and go home. But for Shaw, murder is a living....

SCENT OF DEATH—Emma Page $3.50 ☐
A standard missing persons case soon mushrooms into a horrifying double homicide when Detectives Lambert and Kelsey find two young women in an abandoned shed, strangled. Not available in Canada

CHAOS OF CRIME—Dell Shannon $3.50 ☐
Amid a panorama of fear and evil, Luis Mendoza of the LAPD is up against one of his grisliest cases ever when he searches for a psychotic sex killer who is prowling the city

Total Amount	$ _____
Plus 75¢ Postage	.75
Payment enclosed	$ _____

Please send a check or money order payable to Worldwide Mysteries

In the U.S.A.	In Canada
Worldwide Mysteries	Worldwide Mysteries
901 Fuhrmann Blvd	P.O. Box 609
Box 1325	Fort Erie, Ontario
Buffalo, NY 14269-1325	L2A 5X3

Please Print

Name: _____

Address: _____

City: _____

State/Prov.: _____

Zip/Postal Code: _____

WORLDWIDE LIBRARY

MYS-4

ATTRACTIVE, SPACE SAVING BOOK RACK

Display your most prized novels on this handsome and sturdy book rack. The hand-rubbed walnut finish will blend into your library decor with quiet elegance, providing a practical organizer for your favorite hard-or soft-covered books.

Only $9.95

Approximately 16" x 8" when assembled

Assembles in seconds!

To order, rush your name, address and zip code, along with a check or money order for $10.70* (9.95 plus 75¢ postage and handling) payable to *The Mystery Library Reader Service.*

Mystery Library Reader Service
Book Rack Offer
901 Fuhrmann Blvd.
P.O. Box 1396
Buffalo, NY 14269-1396

Offer not available in Canada.

BKR-ML

*New York and Iowa residents add appropriate sales tax.

Winner of the Grand Master Award from the Mystery Writers of America, Dorothy Salisbury Davis "... has few equals in setting up a puzzle, complete with misdirection and surprises."
—*New York Times Book Review*

Julie Hayes Mysteries

LULLABY OF MURDER $3.50 ☐
When an infamous New York gossip columnist is found murdered, reporter Julie Hayes starts digging and discovers a lot of people are happier with him dead! As murder takes center stage, Julie finds herself caught in a web of hate, deceit and revenge, dirty deals and small-town scandals.

THE HABIT OF FEAR $3.50 ☐
New York columnist Julie Hayes struggles to regain her equilibrium by traveling to Ireland in search of her father after a seemingly random act of violence shatters her life. Her pursuit leads her into a maze of violence, mystery—and murder.

Total Amount	$ _____
Plus 75¢ Postage	_____ .75
Payment enclosed	$ _____

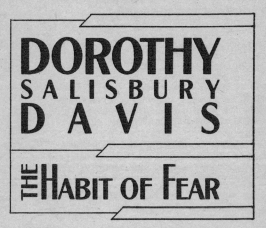
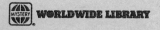